Adam was angry at her, angry with himself.

For a split second he'd wondered how it would feel to wake up with Pat next to him every morning, to hear her footsteps in the house every evening.

He'd been a fool.

She still bore a grudge against the town. And as long as she did, she was a danger to him, to his son and to everything he'd come to cherish. Her values would always be poles apart from his. Given the chance, she would bring the Grove to its knees.

He dare not forget that again....

Dear Reader,

As always, I'm very proud of the lineup of books we're offering this month in Silhouette Intimate Moments. I think every story here is exciting, and every author is writing at the top of her form. But there's one book I'd especially like to discuss in more detail, taking a somewhat more serious tack than I usually do.

For many years I have been closely involved with Silhouette Intimate Moments, having a strong voice in choosing what books we'll bring to you, then scheduling those books, and also handling the reader mail I'm so lucky to receive from so many of you. Over the years, one question has been asked of me many times. Sometimes the letter writer identifies herself as black, sometimes as a woman of color, sometimes as an African-American. But always the question is the same: Why aren't you publishing books about women like me, black women meeting and falling in love with black men? Always my correspondent tells me that she enjoys our books anyway—a compliment I am happy to receive on behalf of all our talented authors—but that just one book about a black couple would make her happy, make her feel that she belongs fully to the fellowship of readers spanning the globe. This month I am proud to be bringing you—all of you, whatever the color of your skin—*Unforgivable* by Joyce McGill. *Unforgivable* is a sizzling novel of suspense, of small-town secrets and sensuous romance. It is a novel for every woman, every reader of Silhouette Intimate Moments, because the emotions in it are universal, just as love is. And I hope that all of you—whatever your heritage, whatever the color of the face that looks back at you from the mirror—will read this terrific book. It is a book I'm proud of, just as I'm proud of every book we publish. But in this case I feel a special sense of pride, because it gives all of us a chance to prove what the sages have told us down through the years: Love is indeed blind. It recognizes no boundaries of color, of country, of language or of age. Love is always love, and all of us can share its bounty.

Thank you all for listening, and for the support you have so freely given over the years. And I promise to be back next month with more exciting—and I suspect unexpected!—news.

Leslie Wainger
Senior Editor and Editorial Coordinator

JOYCE McGILL

Unforgivable

SILHOUETTE·INTIMATE·MOMENTS®

Published by Silhouette Books New York

America's Publisher of Contemporary Romance

If you purchased this book without a cover you should be aware
that this book is stolen property. It was reported as "unsold and
destroyed" to the publisher, and neither the author nor the
publisher has received any payment for this "stripped book."

SILHOUETTE BOOKS
300 East 42nd St., New York, N.Y. 10017

UNFORGIVABLE

Copyright © 1992 by Chassie L. West

All rights reserved. Except for use in any review,
the reproduction or utilization of this work in
whole or in part in any form by any electronic,
mechanical or other means, now known or
hereafter invented, including xerography,
photocopying and recording, or in any information
storage or retrieval system, is forbidden without
the permission of the publisher, Silhouette Books,
300 E. 42nd St., New York, N.Y. 10017

ISBN: 0-373-07441-7

First Silhouette Books printing August 1992

All the characters in this book have no existence
outside the imagination of the author and have
no relation whatsoever to anyone bearing the same
name or names. They are not even distantly
inspired by any individual known or unknown
to the author, and all incidents are pure invention.

®: Trademark used under license and
registered in the United States Patent and
Trademark Office and in other countries.

Printed in the U.S.A.

Books by Joyce McGill

Silhouette Intimate Moments

Through the Looking Glass #347
A Loving Touch #368
Unforgivable #441

JOYCE McGILL

began her writing career by doing articles for her high school newspaper, but soon became more involved with the theater. After winning several state awards for Best Actress, she went on to college to earn her B.A. in drama and literature. For some years, she acted in professional and community theaters and made films and commercials before returning to writing. Ms. McGill previously published young-adult romances under the name Tracy West.

To Karen and Mary Clare and Leslie, for their
patience and understanding;
To my writing group, whose moral support
was unfailing;
To Shirl in the Baltimore Medical Examiner's Office,
for her cheerful advice and cooperation;
And to Bob, my husband, the solar source of all my
creative energies:
THANK YOU

Chapter 1

It was a nice room, poles apart from the cabbage rose wallpaper and claw-footed furniture he'd expected. There were no tapestry-weight draperies blotting out the sun, no dust motes dancing in the air. It was, in fact, a light, airy room, a symphony of organdy, or was it organza? Whichever. Color scheme: deep pink and white throughout the whole wing—the bedroom, the sitting room beyond, the king-size bathroom and dressing area. And plants: Boston ferns, ivies, African violets, their leaves a healthy green. The overall effect unmistakably feminine, a space for a lady. Which probably accounted for the reason he felt so out of place, Adam Wyatt decided.

The delicate white and gilt chairs with the petit point seat covers weren't designed for a man's comfort, especially one who stood six-two and nudged one-eighty-seven; it had been an act of faith that he'd sat down at all. But he wanted to get to know this room intimately, the reasons best left unplumbed since they had kept him awake most of the night. Now that he was here again, the first step in the process was to perch somewhere and just soak up the feel of the place.

It had taken a few minutes to find the right vantage point. There were mirrors of one sort or another on every wall, making it difficult to escape his image. He'd found his masculinity an alien presence among all the frills and flounces, his toasted almond complexion a jarring element in the pink and white color scheme. He'd finally chosen the secretary in the corner, which was the one spot where he could sit without seeing his reflection. He scanned the room, mentally cataloging the personal touches that would enlighten him as to the personality of the owner—the silver-plated comb and brush set on the glass-topped dresser, the mother-of-pearl inlaid jewelry box, the crystal atomizers, the collection of owls, most carved from ivory or jade.

Books, well-thumbed, were scattered around the room; he would check the titles later. Photographs lined the mantel of the fireplace, glimpses of relatives long dead, of a youth long past. And one of a face that, like his, seemed out of place among the faded snapshots of boyish brunette flappers in the short fringed dresses of the twenties, and pompadoured blondes in forties attire. A recent photo, he was sure, perhaps a studio portrait.

To a degree her hairstyle was a twin of the flapper, cut smooth and short, Dutch-boy style. A young woman, her complexion flawless, the anomaly in the color of her skin, milk chocolate with a hint of cinnamon. Not knock-'em-dead pretty, yet attractive in a way that was difficult to define; a gently rounded face, great cheekbones, a generous mouth.

Quite aside from the enigma of her presence on the mantel among several generations of the white, moneyed aristocracy of the Harland clan, however, was the curious magnetism of her eyes. They had an intriguing cant to them and fairly danced with laughter, as if she had something humorous on the tip of her tongue and could barely wait to share it. And by some trick of the angle at which she'd been photographed, her eyes seemed to follow him.

The picture had captured his attention almost as soon as he'd entered the room the day before, even though there'd been far more important matters to attend to; she'd seemed to watch him as he'd moved from one side of the canopied four-poster to the other. The phenomenon was no less pronounced today, along with the feeling, intensifying by the minute, that she was someone he knew. But there was no signature on the picture, no means of identifying her. He was tempted to turn the picture to face the wall. She was a distraction—a pleasant one, but still a distraction he didn't need.

Yes, Adam reiterated, forcing himself to concentrate, definitely a nice room, an easy room to live in. And, evidently, to die in, as well, since Elizabeth Harland had done precisely that two nights before. Which, for Adam, was the problem, one, he suspected, of his own making because in the natural scheme of things, it was not unusual for someone who'd gotten to the ripe old age of eighty-four to die. So why couldn't he shake the feeling that, her age aside, this particular old lady had died before her time?

"Chief? Hey, where are you?"

Adam sighed. Yet another distraction. At this rate he'd never get a handle on the things this room could tell him. "In here, Bo. The bedroom."

Bo Chavis rounded the doorway and, in response to Adam's palm raised in the classic stop-traffic signal, almost skidded to a halt. "Oh, sorry. Did I interrupt something?"

"No." Adam kept his smile in check. As eager and brown as a collie pup, Bo was twenty-three but seemed younger, in part because of a round, boyish face that would always chop a good five years off his actual age. Regardless, if his tendency to let his enthusiasm run away with him could be reined in a bit, he'd be a good cop someday. "Come on in, just don't touch anything."

"Oh. Okay. What are you doing up here, anyway?"

"Just looking around."

"Why?"

Adam didn't want to lie to the kid, but he wasn't ready to reveal his reasons for being here, either. "Since I only met her a couple of times, I'm trying to get to know Miss Harland a little better, and bedrooms usually tell you more about a person than any other room in the house."

"They do, huh?" Bo glanced around, seemingly unconvinced.

"For instance, my first impression is that she had an orderly mind, liked things just so. This wing is packed with furniture and gewgaws, but it's very neat."

Bo grunted. "Come on, Chief. If I had somebody like Miss Lorna to do the cleaning, even my room would be neat."

"That's not what I mean. Everything's organized, has a place, relates to the things around it and looks as if it belongs where it is. So any break in that pattern sticks out. That tells me something, too, only I'm not sure what quite yet."

"You found a break in the pattern?"

"A couple. Check out this space, then take a turn through the sitting room and bathroom and tell me if you notice anything in particular."

Bo's eyes swiveled toward him. "Is this a test?"

There was no way for Adam to restrain his smile this time. "Let's call it a test of *my* powers of observation, okay? No pass-fail involved—for you, anyway."

"Whew!" Bo wiped imaginary perspiration from his broad forehead. "Okay, gimme a minute." Backing up until he stood in the doorway again, he glanced around the room, dark eyes flitting from the four-poster, the flowered sheets in a tumble at the foot of the bed, to the glass-covered nightstand and dresser, then on to other items of furniture. Humming under his breath, he disappeared into the sitting room through the connecting door. Adam, waiting, shrugged his shoulders several times to shake off a sudden tension stealing across his back. The fact that he was relying on his young co-worker to spot the same discrepancies as he had told him just how desperate he was to have his uneasiness justified.

After several minutes Bo reappeared, wearing a puzzled frown.

"What is it?" Adam asked.

"Well . . ." Bo's nut-brown face skewed with uncertainty. "It's like pictures in one of my mother's decorating magazines, with everything perfectly coordinated—the colors and fabrics, that kind of thing. Like in the sitting room, the covers on the sofa and chairs are the same. Throw pillows match the curtains. Bathroom's got little flowers on the window and shower curtains, and the toilet seat cover's part of the set, too. You understand what I'm saying?"

"Yes. So?" Adam felt the tension in his back begin to ease. If Bo, a relative novice at this kind of thing, had noticed the same inconsistencies he had, then he wasn't being paranoid.

"Well, the rug in the bathroom doesn't match," Bo continued, beads of sweat above his mustache betraying his nervousness. "It's pink but a different pink than the others. And in here, the sheets and pillowcases don't match."

"Congratulations. I noticed that, too."

"But... well, so what, Chief? What's it tell us about Miss Lib?"

Adam rubbed his face in thought. "I'm not sure it tells us anything—about her, anyway. But it doesn't fit the pattern, so it bugs me. Just something else to ask Lorna and Miss Hetty about. Was Miss Hetty feeling any better by the time you got her home?"

"I reckon. I walked her to the door like you told me, and she said she was going to lay down awhile. She didn't look so hot, though."

"I'll give her a couple of hours, and then check on her. I really didn't get much out of her, but I didn't want to push. This has hit her hard. Is Lorna still downstairs?"

"No, sir. Said she had to go over to Mr. C.J.'s, something about getting his guest rooms ready for people coming for the funeral. She's kind of miffed that you closed up this wing here."

Adam got to his feet. "Well, that's too bad, because these rooms are off limits to everyone until I've had a chance to go over them, take some more pictures, a few samples."

"But why, Chief? You didn't do anything like that when Mr. Brett died at home, and he was way younger than Miss Lib."

"Grady Brett died with a doctor in attendance. Miss Harland didn't. Truthfully, what I'm doing is called C.M.A., if you get my meaning."

Bo grinned and looked for all the world like a fifteen-year-old kid. "Covering your...uh...butt. Sure. Okay. Anything I can do to help?" He bounced over to Adam, tail a-wag.

"How about bringing me the evidence kit from the trunk of the car?"

"Yes, sir." He started out, but turned at the door. "Chief, you think there's something fishy about Miss Lib's death, don't you?"

Adam met his gaze, chiding himself for selling the kid short. Bo's baby face made it easy to forget how sharp and intuitive he really was; it was one of the reasons Adam had hired him. Bo had been in training for a year. Granted, so far nothing had arisen to truly test him, but Adam had every confidence that Bo would not disappoint him. It was time to trust him in a way he would probably never trust the other two men on his small force.

"Bo, I worked homicide on the N.Y.P.D. for eight years. When you see as many varieties of death as I did, you get a sixth sense about it. I walked into this room yesterday morning and got a churning in my gut I haven't felt in three years. Something told me that nice old lady hadn't just shuffled off this mortal coil in her sleep."

Bo's face became a mask of worry. "Then I messed up, didn't I? But I didn't know what time you'd get back to town," he said, his voice rising, "and I couldn't just leave her lying there. I mean, I guess I could have, but it didn't seem right. It was Miss Harland!"

"Don't sweat it, Bo. You had no reason to do anything any differently. And I'm proud of you for standing up to C.J. and keeping everyone but the ambulance attendants out. Except for their footprints in the carpet, the room is basically the way it was when you answered the 911."

"If you'd been here, what would you have done?"

"I can't answer that," Adam admitted. "If I'd seen her in that bed, there's every chance I might have taken the scene at face value. I don't know why getting here late made such a difference in how I viewed it, but it did, and my edginess hasn't gone away. I'd hoped talking to Miss Hetty might help flush it down the toilet, and maybe it will, when I try again later. In the meantime, I can't ignore it any longer. It won't let me. I'm going over this room with a fine-toothed comb, do a proper examination, as if it were a crime scene."

"Looking for what, Chief?" Bo asked, his eyes intent and solemn.

"Anything out of the ordinary—like the mismatched sheets and pillowcases and a couple of other things I've noticed today. Between Lorna and Miss Hetty, I may find that there are perfectly logical explanations for them. I hope to God I do. But between you and me, buddy, I have a bad feeling about this."

"I'll tell you, Chief, *I* hope to God it's just something you ate. I liked Miss Lib. She was an okay lady. It really hurt me to see her carried out all covered up that way. You need any help?"

"Your shift is about over," Adam pointed out.

"Shoot, if I go home, Tisha's gonna show up lugging those dumb books with all the silverware patterns. I keep saying stainless steel was good enough for my parents, it's good enough for me, and she keeps saying I got no class. If you don't mind, I'd just as soon hang around."

"Up to you. And while we're working, I want you to describe anything you noticed about Miss Harland's body, just in case there's something you might have remembered after you wrote up the report."

Bo's embarrassed expression told him he'd struck gold. "There is one thing. When I bent over her to see if I could hear or feel any breath, I got a whiff of something. Real faint. Sort of like coffee."

"Coffee?"

"Yes, sir. I thought it was kind of funny that she'd drink coffee before going to bed. It would keep me awake for hours."

"Coffee. Okay. Go get the kit."

"Be right back." He bounded from the room and clattered down the steps.

Adam shook his head at Bo's youthful exuberance. The fourteen-year difference in their ages yawned like a gaping chasm. Had he ever been that young? Probably not. At twenty-three, he'd already been on the force a year and a half, finding out how much he still had to learn about a city he'd thought he'd known well but really hadn't. The protective shield he'd needed to survive facing malice, mayhem and murder every day had already formed but was not yet dried and hardened. Hopefully Bo would have no need for that kind of protection, not in Harland Grove.

Several hours later, however, he suspected that his hope was misplaced. Something out of the ordinary had indeed taken place in Lib Harland's bedroom, the only questions being exactly when and why. He needed to talk to Miss Hetty—soon. She knew something, he was sure. Packing away the evidence bags and the items to be sent to the lab for analysis, he glanced up at the mantelpiece and felt the hair on the back of his neck stand at attention. The remarkable eyes in the photograph looked back at him. Only they didn't seem to be laughing anymore.

Pat Chase sat huddled in the cocoon of silence she had spun around herself to help her keep her sanity during the sharp-tinged agony of waiting. Shifting her position on the too soft lounge chair, she allowed a momentary breach of her delicate defenses, allowing the hubbub of Three South to rush in on her, the nurses' chatter, the insistent bleat of the call button register above their desk, the nasal commands of the paging system.

Pat rubbed her eyes, fighting fatigue that gnawed at the marrow of her bones. Her body still vibrated after almost eight hours in the air, five zooming eastward from Seattle to D.C. But instead of going directly to her apartment, she'd stopped by the station to pick up ten days' worth of messages, one of which had precipitated a second flight, from Washington, D.C. to Charlotte.

She withdrew the three pink While You Were Out slips that had been waiting for her at WPQQ-TV, staring at them as if they might reveal something she'd missed. Two from Hetty, logged in the day before—no message, simply requests that she call. Then the third, the one that had set panic bubbling at a roiling boil. "Hetty admitted to Harland Memorial. Come A.S.A.P." The name of the caller: C.J. Pat hadn't needed further identification. Charles Jonas Harland, of Harland Grove's founding family; the last person she'd expect to phone her. Under any circumstances.

Hetty's calls had clocked in the previous day at nine-fifty and four-seventeen, the one from C.J. at eleven this morning. She assumed now that Hetty had phoned to tell her she was sick. The fact that C.J. had placed the call today—C.J., who had to know how low he was on her list of favorite people—must mean that Hetty was worse. God, Pat thought, had that hard-headed old lady refused to go to the hospital, waiting for me to return her call? Had she made herself worse by not coming here immediately?

"Ms. Chase?"

Pat looked up into the cherubic face of the nurse who'd volunteered to find out what she could about Hetty, since the room in which her great-aunt was registered was vacant, the bedcovers undisturbed, the closet and nightstand empty of any personal effects.

"Sorry it took so long," the nurse said, her inflection transforming her statement into a question, a characteristic of the region's Southern accent. "It's been a zoo around here. I just wanted to let you know Miss Melton's downstairs in Radiology. Dr. Vernon's ordered a CAT and a battery of other tests."

"Vernon?" Pat rose in confusion. "Her doctor's name is Trent."

"Well, Dr. Vernon's taking care of her."

"Why?" Pat asked. "What's wrong with her?"

The pleasant, open face became guarded. "Are you a relative, ma'am?"

"Her only relative, Ms.—" Pat checked her name tag "—Ms. Maxwell. She's my great-aunt. Please, I'm completely in the dark. All C.J.'s message said was that—"

"Oh! Mr. Harland called you?" The young woman turned azalea pink and Pat's spirits rallied. Perhaps she'd inadvertently punched the right button. The fluted cap quivered on its perch of strawberry-blond curls. "I wish I could help you, Ms. Chase, but I can't. All I found out is that she came in through Emergency sometime this morning and we were told to get a single ready for her. They've probably been working on her ever since."

Since this morning? Pat checked her watch. It was almost six. Whatever had happened must have been serious. She had to see Hetty. "Where's Radiology?" she asked, and reached for her bags.

"In the basement. But you won't be able to see her until they're finished, and you'd be much more comfortable up here, honest. There's a lounge, but it's always crowded with people waiting for outpatients. Please, ma'am, don't worry." Ms. Maxwell tried a reassuring smile. "They said she's alert and doing just fine. I can see that someone lets her know you're here."

"Thank you. I'd appreciate that." Alert and doing just fine. Pat swallowed her panic and willed herself to be satisfied.

"Oh, and Dr. Vernon called to say he'll be here in about forty-five minutes. He'll tell you everything you need to know. Excuse me, someone's leaning on their call button." She hurried away.

Alert and doing just fine. Pat's sense of relief disappeared, blown to bits by a stiff gust of closer scrutiny. "Alert" told her only that Hetty was conscious. "Doing fine" could mean anything—passing the mysterious tests they were putting her through, withstanding the wait, or perhaps just being a cooperative, undemanding patient. How was she really?

Pat sat down again, hard. Fifteen years before, she'd sworn that nothing on earth could make her return to Harland Grove. Once she'd confirmed that Hetty was indeed registered at the hospital, there'd been no question of keeping her word; she had to come back. Now, she realized, she would have to stay at least long enough to determine the nature of Hetty's problem and what needed to be done. What if it took longer than a day or two? How would she stand it?

Suddenly she was sixteen again, cowering in the corner of a Harland Grove jail cell. Unbidden, its dank musty smell infiltrated her memory and she pressed her fingers against the sides of her nose, as if the act might somehow snuff out the offending odor. She thought she had put all that behind her. She was wrong. Even being in the vicinity of the Grove had strained the scar tissue, ripping open the wound it had protected to expose a festering anger, remembered pain.

Pat pulled herself upright, stiffening her spine. She was thirty-one now, not a frightened teenager. She could take care of herself. But what if Hetty had fallen, broken something and couldn't live alone any longer? She would take care of Hetty, too, convince her to move to D.C. Pat began plotting, desperation driving her thoughts. She'd have to hire someone to stay with Hetty during the day while she was at work. She'd have to cancel the trip to Texas, perhaps cut out traveling altogether. She'd do whatever it took, Pat decided. She owed Hetty Melton.

A thirty-second newsbrief on the monster TV in the corner reminded her of all she'd left undone at work. Milt, a co-host, would have to take over for her. She wished she'd been able to organize the tapes of the Seattle interviews for him before she'd left, but there hadn't been time. Shrugging, Pat dismissed her concern about the advocacy reports she anchored once a week; there was nothing she could do about them for the time being and no way to determine how long the time being would last anyway.

The pace of activity had increased since the last time she'd plugged in on the comings and goings at this juncture of the L-shaped wings. Watching visitors had provided a distraction for the first few minutes of her vigil. The elevator doors wheezed open again, spilling the next round of people onto Three South, several of them in the burgundy and gray jumpsuits worn by employees of Harland Industries. After all these years, the uniforms hadn't changed. Amazing.

Pat's gaze darted to the clock above the nurses' station. Five fifty-two. Of course. The first shift at H.I., the Grove's only claim to fame, was just getting off. She fought the temptation to change seats so her face would not be visible. That, she had to admit, was what she dreaded the most, being remembered, seeing that moment of recognition in someone's eyes. She would not, she promised herself, look away when the time came. She had nothing to be ashamed of, no matter what they thought.

As if inviting the first confrontation, Pat studied the faces of the visitors intently, especially the darker-skinned ones. In the Grove, the age-old jab about all black people looking alike was true. How could it be otherwise in a small town where seven out of ten black residents were descendants of the eighteen slave families who'd labored on the Harland plantation, descendants who, over the years, had seldom found it necessary to stray beyond the city limits to find a mate?

Pat remembered her astonishment years before when she'd arrived to find that even she had fitted the Grove mold. As a Melton, she had cheekbones professional models pulled teeth to simulate, and the liberally freckled mocha complexion of the Chases. She'd seen those same cheekbones in distant cousins on her mother's side of the family and the same freckled faces from those on her father's side. Now, scrutinizing the five brown-skinned people who'd left the elevator, she found they were all familiar to a certain extent.

The sixth, however, was not, and defied categorization. Unfortunately, by the time she'd noticed him, he had skirted the nurses' station to disappear down the far wing, leaving Pat with only a general impression of him. Tallish, twenties, an erect, arm-swinging carriage that smacked of parade grounds and armed forces uniforms. She hadn't gotten that good a look at him but what little she'd seen left no doubt that he was U.S.D.A. Prime. Definitely not a native of the Grove; she was sure of that. Perhaps a doctor, out of hospital uniform.

Reminded, she wondered again about the whereabouts of the elusive Dr. Vernon. Hetty was here, damn it. Why wasn't he? For that matter, where was Lib? She'd tried twice to reach her and had gotten an answering machine at the mansion, and then, maddeningly, at C.J.'s home, as well. Where the hell was everybody?

Stirring restlessly, Pat got up and went to the window. Other than the glorious palette of greens in which June had painted the North Carolina countryside, there was little to see; according to the cabdriver, the Grove itself was several miles southwest of the hospital. It had made the bile rise in Pat's throat to see the name above the front door: Margaret Harland Memorial Hospital. Despite her abhorrence that Hetty was a patient in a hospital named for the woman whose voice occasionally haunted her nightmares, she had to admit that on the surface, at least, it appeared to be a pretty good facility—clean, well-staffed. Well-appointed, too, if it had its own CAT.

"Ms. Chase."

"Yes?" Pat turned around and thought *Mercy!* Confronted with a potently masculine vision in bronze, she had to revise the impressions she'd gotten as this man had disappeared down the hall moments before. He was both older and taller than she'd thought, his skin the color of scratch gingerbread fresh from the oven, a comparison so apt that Pat felt her stomach grumble with hunger. Indecently thick lashes framed eyes of a golden brown that appeared to be engaged in as thorough an examination of her as hers were of him, with an unsettling difference.

Initially she thought she'd detected a flash of surprise across his features. Now, however, there was nothing other than a coolly professional interest in his regard of her, as if he might be a photographer for whom this type of scrutiny went with the territory, an occupational knee-jerk reaction to a new face.

"I'm Adam Wyatt," he said. "The desk clerk told me you're Mrs. Melton's niece, so I..." A puzzled frown etched itself between his thick, glossy brows. "I swear this is not a line, but have we met before?"

Pat's guard went up. It was rare for someone to recognize her off camera but it happened occasionally and she was in no mood for autographs. "I don't think so. I'm sure I'd remember. I'm good at faces," she added quickly.

"So am I—usually." He shook his head, as if he found it difficult to reconcile his mistake. "I just heard that Miss Hetty is here. Is she all right?"

"I don't know. I haven't seen her yet." Pat congratulated herself that at least part of her first take on him had been right on the mark. He was not Grove material. In fact, he sounded like a dyed-in-the-wool New Yorker. No ring on the appropriate finger, but he just had to be spoken for, had to be. The broad, sloping shoulders of a swimmer, narrow waist, lean tight hips. His walking shorts exposed muscular legs, beautifully tanned. He was clean-shaven, something she didn't see often, with a complexion bearing the healthy glow of a physically active man. Not quite handsome, especially with that square jaw, but those clear, amber eyes...oh, Lord! On an attractiveness scale of one to ten, he was nudging eleven hard.

"You know Hetty?" she asked when the silence stretched beyond comfort and he hadn't made goodbye-nice-to-have-met-you noises.

"Only in passing, until yesterday, but she seemed in pretty good shape then. This morning, too, at first, but—"

Pat forgot his legs. "You saw her today? Where? What time?"

"At the Harland mansion, about nine o'clock."

"And she was all right, then?"

He hesitated. "A little edgy. I figured that, under the circumstances, it was to be expected, so I—"

Puzzled, Pat interrupted him again. "What circumstances?"

An imperceptible narrowing of his eyes was the only indication that the question had been unexpected. "When's the last time you talked to your aunt, Ms. Chase?"

"Sunday. Call me Pat, please. She phoned me at work yesterday but I was out of town and didn't get the message until today—hers and C.J.'s saying she was here. I assume she called to let me know she was sick. But if she was okay yesterday... Has something else happened?"

His lips formed a grim line. "Yes. It's Miss Harland. Your aunt found her dead yesterday morning."

Pat felt her face grow cold, her skin chilled and tight. "Lib's dead?"

"I'm afraid so. You knew her well?"

Lowering herself onto the window seat behind her, Pat left his question unanswered. How could she explain what Lib had meant to her? She'd been like family, the difference in their races notwithstanding. Lib and Hetty had been friends for as long as Pat could remember, and caring for Elizabeth Harland these last few years had been her great-aunt's raison d'être. "Gives me something to get up for a'mornin'," was the way Hetty had put it when Pat had urged her to stop working. "Libby, she needs me, what with her arthritis and all. I need to be needed. Not much else to live for, when you get my age."

Lib and Hetty, her only allies in Harland Grove. Now one was gone and the other... Pat closed her eyes, appalled at her selfishness. What would this do to Hetty? Would her friend's death become an excuse for her to give up and "go on home," as she would put it?

Slumped against the windowsill, Pat felt tears sting the corners of her eyes. But if asked, she'd have been hard-pressed to say for whom she cried—Hetty, Lib, or herself.

Adam watched in silence, trying to unravel several different skeins of thought, among them the growing conviction that he had indeed met Pat Chase before. Sooner or later, he'd remember where and when. He just hoped he hadn't given himself away when he'd seen her face; the mystery of her photo on the mantel had been cleared up on the spot.

Almost as surprising as meeting her at all was the fact that her picture was a pale imitation of her. The camera hadn't captured her softness or gentility. She was lovely in a quiet, unassuming way. A leggy five-six, small-boned, perhaps a hundred and ten pounds with a wet brick in her pocket. In the flesh, a strong resemblance to Miss Hetty—the same cheekbones, the same clear complexion, generous mouth. The freckles were another surprise; there'd been no hint of them in the photograph. They added a girl-next-door charm, made it a face to remember. Quite a voice, too, unusually deep and rich with timbre, the kind of soft purr that went straight for the groin and raised havoc. God, what she must sound like on a phone.

Her reaction to the news of Elizabeth Harland's death made him wish he'd been a bit more gentle about telling her. But was she mourning for the woman herself, or for the end of a devoted alliance that must have meant a great deal to Miss Hetty? He was genuinely puzzled about that relationship.

According to C.J., Lib Harland's only nephew, the two old ladies had been very close for years. And Miss Hetty's grief was genuine, he was sure of that. But he'd also sensed something off-key this morning when she'd talked about her friend, something she wasn't saying.

Miss Hetty had been in no shape to tell him much yesterday, other than the fact that she'd arrived at the mansion to fix breakfast and had found Elizabeth Harland dead in bed, her body already cold. A tiny white-haired woman with the kind of

carriage that made her appear twice as tall as she was, Hetty
Melton had exuded a fragility the day before that Adam was
not prepared to test. It wasn't until he'd seen the starch in her
spine and the proud tilt of her chin this morning that he'd felt
comfortable prompting her for details. She'd had little to say,
insisting that she'd told him everything there was to tell. His
interrogation had ended abruptly when she'd stood up, said she
wasn't feeling well and wanted to go home. He'd been suspicious but had asked Bo to take her, making certain she understood he'd need to talk to her later. He'd even stopped at her
house after leaving the mansion to find her gone.

When a neighborhood kid popped over to tell him Miss
Hetty had been taken to the hospital, he'd felt bad that he'd
assumed she'd been faking earlier. On an intellectual level he
knew she might have become ill whether he'd tried to question
her or not. Why then did he feel a little responsible for her being here?

Pat had found a tissue in her purse and wiped her eyes. Even
with tears in them, they were still alluring with a magnetism that
pulled at him. "Sorry," she said. "I just wasn't expecting . . .
God, I wish I'd gotten Hetty's message yesterday. It must have
been awful for her. I just hope . . ."

"What?"

She seemed to be regaining her composure. "Hetty and Lib
must have had a disagreement about something a while ago.
They usually patched things up pretty quickly, but this time it
had been much longer."

"What was the problem?"

"I don't know. Hetty wouldn't say. I just hope they'd made
up before Lib died. If they didn't, this will kill Hetty."

"She seemed to be holding up pretty well," Adam said. "Do
the two of you talk often?"

"Any time the spirit hits. And come hell or high water I call
her from wherever I am, every Sunday." She pleated the tissue
she held. She had beautiful hands, long, slender fingers. "Hetty
said Lib hadn't been feeling too well lately, but I had no idea. . . .
She certainly sounded all right. In fact—"

"You talked to Miss Harland? When was that?" Adam
hoped he'd managed to sound only mildly curious.

"Sunday. Hetty was at the mansion and she'd forwarded her calls there. Lib answered the phone. She was bubbling all over herself, said she was working on a big surprise and would call me soon because she wanted me to be the first person she told about it." Her eloquent eyes lost focus, became clouded with pain. "It reminded me of the old days when we'd hole up together in her sitting room, give each other manicures, and talk for hours." She looked down at her hands, spread her fingers wide, the nails unpolished, perfectly shaped. "Now I'll probably never know what her surprise was."

Adam took a moment to digest this. Elizabeth Harland and Pat Chase as confidantes was hard to imagine; there had to be a fifty-year difference between their ages. Regardless, Pat might be able to fill in some of the information gaps he'd hoped her great-aunt could have cleared up for him. Finding out more about Hetty Melton's niece would be a nice little bonus, as well.

At that point he became aware of a soft rumbling that hadn't registered before. It was a moment before he identified it. "Er...pardon me for asking, but when's the last time you ate?"

Pat's face flamed a lovely bronzed rose. "I was hoping you couldn't hear it. I had a Styrofoam omelet somewhere between O'Hare and National airports. That was about eight o'clock this morning."

"No wonder. Look, there's a dynamite cafeteria in the basement. Jim won't be here for another half an hour. That should be time enough for a sandwich, if nothing else."

"Jim?" she asked.

"Jim Vernon, the doctor. I'm waiting to see him, too."

"Oh." He could see her waver. "I don't think I'd better. I might miss Hetty."

"They'll page you. I promise you, you'll hear it." He was determined not to let this opportunity pass, and the cafeteria was far more conducive to relaxed conversation.

Another insistent protest from the region of her wisp of a waist decided the matter. "All right. Maybe a cup of tea. I'm not sure I should eat anything. When I'm upset, my stomach usually is, too."

"All the more reason to give it something to work on," he said. He retrieved the handsome leather attaché case she'd reached for, then led the way to the elevators. "You are talking to a man who was once that far—" he snapped his fingers "—from an ulcer, so as the old folks say, I know whereof I speak."

Pat chuckled. "Perhaps you do, Adam Wyatt. All right, I'm convinced. Lead on."

Adam punched the down button, startled at the odd things that had happened to his stomach just now, things that had nothing to do with an ulcer and everything to do with the way her deep, soft voice had massaged his name. By the time they'd worked their way past the steam table and found seats, he was sorry he'd suggested the change of venue. He needed to maintain a professional distance that sharing a table and coffee with her would make difficult. She was too attractive, the setting a little too intimate, which, although it appealed to him, was out of place, given the circumstances. He'd be stupid to strike up anything more than a casual acquaintance with Pat Chase. If his instincts proved correct, they might soon be on opposite sides of a very awkward situation.

Pat was a magnet for the curious stares of practically everyone in the room, but seemed unaware of it, staring morosely at the soup and salad combo she'd chosen. "This was a waste of food. I'm really hungry, but I don't have any appetite."

"At least try the soup before it cools off," he suggested, waiting until she'd downed a couple of spoonsful, her face taut with anxiety.

"Hey, Chief." A young blond woman in a Harland Industries uniform stopped at their table. "Excuse me for interrupting, but I wanted to thank you for dropping off my paycheck." Her eyes flicked toward Pat, then away. "Corey's all right, is he?"

"Corey's fine, at camp, having a ball. I just came back from there yesterday. But the next check of yours I find, I keep. Say hello to Bubba for me."

"Sure will. And thanks again, Chief."

He turned his attention back to Pat. "How's the soup?"

"Good, but..." The spoon trembled in her hand and she put it down. "Adam, what happened to Lib? A heart attack?"

He hedged. "Possibly. We'll know for sure after the post-mortem."

"Poor Lib." She sighed. "Poor Hetty. They were so close."

"So I've heard," Adam said. "Isn't that kind of unusual? Employer and cook? How long had Miss Hetty worked at the mansion?"

She tried another spoonful of soup, then pushed the bowl away. "All told, maybe thirty years. She left for a while, took courses to become a nursing assistant, something she'd always wanted to do. She got her certificate in 1978, I think it was."

"But—" Adam performed some mental arithmetic. "She'd have been in her sixties then."

"Right. I was so proud of her. She worked at the Ashland Nursing Home and didn't go back to the mansion until after C.J.'s mother died. Lib's arthritis had gotten so bad that she needed full-time help, which she couldn't seem to keep. Hetty offered to fill in until Lib could find the next hapless soul, and never left."

"Then I guess it was only natural that Miss Hetty would begin cooking for her again."

"It was only natural once she and the cook fought about the fats and sugar in the meals the lady prepared for Lib." She chuckled, a warm, throaty sound that derailed Adam's train of thought once again. "The cook got insulted and left, and Hetty took over."

"I see. So there were just the three of them in the house—Miss Harland, Miss Hetty, and the housekeeper, Lorna Forsythe."

"Right."

Pat began the salad with slightly more vigor as Adam thought over what he'd learned. All things considered, it wasn't much. "How long have you known Miss Harland?"

"Since I was thirteen." She put down her fork, placing it on the tray with more deliberation than he thought the action warranted. "Would I be able to hear a page from outside?" she asked abruptly. "I need to feel some sun."

Adam glanced through the tinted double doors that opened onto an outdoor eating area behind them. He could see heat devils levitating above the metal tables, even from this distance. But if it would keep the flow of conversation going, he'd put up with a little perspiration. She was worth it. "Sure. Lead the way. I'll bring your tray."

"Thanks, I've had enough." She picked up her glass of iced tea, slung the strap of her attaché case over her shoulder and hurried outside. She had her choice of seating. With the temperature in the upper eighties, most people preferred air-conditioned comfort.

Adam followed Pat to a corner where the overhang of an upper floor bathed half of one table with shade. She took a chair on the exposed side, her case in her lap, and sat, eyes closed, her face lifted to the sun. He opted for shadow, and sat opposite her, mesmerized by the way sunlight brushed her skin with a patina of gold. A series of idle thoughts meandered through his consciousness, sneaking up on him before he could squelch them, images of moonlight dusting her face with a silver sheen, or candlelight painting it with patterns of copper and flame.

"This feel wonderful," she said. "I just left Seattle. Two straight days of gray skies and drizzle. It reminded me of London just before spring."

"London." Adam slumped low in his chair and extended his long legs, crossing his ankles. "Sounds as if you've done a lot of globe-trotting."

"With my parents. Dad was career army."

"Which one of them was from the Grove?" he asked.

"Both. You can't tell by looking at me?" She managed a smile that wrapped itself around his heart. "They're home-grown products so they sent me to live with Hetty while Dad was stationed in Korea."

"And you've kept in close touch with her ever since," he prompted, deciding it was time they got back on the subject, which had somehow taken a back seat to his interest in her. "How did you and Miss Harland become such buddies?"

Her expression softened. "I'd go by the mansion after school every day to wait for Hetty to finish making dinner, and Lib would be in the kitchen dishing dirt with her. When she discovered how much I loved to read, she loaned me a few of her books and eventually turned me loose in the mansion's fantastic library. By the time I left, we were pretty close.''

"How long did you live in the Grove?''

"Three years.'' She blinked and something happened behind her eyes, shuttering her thoughts. They were just as lovely as before, almond-shaped, a clear, dark brown, but the sparkle was muted, the humor gone. "By then Dad was stationed in England. I finished high school there. It occurs to me,'' she said, picking up her iced tea, "how did you happen to be at the mansion this morning?''

Adam wondered if the abrupt change of subject was intentional. "C.J.'s expecting a mob for the funeral. A couple of the ladies on H.I.'s cafeteria staff volunteered to help with the cooking and I gave them a ride to the mansion.''

Pat groaned. "Oh, God. The funeral. I guess I'll have to go. Does the Buick dealer still rent cars?''

He couldn't contain his bemused expression. "You have a lot to catch up on. Bill Grimes went out of business years ago. I wouldn't worry about it. People will be falling all over themselves to give you a ride.''

Her features seemed to cool. "I doubt that. I'll go back to the airport later and try for a rental again. There wasn't a single car available when I got in. Some sort of big convention in Charlotte. God!'' she exclaimed suddenly. "How much longer are they going to keep Hetty in Radiology? When can I see her?''

Adam had enough experience with people nearing their breaking point to recognize that Pat's wasn't far away. "Let me go see what I can find out. Maybe I can call in a favor or two.'' He rarely used his position as chief of police as a crowbar. There was really little justification for it now, besides wanting to do what he could to relieve the anguish in her eyes. He wanted to see them laugh as they did in the photograph. Or had that been a trick of the camera? He would be disappointed if it was, since that was one of the things that had intrigued him most.

Once in the cafeteria, he saw there'd be no need to go any further. Jim Vernon, counting out change to pay for the coffee he'd just bought, had spotted him, a finger raised to snag

Adam's attention. He looked tired, with pouches under his eyes the size of garment bags. Adam, however, suspected Jim had probably been born looking like a tired old man. All it took was a hint of his quick wit and the lively interest in his blue eyes to realize that his mind was far from fatigued.

"Can't talk now," he began when they met halfway. "Gotta find Hetty's niece, but—"

"Out there on the patio." Adam pointed. "What's the problem with Miss Hetty?"

Jim peered through the tinted doors. "Be damned. She really grew into a gorgeous woman. Hope she hasn't changed much otherwise. She was a nice kid."

"She seems to be a nice woman, too," Adam said, opting for understatement. "What about Miss Hetty?"

"I'm obligated to tell her first, but don't get lost. We've got to talk."

"About what?"

"It'll keep. Let me go tell Patty the bad news." He strode toward the exit to the patio.

Adam wavered. If Jim had bad news for Pat, he wanted to be there. He couldn't seem to forget the air of vulnerability and isolation she'd exuded upstairs before he'd gone over to introduce himself. If she needed moral support now, he might be able to help. Granted, she wasn't exactly a stranger to the town, but since she hadn't had a chance to hook up with anyone she'd known....

"Chief, you okay?"

Startled, Adam gazed into the puzzled face of one of the Dabney boys, and realized he'd been standing in the middle of the cafeteria staring into space. "I'm fine. Just thinking, that's all."

About Pat Chase, he chided himself, instead of Hetty Melton. He was intensely interested in whatever Jim had to say about the old lady, yet it was Pat who'd been uppermost on his mind. It had been years since the thought of a particular woman had interfered with his job. The last time the lady in question had been a journalist, and she had spelled trouble. He had the sinking feeling that Pat Chase would, too.

Pat had watched Adam leave, fascinated by the ease with which he moved, shoulders straight, his gait smooth and even. Like Dad, she thought, closing her eyes against the glare of the sun. There was a sense of authority about him, of being in control, much as her father had been. Perhaps that was why she felt so comfortable with Adam from the start. She was willing to bet he'd spent more than one tour of duty in the service. Now that she reflected on it, she realized that she'd spent the last half hour talking about Hetty and Lib and herself and had learned nothing at all about him.

He seemed well liked, considering the number of people who'd nodded or spoken to him between the elevator and the cafeteria. Probably an upstanding pillar of the community with a half dozen crumb snatchers who looked just like him and the Grove girl he'd married. Trying to guess which of her schoolmates welcomed him home each night, Pat experienced a stab of envy and recoiled from it in astonishment. She'd fallen in love twice in her adult life, had considered marriage with both men, but had been unable to imagine herself in the company of either of them around the clock. She'd never met a man who'd made her think: Lord, put me on a deserted island with this one. *Please*. Until now. The mental picture of Adam Wyatt in a loincloth, or even better, without one, set off hot flashes that sent her scrambling for a tissue, napkin, anything with which to fan herself.

Well, a little erotic daydreaming never hurt anyone, but that's all it would ever be. Even if by some stroke of luck he was unattached, he could keep his eligible status, as far as she was concerned. He lived in the Grove. Love might conquer all in fairy tales and romances, but it would never triumph over her gut-deep hatred of Harland Grove.

The door opened behind her. "Patty?"

Pat looked back over her shoulder at the lanky figure loping toward her and recognized him immediately. "You're..." She struggled for the names of her former classmates. "The twins' father. Valerie and Vicki."

"My one claim to fame." Dr. Vernon stopped before her as she got to her feet, looking her over. He seemed pleased with what he saw. "We didn't think you'd come." His hair was now completely white but his eyes were as blue as she remembered, his smile still as gentle.

"It's nice to see you again," Pat said, registering mild surprise that she meant it. "Please, how's Hetty? What's wrong with her?"

"Sit down," he said, waiting until she was seated before collapsing in the chair on her left. After removing the lid from his coffee cup, he took a sip and replaced the lid again. "I haven't had a chance to see the results of all of the tests I ordered, but I didn't want you left hanging any longer. Hetty's had a stroke."

The news hit Pat with the force of a body block, the last of her hope that this might be a false alarm, or at most, nothing serious, shattering like fine crystal on cement. There was no question now of hopping a plane back to D.C. in a couple of days. Hetty would need her. And she would stay. She was stuck.

Chapter 2

"How bad was it?" Pat asked, only subliminally aware of Adam joining them. Her voice was hoarse with fear.

"Generally, she's stable now. But there's some hemiplegia and—"

"English, please," she interrupted.

"Sorry. Right side weakness, perhaps some damage to her language center. We'll know a lot more after the swelling in her brain has subsided. How old is Hetty, or do you know?"

"She'll be seventy-nine in August."

He grimaced. "Well, she was a healthy seventy-eight-year-old, so there's one positive aspect in her favor. It's possible she can make a full recovery, but I suspect she's in for a long haul. She's going to need all the support she can get, Patty. She'll get it from us. My question is, will she get it from you?"

Adam shifted uneasily, leaning forward as if to rise. "Maybe I should leave so the two of you can talk."

Pat's response was abrupt, betraying her anger at the question. "We are talking. Hetty will get whatever she needs from me," she said to the physician. "How could you ask that?"

"Think about it, Patty. This is the first time you've been here in—what's it been, fifteen, sixteen years? And I suspect that if this hadn't happened, you wouldn't be here now."

"You're right. I wouldn't be." Determined to confront the subject head-on, she met his gaze, her eyes boring into his. "But it has happened. I'm here. And I'll be here for the long haul, as you put it. Does that tell you what you want to know?"

"Possibly."

Adam stood. "Look, I've got a couple of calls to make. Don't worry, I'll be back." That interjectory appeared to be for Dr. Vernon's benefit. "Can I bring you something, Pat? Another iced tea?"

Warmed by his consideration, Pat managed a smile. "No, thanks for asking."

"Sure." He returned her smile along with a chin-up gesture, and left.

"Patty," Dr. Vernon said, "I want to be clear. When I say Hetty's in for a lengthy period of recuperation, I'm talking in terms of months."

Months in Harland Grove. Pat's breath whistled between her teeth, her resolve beginning to ebb. "There are excellent hospitals in D.C. As soon as she can be moved, I'll take her back with me."

His expression was disapproving. "I'd advise against it. Hetty will have enough to adjust to without the added stress of an alien environment."

"My apartment is hardly an alien environment to Hetty," Pat countered, her irritation barely contained. "She's come to stay with me twice a year for the last eight years."

"Knowing she would eventually be going back to her home, her bed, where she could look out of her window and see her trees, her garden. And don't go off and buy yourself a house up there, because that's not the point. It would still be your house, not hers. Not home. Don't do that to her, Patty. She's an old lady. Let her stay around the things she knows."

"I'll leave it up to her," Pat responded, refusing to back down out of sheer desperation. "If she'll go, that will simplify matters for me. If she prefers to stay here, so be it. I'll be with her until she doesn't need me any longer."

Dr. Vernon's craggy face relaxed. "Good." He rose, carefully balancing his cup. "I'd better get back inside. Give us another half hour and then come on up to her room. As soon as we have a clearer picture of the damage, the staff in charge of whatever therapy she needs will arrange a conference with you to go over her regimen and how you might be able to help."

"Good. I look forward to that." Pat stood and offered her hand. "Thank you, Dr. Vernon. By the way, I didn't realize you were Hetty's doctor."

"I wasn't, but Don Trent retired a couple of years ago. Moved to Alabama. Now I'm everybody's doctor. If you'd prefer someone else . . ."

"No. You've known her for a long time. That carries a lot of weight."

"Fine. Smile, Patty, and keep smiling. Don't let Hetty see how upset you are."

"I'll try."

"That's all I could ask." He turned away, then hesitated. "It occurs to me that you might prefer to be called Honor now."

She started with surprise. "Oh, you've seen the show. Honor's strictly my on-camera persona," she said, explaining her alter ego. She didn't want to think about what this might mean to her job, at least not yet. "Pat—or Patty—will be fine. And so will Hetty."

A smile erased a little of the fatigue from his features. "You haven't changed. I'm glad." With that, he left with the loping walk she remembered.

Alone, her mask of determined optimism began to crack. Hetty had been healthy for so long she'd seemed indomitable. Or perhaps, Pat mused, it had been easier not to deal with the reality of Hetty's advancing age. That had been foolish, she saw now. She'd been ill prepared for the inevitable.

And Hetty. How would she cope? Pat's mind flooded with the image of Hetty, her long white braids flying, flour up to her elbows as she slipped a pan of bread dough into the oven. Hetty on her knees in her garden, her smooth caramel complexion damp with perspiration, swearing a blue streak at the bugs on her tomatoes. Would she ever be as active again? Could she live with a future that precluded a Saturday afternoon of baking for

Sunday church suppers? Would she even want to go to church, knowing she could no longer teach the senior citizens' Sunday School class?

For the first time Pat began to consider what she knew of Hetty's day-to-day activities and how many of them might have to come to an end. It made for a bleak picture. Add Lib's death and by Hetty's lights, there would be little motivation to fight back. She had to feel needed. I need her, Pat thought. Hetty was all she had left, the only remaining link to her immediate family. But would that be enough for Hetty?

"Pat."

She looked up to find Adam at her elbow, with no idea how long he'd been there.

"How are you?" he asked.

"Middlin'," she said, past faking for his benefit. "Just thinking, trying to plan. There's so much to consider..."

"It may not be as much of a problem as you think." He pulled up the nearest chair, angling it close to her. "Hope you don't mind, but I called the head of the Sunshine Club and... You know who they are, don't you?"

"The church group who rally round in time of need," Pat said, thoroughly distracted by the cat's whisper of space between his knee and hers. "Hetty's been a member for years."

"Right. Everything's all set. The two of you won't be going through this alone."

"Oh?" Pat hoped the question didn't betray how much she doubted she could count on anyone in Harland Grove for anything.

"You're on your own for breakfasts, but someone will deliver lunch and dinner every day, so you won't have to worry about cooking. Laundry, either. They'll take turns washing Miss Hetty's gowns. And they're working out a schedule of available drivers who will provide you with transportation, so that whenever you'd like to see Miss Hetty, all you have to do is call."

Pat stared at him and wondered how to phrase her question. "You told them I had come? By name?"

It was Adam's turn for a baffled expression. "Of course. They'll do everything except take care of the lawn, and I'll tend to that until Corey comes home from camp."

That was the second time she'd heard that name. "Corey?"

"My son," Adam said. "He's only nine, but he wields a mean lawn mower."

The fact that she'd guessed right about his familial state almost—but not quite—took a back seat to her astonishment at the response of Hetty's friends and neighbors. It had never occurred to her that she'd be on the receiving end of this kind of support from the people of the Grove. That, she concluded after a bit of thought, was only because their purpose was to help Hetty. If Hetty needed her infamous grand-niece at her side to speed her recovery, they'd see that nothing stood in the way of her getting there.

Adam's puzzled frown reminded her that she had yet to respond. "Thank you so much, Adam. I appreciate your getting in touch with them. But I can do the lawn and garden. You'll be tired after working an eight-hour shift."

"Twelve-hour," he corrected her with a wry smile, "but I said I'll do it, so I'll do it."

"All right, all right." Pat held up her hands, admitting defeat. "Are you always this nice to people you've just met?"

"No. I'm not," he said, meeting her gaze with an intensity she found unsettling.

Flustered, Pat gathered her belongings. "I'd better get up to Hetty's room. I want to be there when she arrives."

"Of course. I'm headed in that direction myself." He walked her back through the cafeteria, his hand cupped around her elbow, a gesture she found more intimate than chivalrous.

As they waited for the elevator, he focused on the floor indicator above the door. "Okay if I check with you in a while, to see how Miss Hetty's doing? And you'll need a ride. I'll be glad to run you into town, unless there's someone else you'd planned to call." He lowered his head abruptly, his eyes scanning her features, this time without the clinical detachment she'd witnessed when they'd met upstairs.

"There's no one. Thanks very much. I'd appreciate it."

"My pleasure," he said solemnly as the elevator arrived.

To Pat's relief, they were not alone during the short trip to the third floor. She homed in on the toes of her sandals, unable to sort through her jumble of emotions—concern for Hetty, apprehension for both their futures, dread at the prospect of an indefinite stay in the Grove, a leaden disappointment that Adam was both husband and father, and disgust that she was disappointed to begin with. It made no sense, especially as, aside from Hetty, she wanted nothing to do with anyone from Harland Grove.

The elevator eased to a halt. When the doors slid apart, Adam stepped into the opening, his back against the rubber guard edging the door until everyone was out.

"You've been really great," Pat said in farewell. "Thanks again for everything."

"Any time." The warmth in his voice matched that in his eyes.

Pat stopped breathing and backed away from him, unmindful of the hazard of a collision with passersby.

"Let me know when you're ready to leave," he said. "I'll be around."

Got to get a rental P.D.Q., Pat decided, as she hurried around the nurses' station toward B Wing. Much more time in Adam's company and she'd be a blithering idiot.

"Oh, Ms. Chase."

Pat looked back over her shoulder to see Ms. Maxwell, the baby-faced nurse, beckoning to her. Adam, on the far side of the station, hesitated.

"Yes?"

"Dr. Vernon's in the conference room at the end of this hall." She gestured toward the other wing. "He needs to talk to you."

Torn, Pat glanced down the hall of B. "Is my aunt in her room yet?"

"On her way, but Dr. Vernon asked that you see him as soon as you got on the floor."

"Is something wrong?" Pat's voice was edged with panic, especially as Ms. Maxwell seemed to be avoiding eye contact.

"I'm sorry, I wouldn't know."

"Come on," Adam urged, rounding the desk to take her arm. "I'll show you where he is."

Her pulse pounding, Pat allowed herself to be escorted in the direction opposite the tug of her heart. Had Hetty taken a turn for the worse? Or died? She must be alive, she assured herself, or they wouldn't bring her up here. Perhaps Dr. Vernon had more bad news. Suddenly Adam's gentle pressure on her arm seemed to be the only thing holding her up.

At the end of the wing, Adam tapped at a door marked Conference Room A—Staff Only, and ushered her in, then stepped back outside a diplomatic few inches, leaving the door ajar. Dr. Vernon, on the far side of a sleek, rosewood conference table, looked up from the folder in front of him.

"What's wrong?" Pat blurted.

"Hetty's fine," he said quickly, his face saying otherwise. "At least, no change. But I wanted to catch you in time. Patty, I'm sorry, but Hetty doesn't want to see you."

A moment of mental confusion passed before that registered. "What?"

"It's probably nothing to do with you. There are stages most patients facing a disability go through. One of the first is being self-centered and chewing on self-pity for a while. Her pride has been damaged, perhaps worse than her body. And, as I mentioned, there is a problem with her ability to communicate, but—"

Adam's diplomatic withdrawal ended. He stepped into the room and closed the door. "What kind of problem?"

"Call it a short circuit in the brain that causes nonsense words to be substituted for the ones she means to use. Sometimes it's temporary. We'll have to wait and see. But she's managed to make herself perfectly clear on this point. No visitors...you included, Patty. She probably doesn't want you to see her in her present condition. She needs time to accept what's happened to her and to regain her fighting spirit. Right now she's pretty low. And we have to remember, she's still in mourning for Lib."

"But—" Pat began.

"I know how badly you need to see her, but my first obligation is to her and her health, physical and mental. I don't want her upset, so I'm obliged to honor her request, for the time being anyway."

"Jim, how long is the time being?" Adam's face seemed taut, his expression somber.

"As long as it takes. I'm hoping a few days, but if it's longer, so be it. Her therapy will begin, visitors or no, but in this early stage, she gets what she wants. Why do you ask?"

"Because she has vital information I need. She wasn't exactly cooperative this morning."

Pat stared at him in confusion, wondering if there was something she'd missed.

"Whatever you need to know will have to wait. And I wouldn't make too much of her reaction this morning," Dr. Vernon said. "She was already under a great deal of stress about Lib. Then you and Bo show up flashing your badges, asking what Lib had to eat and drink before she died. What did you expect?"

Astonishment exploded in Pat's mind, the blast shaking her to the core. "Flashing your badge?" Pat asked, incredulous. "You're a *cop?*"

"Didn't he tell you?" Dr. Vernon's chest swelled with proprietary pride. "Adam is our chief of police. We were lucky to get him."

Adam leaned against the closed door, arms folded. "Granted, the subject of my job never came up, but what did you think I did?"

She glared at him. "I thought you worked at H.I. like everyone else. You said you were at the mansion because you'd given a ride to some ladies on the cafeteria staff."

"I did—as a favor for my next door neighbor. She's the manager of the cafeteria."

Pat realized that the mistake had been her own. She'd been so wrapped up in her own concerns that she hadn't given him a chance to tell her anything about himself. But her anger at feeling she'd been deceived was not allayed. Then, belatedly, Dr. Vernon's defense of Hetty registered. She turned to look at him. "Did Libby die of food poisoning?"

"Don't answer that!" Adam's voice rang with command. "Effective today, this has become an official investigation. Nobody talks to anyone about this without my approval."

Pat, still putting two and two together, finally arrived at the correct answer. "In other words, you weren't just talking to Hetty this morning. You were *questioning* her!"

A mask of implacability dropped over his face. "In my official capacity, yes."

"Your official capacity? I know more than a little about the Grove's police department when it comes to their methods of interrogation," Pat said, slowly losing a grip on her temper. "Did you and—what was his name, Bo?—browbeat that poor old lady?"

Adam's demeanor changed immediately, his nostrils flaring with anger. "Now wait just a damned minute—"

"Did you play good cop, bad cop? Which were you? Mr. Tough Guy? You asked what Lib had eaten . . . ? My God, did you make Hetty think that something she had prepared killed Lib? Is that why she suffered a stroke? You *bastard!*"

"Now, Pat," Dr. Vernon intervened quickly, trying to diffuse a rapidly deteriorating situation. "That's not fair. Adam wouldn't operate that way. Besides, you have to remember, Hetty's suffered with hypertension for years."

"And it's been under control for years," Pat said in rebuttal. "Sure, Lib's death would affect her blood pressure temporarily, but if Adam even hinted that food she'd fixed for Lib caused her death, that's all it would take to blow it sky-high. My God, she must think she killed her dearest friend!"

"Pat." Dr. Vernon placed a gentle hand on her arm. "Lib did not die of food poisoning."

"Damn it, Jim!" Adam exploded, crossing to the table.

"It's important she knows that." Pat moved quickly to the door. "I'm going to see that one of the nurses tells her the truth right now, and short of putting me in jail, Adam Wyatt, which would be old hat for me in this burg, there's nothing you can do to stop me. I won't have her lying there thinking she killed Lib. You stay away from her or I'll see to it that you won't be chief of anything. And if you don't think I can, try me, buddy!"

* * *

Adam shut the door and stared at it as if he could still see Pat's image in its teak veneer. He wasn't sure at whom he was angrier, Pat or Jim. After a mental toss of a coin, Pat won. He'd always put great stock in his ability to size up a person within a couple of minutes and Pat had just shredded that stock into confetti. Not half an hour ago, he'd been thinking that she was one dynamite lady, certainly one of the most attractive women he'd met in a long time.

He turned on his friend. "Damn it, Jim, how could you hang me out to dry like that? Not only does she know food poisoning has been ruled out, which even *I* didn't know, now she believes I grilled that old lady until she had a stroke. And what was that shot about our interrogational tactics and having been in our jail before?"

Jim scrubbed long fingers across his face and lowered himself into his chair again. "Well, I'd always discounted the rumors, you know what it's like in a town the size of ours, but I guess this time they weren't just talk." He lapsed into a contemplative silence.

Adam waited and when nothing else seemed forthcoming, demanded, "Are you going to tell me today, or should I go on home and check in with you tomorrow?"

"Oh. Well. I don't know the whole story, but it seems that the last year Pat stayed with Hetty, she got herself arrested. The next I knew, she was gone, and no one seemed willing to talk about it."

"What had she done?"

"I never heard. I do know that Margaret—C.J.'s mother—was involved, because Hetty left the mansion and wouldn't put foot in the place until after Margaret died. And this is the first time Pat's been in the Grove since."

Adam dropped into a chair. "Whatever happened sure as hell left her with an attitude about police, which..." He scowled at Jim. "... You did nothing to change. Damn it, I did *not* browbeat Miss Hetty."

Jim eyed him speculatively. "I know what your problem is. You really aren't sure whether you caused her stroke. My professional opinion is that the shock of finding Lib's body probably set things in motion. If I'd been around yesterday, I could have taken some precautions against this. But I wasn't. I was whoopin' it up at a stupid class reunion.''

Adam peered at him. "Looks like I'm not the only one with a guilty conscience. And enough's enough. I'm a professional. I treated that old lady as gently as I could, no matter what her hot-tempered niece cares to think."

"Don't judge her by that blowup," Jim said. "It was a purely emotional reaction. She loves Hetty, and, I'd guess, would be relieved to find a reason for the inexplicable. That's what the stroke is to her. When she uses her head, she's smart as a whip, and damned good at what she does. Watch her broadcasts and you'd agree."

Adam came erect. "What broadcasts?"

"You haven't seen them? The 'Honor Bound' spots every Wednesday on—"

"That Public Television network show, *Current Events*," Adam growled, furious at himself for not remembering sooner. "Honor Melton. I *knew* I'd seen her somewhere before. She's a damned reporter!"

Jim shook his head firmly. "Come on, Adam, that's selling her short. She's a journalist and an advocate. She intercedes on behalf of anyone who's been taken advantage of or treated shabbily and can't get satisfaction. She's the reason the '88 Jiffy Bug was recalled."

"Give me a break," Adam said, unconvinced.

"No kidding. Some college kid who'd had an accident and wound up a paraplegic because the seat belt gave way wrote her for help. The lawsuit he'd filed had been dismissed and he wanted justice. Patty tracked down a couple of dozen people whose seat belts had popped loose. The company recalled the buggy and settled a healthy sum on the college kid. When she gets her teeth into a cause, she's a holy terror."

"All right, she's effective," Adam conceded, "but at bottom she's still just a reporter going after a story."

Jim lifted his chin, as if peering at him through the bottom half of bifocals. "Ah. I forgot. Your wife was a journalist. But that was different. She worked for a newspaper."

"Doesn't matter. They're all the same, a distinct breed. The story's all that matters. Christ, did I have her pegged wrong."

"And still do." Jim hoisted one brow. "I find that very interesting."

Adam, scowling at him, stood up. "Forget her. Any news about the autopsy. What killed the subject?"

"The subject has a name, damn it!" Jim slammed his hand against the table, his blue eyes flashing fire. "Elizabeth Harland, a woman I'd known all my life. She was the best Harland of the lot and I refuse to let you reduce her to—" He stopped, a startled expression on his face. "Oh, God, I'm sorry. I knew I was tired, but . . ."

"No." Adam reached across the table and squeezed his shoulder. "I'm sorry. Consider it the automatic reflex of a former homicide detective."

Jim was still chagrined. "That doesn't excuse my outburst. It was just . . . well, hearing Lib labeled a subject."

"I know it sounded cold, but . . ." Adam searched for the right words. "When you deal with violent death day in and day out as I have, the official gobbledygook becomes a protective device, a—a buffer to help put some distance between yourself and the victim. Even more so when it's someone you knew."

Jim nodded. "M.D.'s do the same thing sometimes. And I owe you another apology. You were right to be suspicious. I stopped by the county coroner's office after morning rounds. That's why I was late getting here. The autopsy won't be performed until tomorrow, maybe the next day. They're short-handed and really backed up."

"Damn," Adam muttered.

"However, the assistant who checked Lib in said a couple of things you should know. This is strictly from a visual examination, understand, but according to him—and I agree—Lib didn't die in bed. Postmortem lividity indicates that she was lying on her side on a hard surface. There are imprints, a diamond-shaped pattern, some with what look like flowers in the middle, on her left arm and calf."

"The bathroom floor," Adam said immediately. "Pink and white tile, a few with flowers. So she was moved."

"Yes. She may have slipped and fallen, but that didn't kill her. But why the hell would anyone move her?"

"A good question." Adam paced in a circle. "That sort of eliminates Miss Hetty, unless she had help. I don't like it."

"Perhaps someone found her, thought she'd hurt herself and carried her to the bed. But why wouldn't they have called an ambulance?"

Adam shook his head. "That doesn't wash. She had to have been there a good while for the pattern of the tile to etch itself against her skin that way. Besides, Bo said rigor had begun. Whoever moved her knew she was dead. Damn it, I wish I'd gotten there before they'd taken her away."

"Of all times for both of us to be out of town. So now what?"

"We wait for the postmortem," Adam said. "And I begin trying to find out who moved her and why. By the way, keep that under your hat. Don't tell anyone, not even C.J. I'm serious, Jim."

"You have my word. Well, let me get to Hetty's test results. I'm not sure she's going to survive this, Adam. What I told Patty about the stages a stroke victim may go through was gospel, but what I got from Hetty was different. I honestly don't think she wants to live."

"She's that low?" He looked away in thought. Perhaps Pat's concern about the argument between the two old friends had merit. It might explain the impression he'd gotten that she was holding something back. Or it might not. He would have expected one kind of reaction if she had a guilty conscience about her spat with Miss Harland, but not the kind of stonewalling she'd done. Something else was going on there. He had to find out what and to hell with Pat Chase.

The sign on the door was very clear: No visitors. It was several minutes before all the nurses were occupied with patients and the desk clerk had her back turned. Pat slipped into the darkened room, her mouth sandpaper dry.

Except for her long white braids, Hetty Melton might have been mistaken for a child, her five foot frame barely raising a lump beneath the covers. Her eyes were closed.

"Hetty?" Pat was relieved that her face, at least, bore no signs of the stroke. She was pale, missing the rich cinnamon that normally colored her brown complexion, but other than that, she looked much the same as the last time she'd been in Washington, younger than her years, her smooth skin barely lined. Someone had unpinned her braids and they trailed along her shoulders.

Her eyes, far darker than those of her niece, opened. "Patty."

"I know you said you didn't want to see me," Pat said quickly, "but I found out something I wanted you to know."

Curiosity creased her brow. "What?"

"Lib did not die of food poisoning. Dr. Vernon told me. You had nothing to do with her death. I didn't want you thinking you were responsible.

"Progion. My fault." She seemed to be struggling with her words. "Killed her."

Pat's mouth went dry. "Hetty, you can't mean that."

"Stroke . . . punishment from . . ." She pointed skyward.

Pat frowned. "What?"

"She wouldn't reckish . . . just wouldn't reckish," she said, becoming agitated. "So I tizo corplin."

It was heartrending. Pat groaned to herself as Hetty prattled on, using words that defied translation. It was clear she wasn't aware of the severity of her problem. It was also obvious that she had a great weight on her conscience. Pat, in agony for her, was thoroughly frustrated at her own inability to fathom what Hetty was trying to relay.

"Sinned cawthorn. Got to pay," Hetty said finally, and turned her head away. "Go home, Patty." A solitary tear slid from her left eye and trickled across her temple into her hairline.

"Hetty—"

"Leave be! Got to . . . rone peace with my God."

Pat felt a flicker of panic. "Stop talking like that. Having a stroke is not God's punishment for anything. It just happened. Dr. Vernon says it'll take a lot of work, but you can recover from this, and I'll be here with you until you do."

"No. Judgment. Go home."

Pat moved around to the other side of the bed and knelt so she could look into Hetty's eyes. "Don't you give up on me, Hetty Melton. I'm not going to let you. I'm not letting you off the hook."

"Who are you?" A nurse Pat had not met stood in the doorway, her face stormy with consternation. "Leave, please. Doctor's orders. No visitors."

Hetty nodded, pulled the covers to her chin again and closed her eyes.

Pat fished under the sheet, found Hetty's hand and squeezed it. "I'll be back. You stood by me. It's my turn to stand by you. I'll be back."

Hetty did not respond.

The nurse spoke louder. "Either you leave, ma'am, or I call security."

"I love you, Hetty," Pat whispered. She kissed an ear, the only part of her great-aunt she could reach, and left the room, her thoughts in turmoil. She had to go to Hetty's, sit down, figure out what to do. Getting into town, however, turned out to be more difficult than she imagined.

Harland Grove no longer had a cab company. Referred to one in Leland, the next nearest community, she received no answer. According to the volunteer at the reception desk, one from the airport would require a forty-five minute wait. With no other option and feeling much put-upon, Pat wrote down the number.

"How much is a toll call to the airport?" she asked the receptionist.

"Forty cents," a now-familiar voice responded.

She swiveled to find Adam behind her, his face as unyielding as stone. He was still angry. Well, so was she, with herself. Granted, the accusations she'd hurled at him had been based on her reading of the situation Hetty had faced this morning, but it didn't end there. It had also been an emotional reaction to the revelation that Adam was a member of Harland Grove's finest and therefore firmly in the enemy camp. That she'd been attracted to him, drawn by the warmth and consideration he'd shown her—to say nothing of his blatant masculinity—made her that much angrier.

Still, she'd accused him of something he hadn't done. Fortified by a deep breath, Pat said, "I owe you an apology. I was wrong, and I'm sorry."

His pupils dilated in surprise, which Pat found gratifying. It was obviously the last thing he'd expected. He thawed a little. "Apology accepted." There was an awkward silence before he asked, "Were you able to see Miss Hetty?"

"I sneaked in. Dr. Vernon's right. She might as well be speaking in Martian."

"You couldn't understand her at all?"

"Only about a quarter of what she said. The rest I guessed at and I can't be sure I guessed right."

His eyes filled with regret. "I'm really sorry, Pat. Let's hope therapy will help. Are you ready to go?"

It was Pat's turn to be surprised. She had assumed she'd blown the offer of a ride. "Yes. And thank you."

"No problem. I'm parked outside the Emergency entrance." He removed the weekender from her hand and walked away.

Chapter 3

A heavy, tension-laden silence enveloped the interior of the car for the first couple of miles. Pat, now flooded with second thoughts, regretted her decision to accept the ride, since it hadn't occurred to her that Adam might be driving a police cruiser. At least she wasn't in the back seat like the last time. Unfortunately there were some convincing arguments against riding in front. It encapsulated her with Adam, sealed them off from the outside world, making her, at least, far too conscious of his proximity to her. She could almost feel the heat of his body, and his cologne, clean, crisp, soap-scented, was generating heat of a different sort in her.

Adam's voice punctured the balloon of silence. "What happens to your job if you stay until your aunt has recovered? Won't you be breaking your contract with the station?"

So he'd finally remembered where he'd seen her before. Or perhaps Dr. Vernon had filled him in. She wondered what else the good doctor might have told him. "Actually, my contract is with the syndicate that produces the program. And I could work from practically any place. All I need is my laptop and a phone. My research assistant can anchor the spot. Milt's subbed for me before. If that doesn't satisfy the front office, we'll have to renegotiate my contract, or cancel it. Hetty comes first.''

"I see." He asked no more questions, assuming, she supposed, that the subject was closed, which was just as well, because the mention of her aunt's name had propelled Pat, body and soul, back to B Wing, with Hetty's words etching themselves across her heart: *Killed her.* Hetty was incapable of deliberately harming anyone, but what could have happened to make her feel she should take the blame?

Suddenly the passing countryside had an air of the familiar. "That's the bridge over Ransom's Creek, isn't it?" she asked, recognizing her first landmark.

"That's right."

Pat had told herself for so long how much she hated the Grove, an easy task while she'd been hundreds of miles away. Now that she was here again, the amnesia that had blanked out the good times was already beginning to erode, for beyond the bridge they were crossing was Mr. Ransom's property, where she and Hetty had come to pick strawberries.

In an instant she was reliving her utter amazement at the sight and aroma of acres and acres of the lush red fruit, the first time she'd ever seen them outside a produce bin in a commissary. She would never forget Hetty's expression when she'd said that aloud. It had become an annual pilgrimage for them for three years. She hadn't been around for the fourth. That memory hurt, and it must have shown.

Adam asked with concern. "Something wrong?"

"No. Just remembering," she said, declining to elaborate.

"Tell me about your parents," he prompted after a minute. "Your father was Army, you said?"

"And how." The mention of Colonel John Ezra Chase resurrected the comparison she'd drawn between him and Adam. "I adored him, but it wasn't until he died that I realized he never got over the fact that he'd sired a daughter. The Chases *always* had boys. I was the first girl in four or five generations."

Adam whistled. "I bet they spoiled you rotten."

"Perhaps a little, but they spent most of their time prepping me to survive as an African-American woman, a Melton and a Chase."

He glanced at her, eyebrows raised. "Is that as heavy as it sounds?"

Pat gave a dry laugh. "I can handle being black and female, but let me tell you, I have a great deal of empathy with Prince Charles. By God, I know what it's like to grow up being told constantly what's expected of you because of your family name. As a Melton, I was supposed to be a straight-A student, active in every curricular activity I could squeeze into a twenty-four-hour day. I would be a professional—that's in caps, mind you—the more initials behind my name the better."

"And as a Chase?"

This time Pat chuckled with genuine mirth. "Poor Dad. He had to come up with an amended version of the Chase propaganda line."

"The what?"

"Come on, Adam. You should know by now that every family in the Grove has its own description to live up to. All the Holts are hard workers. All the Grants . . . well . . ."

Adam's rich laughter filled the car and warmed her blood. "All the Grants have an affinity for the grape. I see what you mean."

"With my father's family, it was all the Chases go into the military. My great-great-grandfather and his brothers set the precedent by escaping from the Harland plantation to fight for the North during the Civil War. Every male since has made the service a career. But because my dad was a chauvinist of the first water and didn't believe in women in the military, the best he could do was to revise the family motto and then stick me with a name that reflected the Chase ideals."

Adam frowned. "Patricia?"

"Patrice. Actually that's my middle name. My first is one of the watchwords of the Chases—honor. So here I am, Honor Patrice Melton Chase. No hyphen."

"You're kidding." A grin softened his features again.

"Hey, I'm not complaining. He could have named me Duty, that's the other watchword. Dad leaned hard on honor and duty to country and our people, and Mom leaned on how bright all the Meltons are, and I got caught in the middle, not quite living up to the expectations of either of them.''

Adam turned for a momentary glance at her. "Well, don't take it the wrong way, but you really don't impress me as the type who'd enjoy basic training.''

"I will have you know," she said with mock hauteur, "that I fully intended to become a Marine—"

"What?"

"I thought I could prove something and make Dad proud of me. Hetty made me realize I was being silly. She was the only one who seemed satisfied with who and what I really was. And she knew that wasn't what I wanted to do."

"You wanted to be a reporter."

"A writer," Pat corrected him. "I wanted to be a female Alex Haley and chronicle the accomplishments of my family. Hetty planted that seed in me."

"And living in the Grove."

"No," she said, her tone giving no quarter. "Just Hetty. The Grove had nothing to do with it. Although now that you mention it, my family's story is the story of the Grove and vice versa."

"See? Same difference." He made a left onto McConnell and drove the remaining few blocks in a pensive silence. When he slowed once again, turning left into the short driveway, Pat knew she couldn't avoid the past any longer. They had arrived at 1615.

Close by, a lawn mower growled and a dog barked, its voice shrill with excitement. Steeling herself, Pat looked up. Hetty's small frame house glistened like a pearl in the early evening sun, the forest-green shutters in stark contrast against the gleaming white siding. The boxwoods that nudged the railing of the front porch had been so recently manicured that cuttings still lay strewn at their roots. The grass had just been cut, the clippings scattered across the sidewalk.

Fifteen years had passed, yet little had changed. Marigolds still blazed in the window boxes. The pecan trees still stood sentinel in the deep rear yard, casting leafy shadows across the roof. And, as was the norm in the Grove, the front door stood open, the interior hidden by the dark mesh of the screen. Pat's throat began to ache.

Sliding from behind the wheel, Adam came around to help her out. "You don't look so hot."

"I'm fine. Just a case of acute nostalgia."

He removed her weekender and stood irresolutely. "Well..."

"Patty?" A graying head rose majestically above the hedges separating Hetty's property from the one to her right. Immediately a breach appeared between the bushes and a giant of a woman with skin the color of dark chocolate stepped through, sailing toward Pat under full steam. She was a Ransom and a Ransom, male or female, shorter than six feet tall was considered a runt. "Do Jesus!" she hooted. "It is you! Lord, child, welcome home! Ya'll!" she yelled back toward her house. "Get on out here! Our girl's come home!"

Before she could move, Pat found herself enthusiastically hugged, her nose buried in a more than ample bosom generously dusted with Chantilly talcum powder. "Hello, Miss Sarah," she said, her voice lost in the bottomless V of the woman's neckline.

Sarah Ransom pushed her back at arm's length. "Is it Honor now, or Patty?"

"Still Patty."

"That's my girl," she said with approval. "I declare, that camera don't do you justice. You're plumb beautiful. Why'd you cut all that long pretty hair?"

"That long pretty hair is sitting on a wig stand in my office," Pat confessed with no hesitation. "Off camera, I prefer it short. I didn't realize you saw the show down here." She'd been sending Hetty videotapes of her spots for the past two years.

"We got cable just like big city folk," Sarah boasted. "Mercy, you're so skinny! Us Sunshine girls will have to put some meat on those bones." A sudden creasing of her broad forehead put an end to her greeting. "How's Hetty? Everybody's so worried."

Given the speed of the Grove's grapevine, Pat was surprised her neighbor didn't already know. "She's had a stroke, Miss Sarah."

"Oh, God." After a second, Sarah swooped into her neckline, rooting around in its depths until a white handkerchief appeared. She wiped at the tears welling in her eyes. "Bad?" she asked.

"It could be worse, I guess." Pat told her as much as she knew, then had to repeat it as the yard began to fill with Ransoms and, from the other side of Hetty's, the Campbells, all of whom came only close enough to hear and no further.

Sarah took her hand and smoothed it with such vigor that Pat's skin began to burn from the friction. "Well, don't you worry. Hetty's gonna be just fine, and she won't lack for a thing. Whatever needs doing'll get done, like the lawn. One of my grandsons, Raymond, Junior, is cutting it for you now. Have you had supper yet?"

Pat hesitated, uncertain of the consequences no matter which response she gave.

"No, she hasn't," Adam answered for that.

"We'll fix that." Sarah patted her cheek. "You know you're welcome in my kitchen, but I've got a house full of grandbabies. They'd get on your last nerve, God knows they get on mine. You go on into your house and I'll be over with plates for you and the Chief."

Adam backed away. "Thanks, Mrs. Ransom, but—"

"But nothing. Can't have Patty eating by herself her first day home. I'd keep her company, but like I say, I got all them little people underfoot until Mary Grace and Tanya finish their shift at the plant. Shoo, y'all," she told the crowd. "You can come say hello another time. Be back directly, Patty." She turned and, parting the hedges, disappeared. The others scattered slowly, peering over their shoulders at Pat.

"Talk about forceful personalities," Adam said sotto voce.

Pat stared after her with a puzzled frown. "If I didn't know better, I'd almost believe she was glad to see me."

"Why wouldn't she be? Look Pat—" he placed her weekender on the porch steps "—you probably want some time to yourself. I'll just fade into the sunset before she gets back."

"No," Pat said. "Please. Unless you have something you need to do."

"Not a thing." Adam's eyes, looking down at her, seemed translucent in the sunset. "The truth is, I'm hungry as hell, but with Corey away, cooking for myself doesn't seem worth it. I miss him."

"Good. I mean—" She stopped, flustered. "I'm glad you can stay." Turning quickly, she headed for the house, afraid she'd say something else that wouldn't mean what she'd intended. So his wife wasn't around to fix his meals. Out of town? Separated? Divorced? What difference did it make? That was simple enough to answer. If he was someone's husband, it raised a wall between them, precisely what she needed at this point. God help her if he was divorced.

Opening the screen door, Pat went inside and felt her knees weaken as an aroma as familiar as the sound of her own breathing overwhelmed her. Hetty's house was scented with eucalyptus, several twigs of it in each dried floral arrangement in every room. How could she have forgotten that? And as with the exterior, little had changed. Ornate mahogany and cherry furniture, oak floors gleaming from endless Saturday polishings. Velvet burgundy sofa and chairs, lacy antimacassars on their arms and backs. It was the home of a person who had set up housekeeping decades before with pieces constructed to last.

Moving through the dining room, Pat took a moment to peer into the kitchen. So far, it was the only thing that showed its age; the appliances were the same as when she'd left and they'd been ten or fifteen years old even then. Glancing up, she noticed a big stain in the corner of the ceiling. Hetty must have a pretty bad leak. Pat made a mental note to have it checked.

She moved then into the hallway containing the two bedrooms. Hetty's door stood open, giving her a view of her spindle bed, dresser, chifforobe and rocking chair. It was a utilitarian room with no frills.

"All I do in here is sleep," Hetty had explained. "I want my nice things out where I spend my time and can see them." That meant the kitchen and dining room.

Pat smiled at the memory. Then knowing there was no point in putting it off, she bypassed the bathroom and opened the door of the room she had used as a teenager. It was precisely as she'd left it, dressed in the summer colors she'd chosen, frilly green and white Priscilla curtains, matching spread with green throw pillows. It was all still here, her high school paraphernalia, class photos, pom-poms, all the reminders of her successes. Her good days. And on the dresser, her jewelry box, a reminder of her one bad night and the treachery that had brought her golden years in the Grove to an end. The ache in her throat became unbearable. Reeling, she turned and stumbled from the room.

Adam waited just inside the front door. His stature and build dominated the room, making it seem smaller. His eyes widened at her appearance. "Pat, what's happening with you?"

A shaky smile was the best she could manage. "I stepped into a time machine back there. It threw me. Please, just leave my bag there."

He placed the weekender beside the lamp table and came closer, his gaze never leaving her face. "This hasn't been easy for you, has it?"

"No. I didn't expect it to be." She angled away from him. If he touched her, she'd dissolve, whether in tears or all over him, she wasn't sure.

"Is that why you haven't been back?" he asked quietly.

"It's one of the reasons. But the worst is over—I think." Letting the strap of her attaché case slide from her shoulder, she lowered it to the floor. She needed more room. "If you don't mind, I think I'd like to eat on the back porch." Moving quickly, she led him through the dining room and kitchen, and opening the back door, stepped down onto the screened-in porch. She was not disappointed. The pair of rocking chairs was still on the right side and on the left, the picnic table swathed with a plastic cloth covering, benches on either side of it.

Behind her, Adam whistled in astonishment. "That's quite a yard. It's deeper than I thought."

"It's a combination of Hetty's and my grandmother's." One day it would be hers, she thought, and took no comfort in the prospect.

A lanky teenager was just finishing the lawn. He cut the engine and the sudden silence transformed the back porch into an oasis of serenity. The sounds of the evening became audible, the quiet whisper of a breeze through the pecan trees, the murmur of birds settling for the night, the raucous chirp of crickets now that the racket had ceased. As if drawn by it, Pat opened the screen door and moved down the steps, hearing Adam coming behind her.

The teenager, taller than she'd thought and every inch a Ransom, pushed the mower toward them, his eyes lively with curiosity. "Hey, Chief Wyatt. Evenin', Miss Melton. I'm Raymond. It's getting kind of late, so I'll come back tomorrow and do the raking. How's Miss Hetty?"

It was a question Pat knew she'd hear again and again. She'd better formulate a stock answer. "Resting comfortably, but it looks like she'll be in the hospital awhile."

"Oh." All arms, legs and feet, he shifted awkwardly in his Frankensteinlike athletic shoes. "Well, tell her Raymond Junior asked about her and that we'll be looking out for her place."

"I will. And thanks, Raymond. You did a nice job."

He grinned. "Piece of cake. Are you really Honor Melton?"

"Guilty. Every Wednesday at seven-ten."

"That's the time all right," he said, swatting at a gnat. "Everything stops at our house when you come on." He sobered. "They oughta fix them cameras, though. You're a whole lot prettier in person. Yonder comes Grandma. I'd better git. 'Bye, Chief. See ya tomorrow, Miss Melton."

"I'm sure you will. And it's Chase, but I reckon you're old enough to call me Pat."

"Yes, ma'am, Miss Pat." His look was one of pure delight. He maneuvered the mower to the storage shed.

Pat sighed, reminded of the senior citizen she must seem to a kid Raymond's age.

"You 'reckon'?" Adam asked softly, imps dancing in his eyes.

Pat moaned. "Did I really say that? It took me years of concentrated effort to lose the accent I picked up down here. I'm back half a day and so is it."

"This place does get in your blood, doesn't it?" He sounded smug, proprietary.

For some reason Pat found it annoying. "If that's true, how come you still sound like you just left Flatbush Avenue in Brooklyn?"

Nonplussed, he said, "I do?"

Gotcha, Pat thought. It was time she threw him off-balance for once.

Mrs. Ransom bore down on them, carrying an enormous tray covered by a towel. "Y'all come on and eat this while it's hot," she ordered, marching past them to the steps.

"Yes, ma'am." Adam grabbed the door for her.

Hetty's neighbor, Pat saw, had clearly meant what she'd said when she'd promised to put some weight on her. The mountain of food on both plates would have been more appropriate on the table of a professional football team in training. Baked ham and fried chicken, potato salad, turnip greens and cole-slaw. Iced tea in tall glasses. Dessert was a slab of cobbler, its crust so thick that it was impossible to identify the filling.

Pat knew what was expected of her and complied, sitting down immediately, spearing a slice of ham, nibbling on an end, and groaning with pleasure. To her credit, she was not faking. Adam, following her lead, did likewise, and as she'd antici-pated, Sarah Ransom left, satisfied. As soon as she was out of sight, Pat retreated to the kitchen, found a platter and re-moved half the food Sarah had packed onto her plate. Adam contributed half of his and waited while she consigned it to Hetty's nearly empty refrigerator, before digging in again. The sight of more human-sized portions seemed to trigger Pat's hunger, to such an extent that it almost overrode her height-ened awareness of the intimacy of the setting—and of Adam, sitting opposite her. To her embarrassment, Pat became tongue-tied, and all attempts at conversation ceased until there was nothing left on her plate.

She looked up from her last forkful to find Adam, who had also finished, smiling at her. "I guess I was hungrier than I thought," she admitted. "It's been a while since I've put away that much food in one sitting, in fact, not since the last time Hetty came to visit. It never fails, she shows up and by the time she leaves, I've gained ten pounds. By the time I lose it, she's back again. Lordy, that little woman can cook."

Adam extended his arms above his head in a massive stretch. Pat caught herself staring at the resulting bulge of his biceps and looked away. "Miss Hetty means a lot to you, doesn't she?" he asked.

Never having had occasion to vocalize her feelings for her great-aunt, Pat considered the question before responding. "You have to understand. My parents were real dynamos—brainy, outgoing, comfortable anywhere they went. And then there was me—or is it I?—painfully shy and a complete bust as a military brat. As soon as I'd get used to a new base, new school, new friends, we were packing to move. Then Dad got orders for Korea. Mom decided that considering how much trouble I had adjusting to new environments stateside, a foreign country would probably freak me out. So she shipped me off to stay with Hetty."

"Had you already met her?"

"No. And I'll never forget what she said when I got here—not 'Welcome to my house,' but 'Welcome home.' She walked me all over the Grove that first day, showing me where my parents had grown up, where they'd gone to school, where they'd played, swum. She introduced me to their classmates and friends, all of them full of stories about things they'd done with my folks when they were growing up—pranks they'd pulled on Halloween, in school, and on and on. It wasn't long before I was . . . I don't know . . . connected to a place in a way I'd never been before. For the first time in my life, I felt a sense of having roots and belonging somewhere."

"I think I know what you mean."

The huskiness in his voice surprised her. Pat sneaked a glance at him from the corners of her eyes. The contours of his face seemed different, all the tension gone. What remained was the hint of a soft side she suspected people rarely recognized for what it was, unless they could see beyond the power and masculinity he exuded. That wasn't easy. Neither was it easy to continue to ignore the way her body responded to him, the unnerving quiver in her midsection he could cause with just a smile. Adam was, as her secretary, Iliana, would say, definitely a double-H: a helluva hunk. And I'd second the motion, Pat decided. Just her rotten luck that he was a cop, in the employ of the Harlands, and as such, definitely suspect.

"You were saying," he prodded. "About what Miss Hetty means to you."

"Yes." With effort, she looked away. "Well, once she'd made sure I had a sense of my foundation, she went to work luring me out of my shell."

"How?"

"By making me feel that there was nothing I couldn't do. My mother simply could not comprehend the agony of being shy. She was always pushing me to speak up, volunteering me for this and that. Hetty let me handle things in my own way at my own pace. She just assumed that I'd do what was expected and do it well. Hetty made me feel smart and capable and . . . and loved."

Pat stopped, reminded of the anxiety she'd suffered before showing Hetty her first report card. Hetty's delight at her B-Plus average had been such a surprise, especially in comparison to how her mother would have reacted, that she'd decided on the spot to see how many A's she could earn the next semester.

"Where was I?" she asked, packing the cherished memory away.

"Feeling smart, capable and loved." He grinned and suddenly Pat detected another facet of his personality—a streak of mischievousness. It wasn't difficult to imagine him as a devilish little boy. "By the way." Getting up, he crossed to the screen door to look out over the years. "If you wanted to be a writer, why'd you settle for being a reporter on TV?"

There was something belittling in the way the question had been worded, but she assumed he hadn't meant it to be. "I paid for my room and board in grad school working as copy editor on the house organ of a consumer advocacy group," she said. Stacking his plate atop hers, she took them into the kitchen, found the dishpan and filled it with hot water. "From there I became a research assistant for Don Stanczyk—"

Adam turned so he could see her at the sink. "Wow. The architect of the Department of Consumer Affairs. I'm impressed." His inflection revealed that she'd just made a few points, which pleased her—until she realized it. Why should she care? she asked herself, adding dishwashing liquid to the water.

"When Don was hired to do solve-a-consumer-problem features for a public television station in D.C.," she continued, "he asked me to go with him and I wound up on camera a few times when he was away. When he was assigned a Presidential post, they offered me the slot. I took it on the condition that I could branch out, tackle any kind of problem, consumer-related or not. Voilà! 'Honor Bound.'"

"A catchy name for it. I've only seen the show a few times, but I remember thinking you were very polished and at ease."

"Thanks. It's an act," Pat admitted. "I get such a mean case of stage fright that I overcompensate and come off bright-eyed and bushy-tailed. Fortunately the camera seems to like it." The dishes washed, she rinsed them, stacked them on the drainboard and emptied the pan.

"In the interim," Adam said, "the great American saga about the Meltons and Chases has been tabled."

Once again Pat read a biting criticism into his comment. Suddenly it seemed important to set the record straight. "I started it—the prologue, that is—while I was living here," she said, drying the two plates. "It was an assignment for English Comp and I'd planned to give it to Hetty for her birthday, but..." She stopped, her anger erupting like a mushroom cloud, obliterating rational thought.

"But what?"

"I had to leave before it was finished. I'll get it done one day. That's a promise I've made to myself."

He tipped his head to one side. "Sounds like you feel very strongly about it."

"I do. It's...unfinished business."

"And that irks you."

"Yes." She hoped he was perceptive enough to detect her unwillingness to pursue the subject.

"Pat, I'd like to ask you something."

She knew instinctively what was coming, knew it in the pit of her stomach where a hard knot of tension began to tighten. She put the plates away, closed the cabinet door gently. "So ask."

"What happened to make you leave the Grove?"

"Didn't Dr. Vernon tell you?"

"He doesn't know for certain."

She laughed, a sound coarse with bitterness. "Then he's probably the only person in town who doesn't." She stepped down onto the porch. The evening sky was a charcoal gray with streaks of mauve.

"Would you rather not talk about it?"

Pat considered the question and made a quick decision. She would just as soon he heard it from her rather than someone else. "In brief, I was an overnight guest in your jail for allegedly—" she leaned on the word "—stealing the Harland cameo."

There was no reaction at first. When it finally hit, astonishment exploded across his face. "The fist-sized whopper on display in the lobby of the plant? The model for H.I.'s logo?"

"Is that where they keep it now?" Pat asked with a sardonic smile. "You can thank me for that. It used to be in a glass case in the library of the mansion. Margaret Harland's pride and joy."

"And the town's. Why were you accused of taking it?"

"One—" she ticked off on her fingers "—my mom started me collecting cameos. I loved them, had a dozen or more and everyone here knew that. Two, I was in the wrong place at the right time—or vice versa. Three, no one who could have come forward to say that I hadn't taken it opened their mouths. Four." She stopped for breath, and control. "They found the damned thing in my locker at school."

"Oh." A subtle change in Adam's expression afforded Pat a glimpse of yet another side of his personality—the hardened cop who'd heard it all before and as a result, no longer believed any of it. "So someone set you up."

It was hard not to respond to the overtones of cynicism in his voice. But if she could keep rein on her fury talking to him about it now, she'd be able to hold her own with anyone else in town. "Someone set me up," she said in agreement.

"Then how'd it get into your locker? Did you loan someone your key? Tell someone the combination?"

Hearing echoes of the past, Pat's temper snapped. "Thanks, but I've already been through one interrogation on the subject and I'll be damned if I'll go through a second. I had no explanation then and don't now. All I know is that I spent the night in a smelly little cell in the courthouse with Chet Rowley and Margaret Harland hounding me to admit I had taken it."

"Your lawyer let them do that?"

"I had no lawyer. Not that Hetty and Lib didn't try to roust one for me, but all the attorneys in the area rely on H.I. employees for clients, to say nothing of the Harland family itself. Once they understood who and what was involved, they had other things to do."

"You had no legal advice at all? No rep from Juvenile?"

"All I had, Adam, was Margaret Harland standing over me, ranting about how she had welcomed me into the sanctity of her home and this was how I'd repaid her hospitality—the same woman who'd made it clear from the very first that my place was in the kitchen with Hetty. She was vehemently opposed to my being upstairs with Lib. And dear God, the day she realized that Lib was letting me borrow books from the mansion's library, she literally frothed at the mouth. So thinking I'd stolen the ancestral cameo proved that she'd been right about me all along."

"This is C.J.'s mother you're talking about?" Adam said.

"Margaret Andrews Harland. When she threatened to send me to the state reform school if I didn't admit stealing the cameo, I had no doubt she'd do it. She promised to drop all charges and forget the whole thing if I did. After a night of that, I gave in."

"And confessed to something you hadn't done," Adam said, his voice oddly flat.

"You betcha. I was scared out of my mind and tired and feeling as if I'd been thrown to the wolves. I just wanted to get out of there and go home. And as we were leaving, Her Majesty informed me that, of course, anyone who was a confessed thief had no right to be crowned Miss Harland High the following week, such a shame since it was the first time someone had won who wasn't a native. Under the circumstances..." Pat stretched to her full height, nose powdered with disdain, and assumed the voice of Margaret Harland. "'Under the circumstances, perhaps it would be best if you left town as soon as possible—to spare Hetty the embarrassment, of course.'"

She abandoned her mimicry, reverted to her own pain-filled timbre. "I told Hetty not to bother packing, left in what I'd put on when Chet Rowley had come to take me in—a pair of cutoffs, my high school T-shirt and rubber thong sandals. I haven't been back since. I *detest* this town."

A long silence was Adam's only response until, startling her, he crossed to her briskly, sat her down at the table, then perched next to her, straddling the bench. He was so close, practically imprisoning her between his knees. Pat felt a bead of perspiration ooze down her spine.

He took her hand, holding it firmly. "You were genuinely traumatized by it, weren't you? I have to tell you something. I just hope it helps. What they did was illegal—not only because the law is very specific about the treatment of a juvenile, and because you had no legal counsel, but also because Chet Rowley was nothing more than a security guard on the payroll at H.I. He was not a policeman."

Pat looked at him, lines of confusion etched across her forehead, between her brows, around her mouth. "A security guard?"

"By arrangement with Mrs. Harland, a couple of them cruised the streets of the town instead of patrolling around the plant. A citizen's arrest was the most they were entitled to make. What they did to you was way beyond their authority. Chet was, in effect, impersonating an officer of the law. Harland Grove didn't have a legitimate police force until C.J. hired me."

Pat pulled her hand from his. "But he wore a badge! I saw it!"

"A shield with a star on it, I know. Any H.I. guard in a supervisory position gets to wear one."

"But . . . but . . ." Words eluded her, all her protests tumbling in her mind like numbers in a lottery cage. She turned away to hide the ugliness she felt molding her features into a mask of rage. It seeped through her pores, the smell of her fury inflaming the lining of her nose, making it difficult to breathe.

"Pat. I'm so sorry. I truly am." Adam reached over and brushed the line of her jaw, a caress so unexpected that it rooted to the eye of the maelstrom ripping her apart and extinguished it, leaving her with an urgent need to be held. As if sensing it, he pulled her toward him until she rested, her back against his chest. "It's over, finished," he said. "Forget it. Bury it once and for all."

His voice was soothing, almost hypnotic in quality, and she was sorely tempted to relax and enjoy the solace and security of his embrace. But he couldn't possibly understand what he was asking her to give up. It was the fire, the solar source for the work she did every day. She had been severely wounded by Harland Grove, but at least it had served as the driving force to help others in similar circumstances—the little man and woman cheated, mistreated, or ignored by "the system" or those with the money and clout to do so with impunity. If Harland Grove had done nothing else for her, it had taught her how it felt to be an ant under the heel of a giant. Without that anger, what was she?

"You won't be worth a damn to Miss Hetty like this," Adam said, smoothing her sleek bobbed hair. "And don't forget, the town you detest is the same one that's volunteered to do anything it can to help the two of you through this ordeal. Obviously they don't hold what happened against you, if they remember it at all. It's possible they may not even know about it, if Jim didn't."

"Oh, they know, all right." Pat stood up, unwilling to be persuaded. "C.J.'s mother would have taken great delight in spreading the word about the viper she'd harbored in her precious mansion. Hetty swore she'd never set foot in that house while Margaret was alive, and she didn't. Hetty and Lib were the only ones who stood by me. With Lib gone, the only person I feel an allegiance to is Hetty. Forgive and forget is easy enough to say, Adam, but knowing what I know now? How can I?" Using her empty glass as an excuse to escape him, she went back into the kitchen.

Adam followed her with his own glass and placed it on the drainboard. "At least think about it. Fifteen years is a long time to hold a grudge, don't you think?" He stood looking down at her, a hand on her arm, his face in deep shadow. Outside the sun had dropped below the horizon and the kitchen was dark. Once again an air of intimacy surrounded them, the atmosphere crackling as a current of electricity arced between them. Pat didn't dare move, not trusting herself to overcome the temptation to take one step to her left and plaster her body against his.

Next door one of Sarah Ransom's grandchildren began to wail, shattering the moment, and it was Adam who edged away. "Okay if I use the phone? I'd better check in before the guys think I've skipped town."

"Over there." Grateful for the interruption, she crossed to the door and turned on the overhead light. "I'll be right back," she said, then walked through the house, flipping switches as she went, as if shooing away the dark might short-circuit any further near disasters with desire.

Back in her room with every lamp in it glowing, she perched on the side of the bed and shivered, rubbing her arms against a chill that had nothing to do with the ambient temperature. A host of misgivings nibbled at her psyche. How was it that she'd come very near to throwing herself at a man she'd known less than half a day? Mentally drooling over his physique was one thing, being a second away from eating him alive was another. What was happening to her? A reaction to stress?

Tonight had been the first time she'd ever talked about her fifteen-year-old nightmare with anyone, Hetty included. By tacit agreement, they'd never spoken of that night. Airing her grievance had been draining enough; learning that she'd been at the mercy of a Harland Industries night watchman had left her feeling twice as abused as before. The anger burned brightly.

Adam was right, though. She had to put that on hold for Hetty. Why did Hetty think she'd killed Lib? No matter how put out she'd been with her, she'd loved Lib too much to harm her deliberately. On the other hand, if Hetty felt that the stroke was punishment she deserved, was it possible that she really had . . . ? No. Not Hetty. She had to be misreading the circumstances surrounding Lib's death. And until someone cleared it up for her, she would remain in that bed, willing herself to die.

I have to do something, Pat told herself. But what? She wished Adam would leave. She couldn't seem to concentrate with him around. In fact, she hadn't had a decent thought since she'd met him. And she meant that literally.

Adam left the phone and wandered back out onto the porch. It was dark now, a soft darkness that seemed to undulate from sky to ground before settling in an opaque ebony blanket. That was something to which he'd yet to adjust. In a New York night, except for the occasional power outage, there was no such thing as complete darkness, no matter how late the hour. Here in Harland Grove, however, once the sun went down, night could not be denied. And with night came stars, more than he'd ever seen from the city of his birth. Occasionally after Corey was safe in bed, he'd drag a chair out into the yard and just sit, looking up. Not often, though. The down side of it was that those were usually the times he felt his loneliness most keenly.

There were many pluses working to enhance his life in the Grove, but companionship, especially of the feminine variety, was a definite minus. Most of the eligible women he'd met were either far too old or far too young. Of the few his age, none had been able to hold his interest beyond the first half hour of conversation. And then there was Pat Chase. His uneasiness about Miss Harland's death had kept him awake last night, but when he'd finally slept, the photograph on her mantel had haunted his dreams. And now that he'd met her.... The laughing eyes that had followed his movements were muted by grief and worry, but were still far lovelier than he could have imagined. The smiling lips in the picture had had few occasions to fulfill their promise since she'd arrived, and he yearned so deeply to see that happen. That and more.

Sighing, he left the porch and went down to sit on the steps. She was a problem in more ways than he cared to count. He was moved by her pride in her family, her fierce loyalty to her great-aunt, her willingness to jeopardize her job to take care of her. And he'd been pleasantly surprised by her lack of pretension despite her status as a TV personality. She was bright and perceptive. And hot-tempered, he reminded himself. She was damned attractive, and it galled the hell out of him that he liked her, really liked her. And God, did he want her! For a second back there in the kitchen, he'd almost lost it, had almost reached for her. The kid next door had saved him from making a big mistake.

If he'd only known who she was and what she did for a living before he'd met her. At least then he'd have been able to disregard his first impression of her, ignore the air of vulnerability, the frantic worry in her eyes. He'd have recognized that the strength he'd detected later was part and parcel of the streak of barracuda in her. And the streak had to be there. She was a reporter. One of *them*.

The spots she anchored might reek of nobility and unselfishness, and might even help people, but that, he suspected, was a bonus. The story was the star, the people who were helped minor players. If Pat was a reporter, then the story was the be-all and end-all for which she existed. Seven years of marriage to a kindred soul had taught him that. His son was motherless because of that. Reporters were a breed apart and he wanted nothing to do with them. It was time to rein in his hormones and go home.

"Adam."

He jumped a foot, so engrossed in his thoughts that he hadn't heard her come out. He got to his feet and turned around.

She stood in the doorway, holding open the screen. "What killed Lib?"

Immediately Adam's guard went up, his face hardening. The reporter in Pat, her "nose for news" had finally surfaced, just as he'd expected it would. Well, he was ready for her.

"I'm not at liberty to discuss that with you," he responded stiffly.

She made a gesture of impatience. "Don't go official on me, Adam. It doesn't take a genius to figure out that she didn't die of natural causes if, as you said at the hospital, you were opening an investigation into her death. Why won't you tell me?"

"Don't be coy," he snapped, his irritation rising. "You're a member of the Fourth Estate, that's why."

A frown marred her features. "What's that got to do with anything?"

"What's that...? Give me a break! It's got everything to do with it. Don't think that just because—"

The phone rang, its shrillness interrupting their sparring match. "Hold that thought," Pat said, and disappeared into the kitchen.

She was back in less than a minute, her eyes wide with alarm. "I've got to get back to the hospital. Hetty's had another stroke."

Chapter 4

The next few days gave Pat a taste of hell. Hetty's second stroke was more severe. There was doubt that she would survive, and if she did, serious reservations were raised about the quality of her life. Pat stood watch practically around the clock in the Intensive Care visitor's lounge, allowed to see a comatose Hetty for a few minutes every four hours.

During the agonizing wait, any number of people popped in to ask about Hetty, but for the most part there was much coming and going, family members of other patients in E.C., their only concern for those whom they'd come to see.

Pat tried to keep her mind occupied. She pulled together the notes from her Seattle and Portland interviews and sent them off to Milt. She sorted the mail she'd picked up at the station, weeding out the chaff and marking those pleas for help that warranted further investigation. She arranged to have Hetty's roof checked. She gathered several months' worth of Hetty's canceled checks and balanced her checkbook.

Adam Wyatt was the only constant, dropping by at least twice and sometimes three times a day to check on her and on Hetty. To a certain extent he complicated her life. Each time she saw him, her attraction to him sent its roots deeper, its tendrils invading every niche of her being. She erected barriers, which fell as soon as he appeared. The one occasion when it seemed it might remain intact was the second evening of her vigil when Adam came to the hospital with one of the traitors who'd left her high and dry fifteen years before.

Pat had been reading the same page of a magazine for the past half hour when she heard the asthmatic wheeze of the waiting room door, and glanced up to see Adam holding it open. Charles Jonas Harland walked through it.

Tall, his coarse red hair receding a little at the temples, shadows of fatigue under his gray eyes. Other than that he hadn't changed very much. He was still rangy, with the bouncy walk she remembered. "Patty," he said in a soft tenor. He crossed the room and with no hesitation pulled her into his arms.

Pat reacted with shock and revulsion, backing away, but he did not release her shoulders. "God, it's so great to see you. I stopped by yesterday evening, but you'd just left. How's Hetty?"

"Comatose," she said stiffly, "but they hope once the swelling in her brain has gone down, she'll come out of it. Afterward? Who knows?"

"God, I'm sorry." He slid one arm around her shoulder and sat, effectively pulling her down onto the sofa next to him.

Adam took a chair perpendicular to them, his hands steepled under his chin. "I ran into C.J. this morning. He said he'd be running out here to see you, so I figured we might as well come together."

Pat shot him a steely look before she remembered that he didn't know C.J. was one of those she found impossible to forgive. "I can't tell you how sorry I am about Lib," she said, meaning it.

"Thanks. I still can't believe it. Look, Patty, I don't know what kind of medical coverage Hetty has, but I've told Ewell, he's the hospital administrator, that she's to be treated like a Harland. Single room, specialists, anything. I'll cover any costs her insurance doesn't."

Pat could only stare at him in amazement. It was certainly costing him a lot to ease a guilty conscience. "C.J., that's incredibly generous of you."

He gave her the crooked grin that had precipitated countless fights in the girls' bathroom at H.G. High. There were few who weren't madly in love with him back then, Rena Coleridge among them. "If I didn't do it," he said, "Aunt Lib would haunt me the rest of my life. It's what she'd want. And before I forget it, we've got a car you can use. Don't ask why we have three, but we do. Between me, Rena—she says hello, by the way—and Adam, we'll get it to you."

It was time to be gracious. "I'm overwhelmed. Thank you, C.J. And thank Rena for me."

"Thank her yourself. You are coming to the wake and the funeral, aren't you? Hetty would want that."

As if she needed reminding. "When is it?"

"As soon as they finish the autopsy. Rena's scandalized that it's taking so long, but at least this way the relatives from Colorado will be able to come. Is there anything else you need? Anything at all?"

Pat shook her head. "Nothing. The Sunshine Club's taking care of me."

"Good," he said, then scowled at her. "Though God knows you don't deserve it, sneaking out of town without saying goodbye, then not writing a soul except Hetty and Aunt Lib." He jumped to his feet. "I've got to run. Rena's waiting at Hargitay's. We've got to take a look at the coffin she special-ordered. Nothing in stock was good enough for Aunt Lib. Rena's really taken this hard." Leaning over, he kissed her forehead with a loud smack. "I may not get back here for a day or so, but I'll be calling to check on how things are going. And I'll look for you at the wake."

"Right. Thanks again, C.J."

"I can't believe it. You're finally here. After all the doings are over, we'll have you over to dinner so you can meet our kids and we can talk about the old days. You ready, Adam?" He loped to the door.

Adam got up slowly. "I'll be back to pick you up," he said to Pat, his eyes gleaming with triumph. "Nine-thirty okay?"

"Fine."

He gave her a smug smile. "That's two who didn't know," he said softly. "Jim Vernon and C.J." Then he was gone.

Oddly enough, the subject didn't come up again for several days, primarily because of Pat's concern for Hetty, which overrode all other considerations. At night, however, as she lay in bed, there was time to stoke her anger at C.J. She wavered between gratitude that Hetty wouldn't lack for anything and rage that he thought he could buy off so easily someone he'd betrayed.

There was also her ambivalence about Adam. She knew he'd merely been trying to prove a point, that her anger at the Grove was futile and perhaps misplaced, but she didn't appreciate his efforts being made at her emotional expense. She considered telling him, but held her tongue. The moments with him were her only reprieve from the boredom, agony and fatigue of the waiting.

Pat was disarmed by his thoughtfulness. He brought books, offered to make calls for her, saw to it that she ate and, as promised, delivered the car C.J.'s wife had offered. When she learned that fully half of Hetty's roof needed replacing and that she'd have to move out while it was being done, Adam offered his house, volunteering to sleep at the station. Pat had to say no. There were proprieties to consider.

But she found herself listening for his footsteps in the hall, hungering to see him. He arranged his schedule to arrive at mealtimes, bringing the food prepared by the Sunshine Club. They ate together on the patio outside the cafeteria, which was almost as relaxing as the meal they'd shared on Hetty's porch. And Pat Chase discovered, to her horror, that she was very close to falling in love with a cop from Harland Grove. She had to break this up pronto.

The first opportunity arose the day Hetty began to improve, coincidentally the day of Lib Harland's wake. Adam didn't show, sending instead a baby-faced officer she recognized immediately.

"So *you're* the Bo Adam's been talking about," she said as she took the picnic basket from him. "Celia's little brother."

He grinned. "I didn't think you'd remember. How's Miss Hetty?"

"Improving, finally. Where's Adam?"

"He's been doing paperwork all day. Dern, I see now why he's been keeping you to himself. How come you don't look like yourself on camera?"

Pat laughed. "Just lucky, I guess. How's Celia?"

"Fine. Married to Gus Ransom and pregnant—again. Her fourth. Hope Miss Hetty keeps on improving. You take care, hear?"

"I will. And thanks for bringing lunch."

"Sure. Chief'll probably bring your dinner himself. 'Bye, now."

But he didn't. Another officer came in his place. And Pat, beyond all reason and despite her intention to stop seeing him so often, got mad.

If he was tired of playing delivery boy, all he had to do was say so. If he was tired of *her,* all he had to do was say so. She hadn't asked him to bring her meals, hadn't asked him to do anything. She was this side of irascible when the I.C.U. visitor's lounge receptionist told her there was a call for her.

Mystified, Pat took the phone. Adam.

"Hi," he began. "I've talked to Jim and he told me about Miss Hetty improving. He said they may even move her back up to Three South in a day or so."

That last item was news to her. "That'll be a relief," she said, faking equanimity. "By the way, thanks for sending your stand-ins. That wasn't necessary, if you were busy. I could have gotten something from the cafeteria."

"The Sunshine ladies would have killed me. Look, I thought we might go together to Miss Harland's wake tonight."

Pat's heart soared. Then she remembered. Besides, he'd offered no explanation for his absence all day. Might as well strike while the proverbial iron was hot. "That's nice of you, Adam, but since I've got Rena's car, I can drive myself."

"You could, but why should you? My shift ends at seven. I'm free. You haven't had a chance to see many people. I thought it might be easier for you if you weren't alone."

Pat melted for a second. He could be so understanding. She really was uncertain of the kind of reception she'd get, and being with Adam would make it easier. Once again, though, she remembered, and gave herself a talking-to. She'd be there as Hetty's representative, and for herself, to acknowledge Lib's special place in her life. And she'd go alone.

"Pat? Are you still there?"

"Yes."

There was a slight pause. "I'd really like to see you."

Her heart pumping double-time, Pat made a tire-shrieking U-turn. "What time?"

"Is eight all right? That'll give me time to shower and change."

"I'll be ready." She hung up, disgusted with herself. He'd said he wanted to see her. That's all it had taken. She who rarely backed down after she'd made a decision had just changed her mind so fast she could smell the rubber burning. God, Honor Patrice, she thought, are you that weak for him?

By the time Adam escorted Pat through the doors of the mock antebellum structure Monty Hargitay used for a funeral home, the wake was more than an hour old. After signing the guest register, they headed down the center hall to the double doors at the rear of the building. A sign outside the room proclaimed it the Chapel of Blessed Slumber, reserved this night for Elizabeth Amelia Harland. Pat felt her heart constrict with pain.

The room was jammed, visitors practically cheek by jowl, their voices lowered in hushed conversation.

"Let's express our condolences and get that over with," Adam suggested. Pat nodded, mute, and allowed him to act as battering ram, opening a path to the front of the room. Her progress did not go unnoticed.

"Have mercy! That *is* Patty."

"Yonder's Hetty's girl, the one's on the TV."

". . . Cut her hair. Now why would she go and do that?"

Looking straight ahead, Pat squeezed past the last clutch of visitors in the aisle, coming almost smack up against Lib Harland's bronze coffin. The lid was closed, and she breathed a prayer of thanksgiving. This way she could keep the images with which she'd lived all these years: Lib's eyes sparkling with delight as she smoothed the jacket of a new book, her impish smile at having gotten Margaret's goat—again. Those were the memories she would cherish, minus the veil of death across Lib's features. With that hurdle behind her, she steeled herself for the next: facing C.J. again, and Rena, his wife, a second person for whom Pat held little regard.

C.J. looked drawn with fatigue until he saw them. His lips formed a smile of genuine welcome. "Adam! Patty! Rena, here she is." Rising, he stepped past the stunning blonde sitting on his right, elbowed Adam aside, and took both her hands. "I'm glad you could make it. Reen?" Reaching back, he helped the blonde to her feet.

"Welcome back, Patty—I mean, Honor," the elegant woman said. "I'm so sorry about Miss Hetty. I'll try to see her after we get through . . . all this."

Pat could only gape at her, her animosity momentarily forgotten. "My God, Rena, is it really you? You look fantastic!"

The self-conscious smile she received in response evoked a dim picture of the Rena she'd known, a mousy blonde, tall and painfully thin, sparse brows and almost invisible lashes, her eyes so pale a blue that they seemed almost without color. That person was gone. Rena now had an hourglass figure, and accentuated her height with stiletto heels. Her hair was spun gold, perfectly coiffed, her makeup skillfully applied, her eyes an unmistakable cerulean blue.

"I'm a mess," she demurred with modesty. "But you...you really haven't changed a bit. C.J. said you were still a knock-out, and he was right."

Pat managed something innocuous, remembering how easily she and Rena had become friends her first year at Harland Grove High. In the beginning they'd been much alike, too shy to fit in with the more popular students. That had gradually changed for Pat, but she'd refused to abandon Rena, including her in any group of which she became a part. It had been Patty, Rena, C.J., Celia, and Davie Lucas.

All of them had been with her the day she was sent to the mansion to retrieve the sunhat Lib had forgotten to take to the

May Day picnic. All had waited in the car C.J. had been driving while she ran upstairs, found the hat and ran back down. In and out in less than a minute. She'd been wearing shorts over a two-piece bathing suit. There was no place she could have hidden the cameo without it showing. Yet none of them had volunteered that little detail, only that she'd been the only one to go in.

Pat felt the bitterness tinge the back of her throat and knew it was time to say what she'd come to say and leave.

"Patty," C.J. said, "Adam told me you need a place to bunk while Miss Hetty's roof is being fixed. You're welcome to move into the mansion. The guest wing's available—in fact, the whole damned house."

Pat gasped, stunned and uncertain how she felt about the offer.

"C.J.!" Rena rolled her eyes. "That spooky old place? Stay with us, Patty. You can use the rec room until the cousins leave. Or we could move the kids into the rec room and you could take theirs. . . ."

The mansion began to look more and more attractive, and at the moment she had no other alternatives. "I'll think about it. Can I let you know tomorrow?"

"You don't have to let us know anything," C.J. said. "The door's open and the invite stands. Go and stay as long as you need to."

"Have you forgotten how many things need fixing in that place?" Rena demanded. "Honestly, C.J.!" She never finished the sentence, if it had an ending. Someone who'd been hovering moved in, hugged her and began sobbing on her shoulder. Rena shot an apologetic smile at Pat and sat the woman down, murmuring words of consolation.

"Patty." Pat swiveled around, her elbow in the firm grasp of Sarah Ransom. "Come say hello to a few of the Sunshine girls."

To Pat's dismay, she found herself confronting a smiling mob, almost all armed with paper and pens.

"Miss Sarah," she said softly, "it wouldn't be right to turn Lib's wake into an autograph session."

"Ohmigawd, you're right." Sarah signaled for them to put their pens and pencils away. "But they want to say hello, ask about Hetty. Nothing wrong with that."

Pat looked into their eyes, baffled by what she saw: pride, smiles of welcome, glassy-eyed awe. She'd been prepared to deal with rejection, censure, disapproval, but not this.

"Patty Chase, what is wrong with you?" someone whispered in her ear. "You gonna get hincty in your old age with folks who knew you when?"

It was a voice she hadn't heard in years. Turning, Pat bumped into the protruding midsection of a very pregnant woman. "Celia."

"At least you aren't senile. Lean over here—that's the only way you'll get close to me—and give me a hug. Girl, I don't believe it. You're here. You're home."

Just go with it, Pat told herself, returning the enthusiastic embrace. Now was not the time. It could wait. And she really was sort of glad to see Celia.

"Let's go on out in the hall where we can dish some dirt," Celia said, towing her along.

"Hold it a minute, Cee." Pat stood on tiptoe, craning in an effort to locate Adam. She didn't see him. A careful perusal of the room made it definite. Adam was gone.

Heading for the masked door behind the coffin, Adam watched as Pat was shanghaied by Mrs. Ransom, then by Bo's sister. There was no point in telling her where he'd be; from the looks of things, she wouldn't miss him and he doubted he'd be gone more than a couple of minutes anyhow. Slipping into the vacant chapel next door, he took a pew in the back, grateful to escape from the canned organ music. The sound-proofing in here might be precisely the reason Jim had chosen it for this conference. But what did he want, a further discussion of the results of the autopsy?

Adam had spent a good part of the morning going over it with him. The medical examiner had handed them a surprise or two, the most important being death due to the lethal mixture of alcohol and barbiturates. The verdict: suicide. The problem now became what to do about it. He could leave it alone, and that would be the end of it. Or he could perform the job he was paid to do and probably get fired. He was a cop, damn it. He'd do what he had to. Which brought him back to the subject with which he'd been wrestling for the past twenty-four hours: what to do about Pat?

He had already concluded the night before that he needed to cut back on his visits to the hospital. He could no longer con himself into believing his primary interest was Miss Hetty's progress. It was Pat, had been from the first. The thought of her set his pulse racing, and all the physical needs he'd forced into hibernation leaping—and screaming—into the sunlight again. She made him feel more alive than he had in a long, long time.

Not that she'd done anything to encourage him. She was always happy to see him, but spending the day in the visitor's lounge outside Intensive Care would make her happy to see Attila the Hun. As a result, he chose not to put much stock in her welcoming smile. That didn't seem to stop him from being charmed by the way her hair framed her smooth oval face and the luminous eyes that glowed like topaz.

She was such a refreshing change from anyone he knew, entirely different from his expectations, different even from the image she projected on screen. He didn't know her as well as he could wish, yet liked what he did know. In fact, "like" was becoming too diluted a description of his feelings for her. It was this realization that had precipitated his decision to call time-out to size up the situation.

No matter how far she'd burrowed under his skin, she was in a field he detested, had intensely negative feelings about the town in which he lived and would undoubtedly hit the road just as soon as she could. Furthermore, if he chose the route he felt he had to, his name would top the list of people in the Grove against whom she held a grudge. It was, he'd concluded, time to back off and let their blossoming relationship die from lack of care and feeding.

He'd called her today for the sole purpose of letting her know he'd be too tied up to see her for a while. Just hearing that deep, sultry voice on the phone, he'd wound up asking her to come to the wake with him. Well, no harm done. Considering the reception she'd received, there'd be plenty of people to keep her company from now on. She'd be crawling with allies. He'd be the enemy. The result would be the same, the severance of any ties between them.

A door behind him opened, letting in the murmur of voices and taped organ music. C.J. peered in at him. "Hey. Doc'll be here in a minute."

"Okay." Jim had said he needed a word with him. To C.J., too? What was going on? Adam wondered.

"Evenin', son. Doc here yet?" another familiar voice asked.

Adam groaned. If Wallace Quinton, Mayor of Harland Grove, had been invited, they might as well plan to spend the night.

"Not yet." C.J. held the door open for him. "He's on his way."

Quint, spotting Adam, nodded a greeting. "Evenin', Chief. A sad day. How'd Rena take the news, C.J.?"

"This has been hard enough on Reenie without her knowing Aunt Lib killed herself. So I lied, said it was a reaction to her medication. I'll tell her the truth after the funeral."

"Smart move. Sometimes you have to mangle the truth for the little woman." Quint settled in a pew opposite Adam and folded his hands over his paunch to wait for Jim Vernon. Wallace Quinton had been mistaken for the actor who portrayed Otis, the town drunk on *The Andy Griffith Show,* so often that to counter it, he'd grown a beard and bought a toupee the color his hair had been twenty years ago. It succeeded in making him look like Otis with a beard and a remnant of a fur piece on his head.

Jim Vernon entered through the door behind the choir loft. "You're all here. Good. Let's get straight to the point. Adam, this little meeting is Quint's idea."

Adam, surprised, became poker-faced. "Oh?"

The mayor cleared his throat. "Jim tells me you thought something was fishy about Lib's death from the very first, and that the Medical Examiner's verdict hasn't changed your mind. Is that true?"

Adam peered at Quint, not because of the question, but because it hadn't been couched in his usual country-boy drawl, the one that invariably evoked a smile from his listeners, and for the last ten years, won their votes. His diction had been crisp, almost accent-free. Quint met Adam's gaze, his eyes betraying a steely intelligence and purposefulness Adam had never seen before.

"That's true," he responded.

"I can hardly believe it myself." C.J. turned sideways in the pew. "Aunt Lib never drank. Mom couldn't even serve wine when we had company because Aunt Lib didn't approve."

"C.J., son," Quint rumbled softly. "It's about time you found out about a couple of skeletons in your family's closet. Of your granddaddy's three children, two were alcoholics, your Uncle J.D. and your Aunt Lib. J.D. died young and saved your folks a lot of embarrassment. And truth be told, back in Lib's chippy days, she could drink any man in town under the table."

"*My* Aunt Lib?" C.J. seemed to be having trouble with his lower jaw.

"Old Doc Ringwold finally warned her that she was killing herself, so she gave up the bottle, but your daddy was terrified that one day she'd start sipping again. Lib was your daddy's heart. That's the way it is with twins. Your mother had to share the mansion with Lib after your daddy died because he was making sure there'd be somebody to look after her and keep her in line. I'll give your aunt credit, she stayed sober for damned near sixty years. But Doc Ringwold was right. She tumbled off the wagon and the fall killed her."

"That and a massive dose of barbiturates," Adam reminded the mayor. "Several different kinds, at that."

"None of which *I*," Jim interjected, "prescribed for her. There's something I didn't get a chance to tell you, C.J., something I didn't know until Adam showed me the report. If Lib hadn't died when she did, she'd have been dead in a few months anyway. She had cancer of the liver."

"Oh, God." C.J. paled, his red hair seeming twice as bright.

"She had to know there was a serious problem," Jim went on. "There was no ignoring the symptoms."

Clearly C.J. was having difficulty absorbing it all. His face settled into a grieving acceptance. "She always said she'd rather die than become one of those feeble old women who couldn't remember their own names. And Reenie will tell you, she'd become very forgetful. The liver thing on top of everything else must have pushed her over the edge. God, this will kill Reenie."

Quint cleared his throat again, a clue he was slipping into an oratory mode. "Looks like she felt she had more than one reason to do herself in. But I imagine the Chief there has some questions he'd like answered. For instance, where'd the barbiturates come from? It's a cinch Lib didn't walk into Heck's drug store and find them on the shelves beside the aspirins and the diapers. The same goes for the liquor. So I have to ask, how could she have pulled this off without help?"

Adam levered himself to his feet. "I'm sure a second person was involved, the question being to what extent and when. The answers will determine if Miss Harland committed suicide with help or didn't commit suicide at all."

"Didn't commit..." C.J. looked sick. "What are you saying?"

For Adam, C.J. presented a dilemma. Whatever was said in this room would go right back to Rena. She was at heart a nice woman, bright, and well-intentioned, but the only other person more free with advice than Rena Coleridge Harland was Ann Landers. He neither needed nor wanted her help in this matter.

"I want everyone's assurance that what is said in here tonight will go no further." He waited until he'd received various indications of agreement before continuing. "Miss Harland may well have taken her own life, but she had to have had help, perhaps from someone who had no idea what she planned. If that person knew what she intended, there are legal ramifications. It's against the law to aid and abet suicide."

Jim scowled. "We all know there's only one person Lib would ask to help her and that's Hetty. But it'll be a cold day in hell before I'll believe Hetty'd go along with it."

"Unless," Quint said, with obvious reluctance, "she thought it might spare Lib a painful death later on."

"My job is to make that determination," Adam said, refusing to give up the floor. "Also, whether Miss Harland enlisted help or didn't, someone else became involved after her death.

Miss Harland died in her bathroom. Someone moved her, put her body in her bed, knowing full well that she was dead.''

Quint's grizzled brows climbed an inch. "Say what?"

"It may have been done with the best of intentions, perhaps a sentimental gesture, or someone protecting her modesty, something like that . . . but so far, no one has come forward to say they did it.''

"Why is that important?" C.J. asked.

"Whoever moved your aunt didn't stop there. She . . . or he . . . also tried to mask what killed her. I have to find out why.''

"Adam." C.J. was suddenly clear-eyed, alert. He stood, slowly, as if the simple act of getting to his feet was painful. "You think Aunt Lib may have been murdered.''

A lie might have made his friend rest easier, but Adam couldn't do it. "I'm sorry, buddy, but I can't rule it out, at least not yet.''

"Oh my God." C.J. plopped down again and sagged like a balloon leaking air.

Quint harrumphed for attention. "Is Hetty a suspect?"

Adam nodded. "At this point, everyone is.''

"But she'd be near the top of the list? If not the very top?''

"Yes." Adam was annoyed at being pinned down. "As close as she was to Miss Harland, she fits easily into any of the scenarios we've discussed, as an accomplice to suicide or to euthanasia. And either way, I can see her trying to cover it up.''

"*That's* why we're here," Quint announced. "If Hetty's a suspect, we've got trouble . . . Patty. She'll defend that old lady by every means in her power . . . lawyers, perhaps even—''

"Gawd a'mighty," C.J. said breathily. "She and Walt Callaway were a hot item before he moved down here to Raleigh.''

Jim blanched. "Not the guy who's about to run for State attorney general?''

"You got it. With him practically next door, he's the one she'll hire. That means publicity. The papers follow everything he does.''

Quint wore a grim mask. "That's small potatoes compared to the kind of stink Patty herself could raise. I'm talking the court of public opinion here, public television, *nationwide*. Think back to the guy she helped free, the one about to go to trial for a crime committed by a bail jumper with the same name. She'll take on the law in a minute."

"If I have occasion to arrest Miss Hetty," Adam said, irritated by the implication, "you can bet I'll have an air-tight case against her. Everyone in this investigation will be treated fairly and within the letter of the law."

Quint hitched up his trousers with his elbows, no mean feat sitting down. "It might help a lot if Patty could see that for herself."

Adam squinted at him sidewise. The mayor had something up his sleeve and he suspected he wasn't going to like it. "How?"

Quint cleared his throat. "Chief, we can't afford any negative publicity right now—"

"Because of Tyler," Adam finished for him.

"Exactly. Asa Tyler will only move his shampoo factory to a place with a strong sense of community, room to build his plant, land for the workers who relocate to build their homes. He's looking for peace and quiet and neighborliness. We're exactly what he wants. We need his factory, his workers and his money."

"So?"

Quint got up and took the aisle, hands locked behind his back. "I made a few calls today, found out that Patty's got sound credentials as an investigative reporter. She's a good detective. Why not let her help you?"

Adam began a slow burn. "Are you implying that I don't know how to do my job?"

"No, sir. Hear me out, now." Quint extracted a wrinkled handkerchief and mopped his forehead. "What we're suggesting is that you let Patty do a ride-along. You know, like—"

"I know what you mean, Quint. Every time some hotshot reporter dreamed up an article about New York cops, we wound up stuck with them in our back seats, getting in the way, disrupting interrogations. If that's what you've got in mind, forget it."

Jim leaned forward. "It's a good idea, Adam. She'd see how impartial your investigation will be."

"This is stupid," Adam said flatly. "Why are you going to such lengths to prevent something that probably won't happen?"

Quint glanced at C.J., then back to Adam. "Because unless I miss my guess, Patty Chase has a grudge the size of Texas against our little town, with good reason, I might add. This would be the perfect opportunity for her to get back at us."

"Patty? A grudge?" C.J. frowned. "Why?"

"Just take the word of an old man who knows where all the bodies are buried, so to speak."

So Quint knew what had happened. "A grudge's too mild a word for what she feels," Adam admitted, "but she's too smart to raise a ruckus if there's a possibility Miss Hetty's an accessory before or after the fact."

"Then why not provide the chance to be a participant in establishing Hetty's guilt or innocence? That way she'd have no excuse to make a case for poor old Hetty being picked on while lying yonder in the hospital half paralyzed."

"No." Adam was firm. "There are people who might open up to me but wouldn't with Pat there. Besides, all sorts of dirty laundry comes to light during something like this. If it has nothing to do with the case, as far as I'm concerned, I never heard it. Pat has no right to hear it at all. I'm sorry. No."

"Chief." Quint planted himself in front of Adam, his expression grave. "I hate to remind you of this, but as Mayor, I could order you to do it."

Adam gazed down into the pudgy face and saw the seriousness of purpose in Quint's eyes. He couldn't believe it. For the second time in his life he'd be making a career change because of a reporter.

"Then you'd better take this." Reaching for his I.D. wallet, he opened it, unpinned his badge and slapped it in Quint's hand. "Perhaps you can find someone who'll compromise his principles for you, but I won't do it. Gentlemen." Turning sharply, he started for the door.

C.J. grabbed his arm as he passed, stopping him. "Adam, listen, please. If you think we're overreacting, let me tell you what's at stake. H.I. is for sale."

"For *sale?*"

"Right. I've had plenty of offers for the site alone or the Cammio formula, but Tyler's the only one who'd keep the plant going and let all our people stay on. If he decides on some other town, I'll have to shut down and declare bankruptcy. Without Tyler, we're out of business, six weeks tops."

"If she decided to play dirty and make this a black-white issue, we could kiss Tyler goodbye for sure." Quint seemed to have gotten his second wind. "Without the plant, the Grove will be a ghost town in no time. A century and a half of history, of black and white folks working, worshiping, living together, putting out a quality product. Cammio Cosmetics survived because of our people and vice versa. If Libs' death isn't handled with kid gloves, the Grove's as dead as Lib is."

"The girl I remember," Jim said quietly, "loves that old lady so much that she'd do anything to protect her, including blasting the Grove's good name to hell and gone on public TV."

"Adam, I'm going to hit you with a low blow," C.J. said, the strain evident in the pallor of his skin. "If you won't do it for anyone else, do it for Corey."

It was a sucker punch he should have seen coming, but hadn't. And it had exactly the desired effect. Without the stability and nurturing of Harland Grove, Adam knew Corey would still be a basket case, having nightmares in which he heard the report of the gun, saw the giant red blossom spread across his mother's white blouse, saw her collapse in a heap in the middle of the street, clutching her notepad in a death grip to the very last. The Grove had massaged away the night terrors, introducing him to an entirely different mode of living. Corey loved the place. How could he risk contributing to its demise?

"All right," he said, hating them for putting him in this position, hating himself for the pinch of pleasure he took in thinking that Pat might be working with him, sitting next to him, riding with him. "But if Miss Hetty's guilty, all bets are off. I'll arrest her. What the courts do with her is not my business."

"Understood." C.J. seemed worried, as if he suspected he'd done their relationship irreparable harm.

"Put it to her soon, son," Quint said. "Time's critical."

"I know that. Good night." Adam had nothing more to say to them.

Chapter 5

The crowd had thinned appreciably while Adam was gone, but Pat seemed to have disappeared. I should have told her where I'd be, he thought; then with illogic born of his irritation at the tight spot his friends had put him in, reversed his position. Why should he have had to tell her anything? She had to know he wouldn't run off and leave her. He checked the center hall, then outside. Nothing and nobody, aside from a couple of Hargitay's dark-suited employees sneaking a smoke behind their limos.

Then he spotted her on the grassy island that separated Hargitay's property from that of the New Jerusalem Methodist Church. A row of weeping willows lined the strip, perhaps to mark the boundary between the living and the dead. Pat, barely visible in the darkness beyond the parking lot, stood under the second tree, more shadow than substance, wrapped in solitude.

Adam wound his way between parked cars, wrestling with the trichotomy of his emotions. On the one hand, he resented highly the imposition foisted on him, and the necessity of proving his integrity and professionalism to Pat or to anyone, for that matter. On the second hand, he could not deny the rush of pleasure and anticipation at the prospect of having her as a partner in solving his first challenging assignment in three years. On the third hand...

He slowed to a stop, spellbound by the picture she presented: head bowed, arms behind her back, the soft, flowing fabric of her dress molded against the swell of her breasts and thighs, under the pressure of a playful breeze. All he had to do was look at her to be reminded of the breadth of problems he'd be facing, not the least of which was a gnawing, gut-cramping hunger for her. He wanted Pat Chase, a want that would have to go unsatisfied.

The conference in the chapel might have derailed his decision to see as little of her as he could, but it had not changed his mind about the boundaries of any relationship with her. The most he could allow would have to be platonic in nature. With Miss Hetty as a suspect, he doubted he'd be that lucky. He would ache for her, take cold showers by the dozen, but he wouldn't touch her. He was no masochist, saw no reason to put his heart in a mangler for a woman who was here today, but sure as hell would be gone tomorrow.

Dodging the branches, Adam joined her under the tree, but keeping his distance. The wispy foliage formed a lacy tent around them, like intricately woven mosquito netting, projecting a sense of sanctuary.

"Did you know," Pat said softly, acknowledging his presence for the first time, "that the original name of this town was Willows Grove?"

"No, I didn't. I can understand why. We've certainly got enough of them."

"They're Hetty's favorite tree. She says that whenever everything seems to be going wrong, find the nearest weeping willow and sit under it awhile. Listen to the wind through the leaves, let it sing to your soul and before long, things won't seem so bad anymore. In fact..." She turned, her eyes reflecting the amber spotlights in Hargitay's parking lot. "Can you leave now? There's some place I'd like to go."

Curious as to the cause of this change of mood, he said, "I'm ready to leave when you are. Here." He dug in a pocket and handed her the keys. "You drive."

That pleased her. "Thanks. I'd like to."

Taking the unaccustomed role as passenger, Adam watched as she adjusted the seat and the mirrors, and checked to see what was where on the dashboard, before exiting the parking lot. She appeared to get the feel of the car very easily.

He sat back, admiring the relaxed assurance with which she drove. She seemed taut with anticipation, a half smile on her face. He wondered what she thought of the mob scene at Hargitay's. "Everyone certainly seemed glad to see you tonight."

"Yes, didn't they? I felt like a hypocrite, all that smiling. I imagine they did, too. That's why I went outside, to give everyone a breather."

Adam's disappointment ran deep. Why was she having such a hard time accepting the olive branch the Grove seemed to be extending to her? Why couldn't she bury the hatchet? It would be one less thing for him to worry about.

The route she took, over to a less populated side of town, puzzled him at first. By the time she slowed to hunt for an unmarked road off Burlington, Adam felt a jolt of recognition. The bank above Marble Creek. He should have guessed that's where she was going. Any plans he'd had to propose the mayor's ride-along were immediately tabled. It wouldn't be right to do it there.

A half a mile in, Pat maneuvered the car into a recess well off the narrow country lane. She cut the engine, doused the lights and was out, closing her door, before he'd had a chance to release his seat belt. She cut through the trees with a sure sense of direction, even in the dark. When he caught up with her, she was under a massive willow some thirty feet from the edge of the bank. Head thrown back in abandon, arms outstretched, she turned in small, slow circles. Adam watched, enchanted at her eloquent affirmation of joy at being there.

"This was my very favorite place," she said, turning, swaying the full skirt of her dress billowing around her. "I used to pack a lunch and whatever book I was reading, and spend all day, right here."

"Great minds," Adam, beyond the canopy of branches, responded. "This is where I usually head when I want to get away. Miss Hetty's right. Weeping willows are better than sedatives."

Her dance ending, she hugged herself. "I'm so glad you found it, too." With only stars as illumination, he couldn't actually see her smile, but he could swear he felt it. Her vibrant contralto shimmered with her pleasure at their shared affection for this woodland retreat.

"Pat," he asked on a whim, "did you enjoy living in the Grove?"

For a second he wasn't sure she'd heard him, or if she had, that she intended to answer.

"I *loved* it," she said finally, her voice husky with emotion.

For the first time Adam began to sense the deprivation she must have suffered for so long. After thirteen years of a nomadic life, the shy child had been welcomed by open arms, nurtured in much the same way Corey had been, offered a place to call home, with all the nooks and hang-outs that take on a special glow in the memory when one has moved on in years or in distance. The difference was that Pat had been ejected from her Eden before the time she normally would have moved on, making the loss that much more painful and her memories of it that much sweeter. It helped explain the intensity of her bitterness. She'd been robbed of her adolescence.

Pat moved from under the tree and strolled to the bank, where far below in the deep ravine, Marble Creek bubbled its way toward the east. The rear of the Harland mansion stood directly opposite them, its exterior lights bathing the veranda and Doric columns in a white haze. For Pat, Adam mused, another symbol of sweeter times. She gazed at it in silence for a long time.

He joined her at the edge of the bank. "What are you thinking?" he asked.

Pat slipped an arm around his waist as if it were the most natural thing in the world. He felt he had no choice but to reciprocate, and encircled hers warily. Lord, she was so slender!

"C.J. offered me the guest wing of the mansion," she said.

Distracted by the pressure of her side against his, he could think of no more to say than, "And . . . ?"

"I told him I'd think about it. Rena wants me to stay with them, but . . . I don't think so. A couple of days at the mansion might be a good way for me to say goodbye to Lib and let her go."

"Instead of at the funeral?"

"That hasn't seemed to work for me so far. It's one of my biggest failings, letting go. But it's a no-win situation, Adam. It hurts if you do, hurts if you don't. When I have to choose between one brand of agony or the other, I usually wind up with the one that comes with hanging on for dear life. Stupid, huh?"

Helpless to stop himself, Adam reacted to the undertone of pain in her husky voice, pulling Pat to face him until he could hold her in both arms. He told himself later that all he'd meant to do was give her a hug of sympathy, understanding. At least that's the way it began, a quick, friendly squeeze, except that once he felt her arms around his waist, he couldn't seem to let her go, even when her hold on him loosened. She looked up at him questioningly, and with her face tilted toward his, he simply lost it. Her lips seemed to be pulling his down to hers like a magnet. By the time the voice of reason began yelling that he couldn't handle this, his mouth had settled over hers, gently— he'd give himself that. He felt her stiffen with shock, then relax a bit, and the voice said, *All right, jackass, you're kissing her and she hasn't kneed you yet, so don't push your luck. Keep it light and friendly, cut it short, and there's no harm done.*

Unfortunately the voice couldn't share the luxury of velvet lips as they yielded to his, feel her sweet, warm breath against his face, smell the pure clean scent of her. He slid one hand to the nape of her neck, found her skin like silk under his fingers. Then her lips parted and he felt his whole being expand with sensual pleasure. He explored the smooth, satin inner surfaces of her lips, his heart skittering erratically when his tongue danced against hers. Perhaps emboldened, Pat advanced, sought the tender tissue inside his lower lip, teased his tongue, the taste of her like summer honey. Then it was over. Closing her mouth against his, she ended the embrace, her fingers stroking the angle of his chin. The breach of contact was the same as though he'd lost something precious, something without price, like oxygen, blood, the substances that gave him life.

Pat stepped free of his arms with a sweet, sad smile. "Thanks. I needed that. In case I haven't said so, you're a nice guy, Adam Wyatt."

"And you are a dynamite lady. You'll be all right, Pat." He played that back to himself, congratulating himself for making it sound like a morale booster from a friend. She appeared to have dismissed the whole incident as having little or no meaning. Good. He'd fooled her, but he couldn't fool himself. Kissing Pat had only whetted his appetite—the single potato chip or kernel of popcorn to a starving man. Now, with a taste of what could be, he wanted it all, the feel of her silken skin warm and smooth against his, the pressure of her breasts against his chest, the grip of her thighs as she cradled his weight.... God, that kiss was a big mistake.

"We'd better go," Pat said, and sighed. "I have some material to look over tonight and a decision to make."

"After you." She started back toward the car, slowly, as if she hated to leave.

"What kind of decision?" he asked.

"About a rehab center for Hetty," she said, ducking under a low-hanging branch. "Whether the one up by High Point would be best for her or one of the two in the D.C. suburbs."

Something shriveled inside Adam. "I thought you'd agreed with Jim," he said, opening the car door for her, "that her recuperation would be easier if she stayed in familiar territory."

"No. I agreed to leave the decision to Hetty, but as much as I hate to do it, it looks as if I'll have to make it for her."

They reached the car and she handed him the keys. He took them without comment, opening the door for her, the mood now completely destroyed for him, his hunger for her an unpleasant ache. He drove her back to town in silence, kicking himself for having misjudged her again. How could he have believed she'd put her job at risk to see Miss Hetty through her recuperation? He should have known what her priorities were. Hadn't he lived with a woman for whom being a reporter and getting the story were more important than her responsibility as a mother and the safety of her own child? How could he have forgotten so soon?

Well, that was his second mistake of the night and there wouldn't be another, not again. And he had to make sure Miss Hetty remained in the vicinity, especially as long as there was any chance that she was a prime player in the mystery surrounding the death of her friend. And, he reminded himself, he had to prevent her niece from making him and the whole town look like a bunch of heartless brutes persecuting a helpless old lady while he tried to find out. It was time to propose Quint's idea.

When they pulled into the driveway at her aunt's house, Adam turned off the engine and released his seat belt. As he reached for the door handle, Pat stopped him, a hand on his arm.

"Wait, Adam. Don't get mad, but this is another example of how hard a time I have letting go. I asked you a question the night Hetty had the second stroke and never got an answer—at least one I can live with—about the results of the autopsy." She looked at him expectantly, her jaw set pugnaciously, as if anticipating his resistance.

He almost smiled. She was going to make this easy for him. "Will you give me your word that you'll keep it to yourself until I say otherwise?"

"You have it."

"Miss Harland died from a deadly mix of alcohol and drugs."

Pat gasped. "Alcohol and . . . But Lib didn't drink!"

"Well, she did that last night. Her blood alcohol was almost point four, enough to have killed her without the added knock-out from barbiturates."

"*Barbiturates?* Lib took barbiturates?"

"Yes. The combination left no chance that she'd survive. The coroner's verdict is suicide."

Pat's eyes saucered with horror. "Adam. Suicide? No." She shook her head firmly. "No. Elizabeth Harland loved life, *all* life. She wouldn't do it. Especially not now."

Adam wondered if Pat knew something he didn't. "Why not now?"

"I told you. When I talked to her that Sunday she said she was up to something, remember?"

"So?"

"Lib was famous for her hobbyhorses, like the time she decided that what the bell tower in the town square needed was ivy—"

Adam came erect. "*She's* responsible for that? It got so thick it destroyed the grout between the bricks."

"That's...that was Lib. She'd act first, think second. She'd throw herself into whatever her latest bright idea was and wouldn't leave it alone until she'd completed it to her satisfaction."

"Well, if the ivy's an example, I believe you, but what's your point?"

"That if I believed the idea at all—suicide, which I don't—but if I did, I might...*might* be willing to entertain the notion that she'd do it once she'd finished this latest project, but *before?* No."

"How do you know she hadn't?" he asked.

That stopped her, but for only a moment. "Because she didn't call me. She specifically said she wanted me to be the first to know what she'd been working on. I went through all my messages and there was none from her. Lib Harland did not commit suicide, Adam."

"Excellent reasoning," he said dryly. "She didn't call, so she couldn't possibly have committed suicide."

"Don't patronize me," Pat snapped. "Just because I haven't been here doesn't mean I don't know what I'm talking about."

Adam's first reaction was, he had to admit, a chauvinistic lapse, a cliche. She was attractive when she was angry, eyes flashing, color high. But he didn't dare voice it and antagonize her further. "Pat, believe me, I hear you. But that's the Medical Examiner's verdict, unless toxicology tests say otherwise."

"When will you have that?"

"Not for another week or ten days. It's not like television. Lab results take time."

"Wait. You'll see," Pat said stubbornly.

"But you understand that if I accept your premise, that narrows the options. Have you stopped to consider what the remaining options are?"

"There's only one that makes sense—it was an accident. Lib could be genuinely ditzy, it was part of her charm. She didn't normally drink. I can't imagine why she decided to start now, but she wouldn't be used to it. It probably went to her head almost immediately, and she took the wrong medication. That happens all the time."

"There are problems with that theory," he said carefully. "One, Jim says he has never prescribed any sort of barbiturate for her. Where they came from is a mystery. Two, according to Miss Hetty there was a routine the two of them followed religiously—just before she left for the day Miss Hetty saw to it that Miss Harland took her medication. Lorna witnessed the transaction the day before her death. So there was no reason for Miss Harland to think she'd forgotten to take them earlier. Three, it seems that years ago, she had a very serious drinking problem."

"Lib?" Her eyes were huge with surprise.

"Yes. Lastly, and this may support the suicide theory more than anything else, Miss Harland had inoperable cancer. She didn't have long to live."

"Oh, God, poor Lib." Pat turned away and stared blindly out of the front windshield, her features taut with grief. Adam watched, aching to hold her, comfort her. He gripped the steering wheel as tightly as he could.

A new thought must have filtered through her anguish. Slowly she sat up straight. "Hetty didn't know Lib had cancer," she said, as if speaking to herself. "She couldn't have known or she'd have told me."

"Are you sure? Miss Harland might have sworn her to secrecy."

"I—I don't know. She didn't leave a note?"

Adam switched gears smoothly. "If she did, we didn't find it."

"Then Lib didn't commit suicide," she said, on firm ground again. "If she had, she'd have left pages and pages of explanation. It must have been an accident."

She believed the first, he saw. He was not, however, convinced that she believed the latter theory. She was too smart for that. It was time for him to stop stalling and bite the damned bullet.

"Pat, I have a proposition to put to you."

Another mercurial change. She turned to look at him, her lips stretching slowly in an enticing smile, her eyes dancing with mischief. "I may have let you kiss me, Adam Wyatt, but I'll have you know I'm not that kind of girl."

He frowned, so intent on fulfilling his onerous mission that it was a second before he caught the joke. He struggled with a smile of acknowledgment. "Let me rephrase that. I have an idea." That was true. He'd just come up with a wrinkle that might make a critical difference in being saddled with her.

"The proposition was much more flattering, but I guess an idea's better than nothing. What is it?"

Pat as coquette was playing havoc with his concentration. He buckled down, focused. "I have to find out where the barbiturates came from; there was more than one kind in her system. As for the alcoholic beverage—a coffee liqueur—personally, I can't see her waltzing into the liquor store without setting this town on its ear."

"Me, either."

"You're in a unique position. You know almost as much about Miss Harland as anyone in town, but from a different perspective, as a friend in very special standing, but one who's been gone long enough to be more objective about her than we might be."

"Perhaps. I'm not sure." Adam heard caution in her voice.

"You could probably answer most of the questions I'd have asked Miss Hetty, perhaps even come up with ones I might miss. What I'm proposing, badly, is that you work with me."

She stared at him so long that he became lost in the look of her. The moon had made its appearance, casting its beam into the car's interior, highlighting the bridge of her nose, her cheekbones. She seemed to glow.

"Work with you how?" she asked.

"You're an investigative reporter. Considering the variety of cases you've handled for your show, you probably have five times the experience of anyone on my force. They're good guys but all they've had to do is write tickets for speeders, break up Saturday night brawls at Buster's Roadhouse, and haul in drunks. I'm trying to train them, but they've got a long way to go."

"Here's a perfect opportunity for them to get some experience," Pat said.

"I'll use them where I can, but this involves the death of everyone's favorite Harland. I need someone who doesn't have to be told how to read body language, how to read between the lines and pick up more from what wasn't said than what was. So, what do you think?"

She took her time making up her mind, and Adam's stomach knotted. Finally she sighed. "Okay. When do I start?"

He paused before dealing what he considered his ace in the hole. "Tomorrow morning as soon as you've been sworn in."

"Sworn in?"

"Of course. I have to deputize you if you're to have access to official documents and confidential information. You'll have a badge, a real one. No gun, though."

"I'm relieved to hear it," she said dryly. "Well. Wearing a badge is more than I bargained for, but if you feel it's necessary..."

"It is. Is nine o'clock tomorrow too early for you?"

"No."

"Great. Meet me at the station. I'll swear you in and let you flip through the file before we go to the mansion."

"The mansion."

"To see Miss Harland's bedroom."

"Why? I've been there, remember?"

"Not since she died," he pointed out. "You'll understand once you've been through the file."

She shrugged. "I guess that decides it then—staying there, while the roof's being fixed, I mean. It seems preordained or something. All right. I guess I should go in and pack. Thanks for tonight, Adam—accompanying me to the wake, letting me drive to the creek. I really appreciate it."

"My pleasure." It was an automatic response, but he'd never meant it so intensely, Adam mused as he headed for his own empty house. God, what a mess. He was satisfied that he'd handled things fairly satisfactorily, except for the one slip at the creek, and he thought he'd managed the aftermath of that pretty well. Now if he could only find a way to cancel out the threat she presented as a very desirable woman who'd ignited a pilot light in his gut that he suspected would never go out.

Pat turned off the living-room light and stood in the safety of the dark until the car had disappeared. Too much had happened today, tonight. Hetty improving, the wake and people acting as if forgive and forget was the watchword. The autopsy results. Adam asking her help. Adam, period.

Pat locked the house and flopped across the bed, remembering the kiss. She hadn't expected his embrace, hadn't even seen it coming. After the initial surprise, however, she'd found herself responding, couldn't stop herself from answering the gentle invasion of his tongue with a tentative probing of her own. His kiss had been so tender, the circle of his arms so strong, the hard, muscular planes of his body so enticing. She'd caught herself just in time, had turned in an Oscar-quality performance afterward. Had he known how his touch, his fingers caressing the nape of her neck, had so completely set her afire, circumvented all her defenses . . .

She couldn't let it happen again. She had to focus her energies in one direction from here on. It was imperative she find out the reason for Hetty's "confession." She had to protect her, at all costs. Nothing else mattered. Including sweet, generous, virile Adam Wyatt.

Chapter 6

Police headquarters took up half of the ground floor of the courthouse, one large room on the front for Adam and his staff, one small room used, she assumed, for interrogations or private conversations, and behind that, three cells, all of them empty for the moment.

It was not the layout she remembered. It had been renovated since her previous visit. The depressing tan walls were now ivory, with brown, beige and orange curtains at the window. The furnishings were nondescript, but well cared for—no scarred arms on the chairs, no carved initials or gouges in the desktops. And someone on the force had a green thumb. Spider plants and pothos were suspended from the ceiling panels, leaves glistening with health. All those elements made for a non-threatening environment, alleviating the dread Pat had harbored at the prospect of being here again.

She'd felt more than a little hypocritical as she'd read and signed the oath for Adam. Thanks to this arrangement, she might be able to find out precisely what part Hetty had played in Lib's death. She'd convinced herself that she wasn't really withholding evidence. Hetty's garbled admission of guilt wasn't evidence. She couldn't have meant what she said.

Still, the fact that she was entering into this arrangement with a hidden agenda made Pat very uncomfortable, even though she suspected Adam had one, too. Being asked to help him in an official capacity was the highest form of flattery, but no matter from which angle she looked at it, it didn't make sense. If he felt his staff was that inexperienced, he could ask for help from the county police. Something fishy was afoot, she was sure of that.

"How's it going?"

Pat jumped, startled. Behind her, Adam sat perched on the railing that separated the waiting area from the rest of the room. God, he was gorgeous in uniform, broad-shouldered, narrow of waist and hip. His light blue short-sleeved shirt and slacks fitted as if custom-tailored. His dark hair, slightly curly, his thick dark brows, his clean-shaven, sun-bronzed complexion made his amber eyes that much more startling. A face with which men were probably very comfortable, and women probably loved. He was the picture of openness, trustworthiness. Why then didn't she trust him?

"I haven't gotten very far," she responded. "There's so much of it. I've read through the 911, situation reports, and the initial interview with Lorna. Where's Hetty's?"

"Never got one," he said. He took the chair beside her desk. "That's what I was working toward when she said she didn't feel well and wanted to go home. All we have is what little she gave us that first morning. She arrived at the mansion to fix breakfast, went upstairs and found Miss Harland still in bed, her body cold."

Eyeing the 911 computer printout, Pat frowned. "Lorna called for help at eight-forty? What took her so long?"

"How do you mean?"

"Well, Hetty would have shown up at seven. If she'd fixed Lib's breakfast before going upstairs to wake her, that would take only ten or fifteen minutes. Hetty's fast, and Lib rarely had more than cereal, juice and toast."

"Oh. Miss Hetty said she'd overslept and hadn't gotten there until around eight-fifteen. When Lorna arrived from C.J.'s a few minutes later... Well, you read what she said."

Pat flipped back to Lorna Forsythe's statement again.

Miss Hetty was sitting near the bottom of the steps, all out of breath. I thought she was having a heart attack or something. She told me she'd just come from upstairs and that poor Miss Lib was dead. I ran up to see, just in case, don't ya know. She looked like she was sleeping, so peaceful and all, but she wasn't. Soon's I touched her I knew Hetty was right. So I called y'all.

Pat returned the typed sheet to the folder, lined up its edges with those of the other material, neatened the small pile. It was something to do while she composed herself. Because Hetty Melton never overslept. Weekdays, weekends, no matter, she awoke at five, without benefit of an alarm. Her internal clock sufficed. To believe that on that morning of all mornings she had overslept was stretching coincidence to the breaking point. Hetty Melton had lied, and there was roughly an hour and a half unaccounted for.

"Here's your coffee, Pat. Just brewed." Bo bounded into the room and slowed to a more decorous speed when he saw Adam. "Uh, hi, Chief." He placed the cup in front of her with great ceremony.

Adam gave a long-suffering sigh. "Bo, suppose you tell me who manned the radio and the phone while you were gone?"

Bo's mouth opened in a silent *Oh*. "I was only gone a couple of minutes. But I shouldn't have," he added, the picture of contrition. "I'm sorry. It won't happen again. That's a promise."

"Keep it," Adam said gently.

"Yes, sir." Tail between his legs, Bo moved back to the front of the room where an oversized desk contained the communications console.

Adam rolled his eyes toward the ceiling and shook his head. "Kids," he said under his breath. "What's your schedule today?"

"Lib's funeral at eleven, then a conference with Dr. Vernon. And I have to be near a phone at three for a conference call with my assistant and the producers to talk about letting me off the hook for the next couple of months. After that, I'm all yours." She felt her face redden.

He let that pass without comment, for which she was grateful. "I put your suitcase in the cruiser, so why don't we run over to the mansion now and get you settled in the guest wing before you take a look at Miss Harland's suite. Afterward I'll have Troy bring you back to pick up your car. He's stationed at the mansion and probably needs a break."

"Aren't you going to the funeral?"

"Yes, but in a working capacity. Police escort for the funeral procession."

"Lib's funeral." Pat gathered her purse and notepad. "It's still so hard to believe."

"She seemed like a nice lady," Adam said, opening the gate for her. "I'm sorry I didn't know her better. You've got the watch, Bo."

"Yes, sir." He snapped a salute for Adam and a grin for Pat.

"Why do you have someone stationed at the mansion?" she asked, once she was buckled in the cruiser.

"Didn't want people stomping all over Miss Harland's wing, that's all."

Pat wondered about that as they circled the town square, but lost her train of thought as they drove through Harland Grove's downtown area. Every third commercial establishment was closed and a good many of those still open bore signs advertising going out of business sales. "Adam, what's been happening around here?" she asked. "Did the recession hit the Grove that hard?"

"It didn't help. The town's been in a decline for the last several years."

"But why? H.I.'s the lifeblood of the Grove. If it's still working two shifts—Miss Sarah mentioned it when I returned her dishes—the demand for Cammio must be pretty high."

"Not high enough," Adam said, slowing to pull abreast of a step van about to park in front of a fire hydrant. Rolling down the window, he stuck his head out and called to the driver. "You don't really want to do that, do you, Polk?"

"Reckon not, Chief." The driver gave him a sheepish grin, then signaled to pull away from the curb.

"Jackass," Adam muttered, and picked up the mike. "Unit One to Central."

Bo's voice responded, accompanied by a symphony of static. "Central to Unit One. Something wrong, Chief?"

"Call Maceo and tell him today's the last time I'm warning Polk about blocking the fire hydrant in front of the cleaners. Either Maceo sees that his driver obeys the traffic laws or he can figure some other way to have his goods delivered. Let him know I'm not kidding, Bo."

"Yes, sir. Central out."

Adam glanced at Pat. "What were we talking about?"

"Harland Industries and its double shifts," Pat said, impressed by the fact that at no time had Adam raised his voice, neither at Polk nor when talking to Bo, yet the overtone of command had been unmistakable. She liked his management style.

"Evidently," he was saying, "H.I. suffered under Margaret Harland's leadership. C.J. has been playing catch-up ever since she died. Those two shifts are a slowdown. At one time, there were shifts around the clock."

"But Cammio is fantastic stuff," Pat responded with feeling, "from cleanser to face powder. And, I hesitate to add, it ain't cheap."

"Maybe so, but she wouldn't let the business grow. Damn," he growled as they approached the railroad tracks at the end of Main. The warning light began to flash, its bell clanging, and the crossing gate lowered, blocking their path. Adam glanced in the rearview mirror. "Too many cars behind me for me to back up. We're stuck until this freight goes by."

A pair of diesels eased into view and the parade of boxcars and coal tenders rumbled past at a leisurely pace. Adam engaged the emergency brake, put the cruiser in neutral and relaxed. "Anyhow," he continued, "C.J.'s done the best he could to keep the plant going, but he's fighting a losing battle. It's really aged him."

"How long have you known him?" she asked.

"Seven or eight years. Met him on a red-eye flight from L.A. We got to talking and stumbled onto our mutual love of jazz. The next time he was in N.Y. on business, he called and we wound up closing a little jazz club in the Village. It just grew from there."

Their friendship ran deeper than she'd thought. "So you became buddies, fine, but what kind of inducements could he offer to lure you away from New York? From the Big Apple to the Grove? That's a big jump."

"It didn't take much," Adam said. "My wife was killed three years ago."

Pat gasped. It had never occurred to her that he might be a widower. She'd assumed he was divorced. "Oh, Adam, I'm sorry."

"Thanks. Time helps. What made it worse is that Corey, my son, saw it happen. It traumatized him. I was on leave, trying to find a therapist for him, when C.J. called to ask if I could recommend a private investigator who knew something about industrial espionage. I'd wanted a complete change of scene for Corey anyhow, so I volunteered. We camped in C.J.'s guest rooms while I familiarized myself with the operation of the plant and tagged the culprit inside a week. Meanwhile, I was seeing a change for the better in Corey. He'd had a ball playing with C.J.'s kids."

"How old was he then?"

"Six. That's when I decided I wanted him to know what it was like to live in a house with a yard, among neighbors who were more than names on a bank of mailboxes in an apartment lobby. By that time, C.J. was trying to make the Grove more attractive to businesses looking to relocate. One arm of his plan was to put in place a proper police force. He asked me if I'd consider helping him start the process. That was three years ago. I've got an infuriatingly normal nine-year-old now, thanks to the Grove. I owe this place a lot."

Pat decided to keep her mouth shut. So far the Grove had been generous with what he and his son needed. She just hoped they didn't fall into the same trap she had, feeling themselves one of Them, only to find that when the chips were down, the town would close ranks, with him and his son outside the circle of wagons.

"I'm glad things have worked out for you," she said. "The Grove is a unique place, I have to admit."

"But you wouldn't want to live here. Don't think you could be happy in a town this size?"

"Size has nothing to do with it," Pat said firmly. "I'm not as rabid as I was when I first got here, but make no mistake, I have no great love for Harland Grove. Another thing—this community exists for one purpose, the manufacture of Cammio Cosmetics. Either you work at H.I., or for a business that supports the plant, or the Harlands, in some way. What would I do here?"

"But that's part of the problem," Adam said. "The Grove needs new people with fresh ideas, new industries. C.J.'s trying, I'll give him that."

"Has the herbal shampoo guy made a decision yet?" Pat asked.

Adam was surprised. "You know about that?"

"Of course. Hetty told me."

"We'll know something by the end of the month. But that's the kind of thing that could make a big difference around here."

The last of the freight train rumbled past and the crossing gate jerked upright again. Adam led the procession of waiting cars across the tracks and turned onto Harland Avenue, a broad tree-lined thoroughfare far too pretentious for a town with only three traffic lights. The homes on this stretch were large and imposing, with sculptured gardens and impeccable landscaping.

Adam pointed toward a low-slung brick rancher that nestled on the lawn as if it was growing roots. Behind it was a latticed gazebo, and a sizable playhouse. "That's C.J.'s."

Pat wasn't surprised. "He's the only Harland left, isn't he?"

"Except for distant cousins in Florida and Colorado, I think. I feel a little sorry for him. He's a good guy. And a good friend."

Which I'd be wise to remember, Pat told herself. It made Adam a double threat. Not only did he work for C.J., he felt a personal loyalty to him, as well.

Adam signaled for a right and turned into a wide, brick-surfaced driveway. Pat had tried to steel herself for her first close-up view of the mansion, but it didn't help. Even though Margaret Harland had made it clear she was not welcome in the private domain of the west wing she shared with C.J., this had been Pat's second home, thanks to Lib, who'd allowed her the run of her suite and the main part of the house: parlors, dining room, library, solarium and kitchen. And Margaret could do little about it except complain, because Lib was the Harland by blood. It was Lib who'd inherited the property when her brother, C.J.'s father, had died. Margaret might run things at the plant, but at home Lib called the shots.

Adam started to introduce her to the young man standing sentry at the front door, but was interrupted when he grinned and waved off Adam's attempt. "Don't bother, Chief. Patty and me, we go back a long way. She's the only female ever kicked my butt and got away with it."

Pat stared at him, took in the butterscotch complexion, sandy hair, and the gap-toothed smile. "Troy Lee Graham," she said, and burst into laughter. "A cop? You?"

"Yes, ma'am. It's good to see you. She used to baby-sit me," he explained for Adam's benefit. "I loved her, decided I was gonna marry her someday." He reached for her ring finger.

"I was too much woman for you then and still am," she said, and slapped his hand away. "How's your family?" That was as specific as she dared be; she couldn't remember whether his parents were still alive.

"Everybody's fine. How's Miss Hetty?"

She gave him her stock answer, which opened the door for Adam to outline Troy's assignment as her temporary chauffeur.

"Be right out here waiting," Troy said, ogling her outrageously. "Hot damn! Gonna be driving a TV star around."

"Gonna be driving your baby-sitter around," Pat corrected him. "And don't you forget it."

"Yes, ma'am." He bowed, and opened the door of the mansion for them.

"That's two of my men you've wrapped around your finger," Adam said once they were inside. "I've only got one left. Thank goodness he's married with three kids."

Pat's responding smile was automatic and perfunctory, as her attention was, in reality, focused on her surroundings. Nothing remained of the furnishings she remembered. Pat doubted, however, that the present decor was of Lib's choosing. The

sleek Scandinavian rosewood chairs and tables were as out of
place in the hundred-and-thirty-year-old house as a rap group
at a cotillion. The only familiar item was the enormous crystal
chandelier that dominated the foyer and bounced tiny rainbows of light off the treads of the broad curving staircase.

"Do you remember the way?" Adam asked.

Nodding, Pat climbed the steps, and at the top, turned right.
She opened the door of the guest wing and grimaced. Chinoi-
serie. In itself, attractive enough, but it simply didn't belong.

Adam placed her luggage on the intricately patterned dresser.
"Do you want to unpack first?"

"It can wait." There was a painful chore to be done and she
wanted to get it over with. Leaving the wing, she crossed to the
one opposite and stopped at a set of ornately carved double
doors. Yellow tape barred what lay beyond and warned against
unlawful entry. Adam removed it and opened the doors.

Pat stepped into Lib's sitting room. Once inside, the experience wasn't as painful as she'd anticipated. Lib's furniture
was new to her, making it easier to maintain some distance. The
color scheme, her favorite pink and white, and the collection of
owls were the only sources of discomfort, those and all the
books. Then she saw her picture dead center of the mantelpiece and the reality of her loss became too intense to anesthe-
tize.

The morning sun filtering through the glistening white sheers
triggered memories of afternoons nibbling on sugar-dusted tea
cookies and sipping iced tea, Lib lounging on her chaise, she on
the rug, both with noses glued in their books. Tears stung her
eyes and she quickly blinked them back.

She felt a touch on her arm and found Adam at her elbow,
his eyes warm with sympathy. "Pat," he said, his voice so
gentle that she found herself swaying toward him. Horrified,
she moved away, her back to him. "I wouldn't ask you to do
this," he continued, "but I'm counting on you to home in on
things I might not notice because I'm not familiar with Miss
Harland's personal preferences and habits, things that were
particular to her. And what you don't know, Miss Hetty may
have mentioned to you." He pulled her around to face him. His
cologne, an enticing blend of woods and spice, was a phero-

mone, making her blood sing. "I realize this isn't easy for you. I wouldn't ask you to do it if I didn't think it would help."

"And it goes with the job," she responded, her voice husky. She cleared her throat and, finally, her mind. "Okay." The question was, she thought, who would it help most, him or Hetty?

"I've got to run down to the car, but I won't come back in until you're ready for me," Adam said, leaving and easing the door shut behind him.

Pat gazed at the closed door, the generosity of his gesture warming her. She wished he'd stop surprising her. He was thoughtful and considerate in ways that betrayed how perceptive he was. Still, she'd be well advised not to underestimate his intelligence and dedication to duty, to the Harlands in the person of C.J., and to Harland Grove. With that in mind, she turned her attention to the assignment she'd accepted.

The bedroom, even larger than she remembered, was immaculate, except for a residue she recognized as the medium for lifting fingerprints. Lorna would be furious. Lib's wing was her bailiwick when it came to cleaning and, according to Hetty, she kept it spotless.

The nightstand held a ceramic lamp with fluted shade, a paperback book open, facedown, a small brass carriage clock, a box of tissues, and Lib's reading glasses. The pillow still held the imprint of her head, the sheets pulled back toward the foot of the bed. Pat's heart contracted, and she hurried into the bathroom for a quick look around.

Lib's signature pink and white were in evidence here, too, in the tiny floral pattern of the curtains and tank cover. Hand and bath towels were draped neatly over their holders, with matching facecloths stacked on a tray on the counter surrounding the washbasin. Pat went through the rooms on automatic pilot, looking, cataloging, filtering out, placing mental asterisks next to those things she considered deviations or surprises, considering her memory of Lib's mode of living, which she doubted had changed, except where her arthritis might have affected her activities. Twenty minutes later she sat down at Lib's secretary and listed the asterisked items. She'd done the best she could.

Finished, she found Adam sitting on the floor outside the door, a folder at his side. He seemed completely relaxed, patient. "I'm ready," she said.

Springing to his feet, he retrieved the folder and followed her back in. He stood behind her, his hands on her shoulders. "First, tell me the little things you noticed that you figure don't mean anything, for instance the general condition of the room."

Damn it, Pat thought. She had examined the anomalies she had seen with an eye toward whether or not he might have noticed them previously, and how bringing them to his attention might impact Hetty. He had pulled a fast one, approaching from an angle she hadn't considered.

And she'd have to move away from him as soon as she tactfully could. On the face of it there was nothing out of the ordinary about their positions, but since just being in the same room with him now bordered on the intimate to her, she wouldn't be able to think straight if he remained this close.

"The general condition of the room?" she said. "Lorna's going to shoot you for leaving all this fingerprint powder. She'd just cleaned up here."

"Why do you say that?"

"You can still see the vacuum cleaner tracks in the carpets. The only footprints in the pile are around the bed and out to the hallway. From the size of them, I assume they're the ambulance attendants' and the little ones would be Hetty's. But considering how tidy things are on the outer perimeters of the room, Lib hadn't had a chance to mess it up. She was a clutterbug."

"She was?" To her relief, it was Adam who moved from behind her. He circled the room and stopped some distance away, his brows saluting with surprise.

"Miss Harland a clutterer?"

"In spades. You could track her progress through a room. Wherever she went, she left a path of chaos in her wake—books, pencils, glasses, teacups. And smudges. She was a toucher, like me."

"Oh?"

"Super-tactile, I guess. We sort of relate to things by touching them."

"Does that go for people, too?" His voice was low, rich with meaning.

Pat grabbed her resolve, held on tightly. "In Lib's case, it did. She was a hugger. But in here, for instance, she'd trail her hands over flat surfaces as she went by, patting this, fiddling with that, a fingerprint expert's dream, so I'm sure you picked up plenty of them."

"Well, well," Adam said, a bemused expression on his face. "I had pegged Miss Harland as pathologically neat, an organized person."

Pat burst into laughter, relieved that he was back on track. "Not on your life. And she was a spiller." She pulled back the fringed throw rug beside the bed. "See? Lib spilled something here. You can see where it was wiped up. What surprises me is that she'd use a salmon pink throw rug to hide it, instead of white, or a shell pink that matches the other tones in here."

Adam smiled tightly. "Very good. Anything else?" He watched her with an expectant air.

"I don't know if it's important . . ."

"Tell me anyway."

"Lib loved to match and mix patterns, but she would never countenance pillowcases that didn't match the sheets, and these pillowcases don't."

"I noticed that myself. So did Bo."

"And the books," she said, moving around the bed to the nightstand. Its contents had given her a moment of anguish while she'd been in the room. "Lib rarely read one book at a time, so she used bookmarks. She had dozens of them. She would never have left a book open and facedown like this. She'd have said it put too much stress on its spine. That's how much she cherished books."

"Even a paperback romance?"

So he'd noticed. "A paperback's a book. That's all that mattered. And it's one I sent her, so she'd have treated it with special care."

He came to the nightstand, picked it up. "You read these?"

"Sure, why not?"

He gazed down at her, puzzled. "It would never occur to me you'd go in for this kind of thing. I wouldn't think you'd need it."

Pat took umbrage at that. "I don't *need* them. I enjoy them. They'd never admit it, but men have been known to read them, too."

Adam snorted. "Bull! Men like realism. These are pure fantasy. People making love with such passion that the earth moves? Give me a break. They're obviously written by and for women who're . . . well, unfulfilled."

He had hit below the belt. Insulted anew, Pat went for the jugular, dropping the mask that hid her hunger for him. "How sad," she said, her voice low and husky. She knew she was treading dangerous ground, but he'd asked for it. "It's obvious you've never experienced the kind of lovemaking that would melt the fillings in your teeth."

Adam blinked, unable to hide his surprise. "I . . . don't have any fillings."

"Pity. It might be worth a couple."

His eyes filled with curiosity—and heat. "Is that what it's like making love with you?" he asked softly.

She let him wait, holding his gaze squarely. The air sizzled. "Yes." She picked up the book and handed it to him. "Read one sometime. Find out what you're missing." She moved away from him.

"Pat."

Turning, she looked back over her shoulder, her face without expression, she hoped.

"I went too far, didn't I? I'm sorry. The truth is, there's nothing I'd like more than making love to you. But—"

"But nothing, Adam," she said gently, masking her utter astonishment at his admission. "It's not going to happen. I won't play games with my body or my emotions. Being intimate to me implies commitment and for us that's not in the cards. So there's no point in this discussion, is there? Can we get back to business now?"

He took a deep, button-stressing breath, his face seamed with sadness. "Perhaps we'd better." Crossing to the window seat, he sat down, elbows on his knees, his head lowered.

It took some doing, but Pat finally switched gears, filing away their previous conversation. She could mourn what would never be when she was alone. "This is the way the bedroom looked the morning Lib was found?"

He glanced up. "Yes. As far as I could tell, nothing had been touched when Bo and I went over it the next day."

"But you did remove the bottle of whatever she'd been drinking and her glass. There had to be a glass. Lib would never have drunk from the bottle. She was a lady."

Adam appeared to have recovered. He smiled. "Good for you. There was no bottle, Pat. No glass, no alcohol anywhere in the house. And no pills up here. Her arthritis medication was downstairs."

Chilled by a sudden foreboding, Pat rubbed her arms. Removing the bottle was something Hetty might do to protect Lib's good name. Or perhaps to protect her own? another voice asked. Something was stirring in a remote corner of her brain, an unpleasant memory sent scurrying into and out of the light. The stealth of it perturbed her, didn't bode well.

"Pat?" She came to, to find Adam snapping his fingers. "Where were you?"

"Sorry. Just thinking. That reminds me. I didn't see the autopsy report."

"When you've finished. Or are you?"

"Not quite. The rug in the bathroom doesn't match anything else in there and a couple of hand towels are missing."

"Hand towels?"

"Lib liked her bath towels draped over the towel rack first, on top of them, hand towels, then facecloths. There are a pair of hand towels missing. That's everything. Did that help?"

"Definitely. I'll tell you how much a bit later. I brought in the autopsy report from the car. I'm going to ask you to read it in here because I want you to be able to visualize what happened."

"I . . . don't understand."

"You will. Here." He placed the file folder on Lib's delicate secretary and pulled out the chair for her. Dreading what was to come, Pat sat down. Adam's eyes filled with understanding. "Don't worry. I removed the photographs of her body."

"Thanks. I appreciate that." Suppressing a shudder, she began to read, but after the initial narrative, which related facts she already knew— Caucasian female, height: sixty-five inches; weight: one hundred two; age, physical marks, etc.— Pat realized she'd need an interpreter, especially when the subject of lividity began. "This is Greek, Adam. What does it mean?"

He knelt beside her, pointing at entries as he explained, one arm around the back of her chair. There was no physical contact between them but it was still distracting. With a stab of pain in her midsection, she realized Adam would probably never touch her again.

"A lot of the entries probably aren't important," he said, "but this is. Her blood alcohol level was such that even if that's all she'd had, she'd have lapsed into a coma and eventually would have died. But because the barbiturates had been dissolved in the liqueur—"

"Dissolved . . . ?" Pat interrupted. "Rather than swallowed whole?"

"Right. One was short-acting. The combination hit her hard and fast. The second important piece of information is here. The location of the lividity and the indentations on her skin."

Pat read through the section, read it again. She got up and crossed to the bathroom door, her eyes glued on the tile floor. "Lib died in here?"

Adam, still on one knee, didn't move. "Yes. Another thing. At some point she spilled some of the liqueur in her lap. There was residue across her thighs and some in the hollow of her neck, so her gown should have been soiled in a couple of places. The one she was wearing when we saw her was fresh, clean, not a stain in sight."

Pat leaned against the bookcase, a chorus of hallelujahs echoing through her mind. Hetty could not have lifted Lib. "Whoever carried her to the bed must not have realized she was dead."

"They had to have known. The air-conditioning's on, so her body cooled faster than it would under normal circumstances. And she had to have been on the floor for a considerable length of time for the pattern of the tile to have become etched on her skin."

"But why change her gown?"

"I'm not sure," he said, getting to his feet. "Probably for the same reason someone removed the bottle of liqueur. And if you'd gotten a little farther in the case file, you'd have picked up a few other things: the reason for the off-color bath mat, for instance."

"Why is it there?"

"Lorna cleans top to bottom every Saturday, and makes do with dusting every other day during the week. I checked with her. When she dusted the day before Miss Harland was found, everything in this suite matched. The next morning it didn't. Someone removed them and substituted the others."

"But why?" Pat asked.

"Lorna uses a liquid cleanser on the floor tiles, because scouring powder would mar the finish. Run your fingers across the tile and examine the grout closely, and you'll see that someone scrubbed that floor with scouring powder, probably with the missing hand towels. As for the bath mat, it might have been stained."

Shuddering, Pat moved away from the bathroom door and sank down on the blanket chest at the foot of the bed.

Adam wasn't finished. "Think about it, Pat. They moved her, changed her gown and the pillowcases. They scrubbed the john, then vacuumed from the john all around the bed and out into the hallway. That's why you can still see the tracks the vacuum made. The tracks Lorna had left the Saturday before would have been gone."

Looking back over her shoulder, Pat realized he was right. "Adam, this is crazy."

"And if you'll take a closer look at the fingerprint powder," he continued, "you'll see that there isn't a single print on the nightstand or anything on it, no prints on the bedposts, no prints on the light switch by the door. The bathroom was just as clean, too. Put all those things together and the picture begins to take a very different shape.''

Slowly, Pat raised her head. It was time to stop ducking the issue. "You think Lib was murdered?"

"You disagree?"

She stared at him, her thoughts spinning through the mazes of possibilities, hitting dead ends, blind alleys, resisting his line of reasoning at every turn. There had to be another explanation.

"But who would want Lib dead, Adam? And why? She was no danger to anyone. What was there to be gained?"

"Motive, you mean." He turned and walked back to the window, moving a curtain aside to look out. "I'm glad you brought that up. Leland Stokes, the family attorney, said Miss Harland called him and said she was thinking about changing her will. She evidently wrote a codicil, because Lorna and Pete, the yardman, were asked to sign as witnesses. They didn't read it, so they have no idea what it said. It has disappeared, too. The fact that she wanted to change it might be a motive for somebody."

"Then it seems to me," Pat said, "that the only persons who stood to lose anything were her family."

"There were token bequests for Lorna and Pete."

Despite how it would sound, Pat had to ask. "Nothing for Hetty?"

"Quite the opposite." He stood, arms folded, his eyes holding hers. "Miss Hetty receives a nice piece of change. Fifty thousand dollars."

"Fifty—!" Pat ran out of breath.

"'So that,' I'm quoting, 'my dearest friend can live her remaining years in comfort.' Losing that much money constitutes one hell of a motive."

"Losing . . . ?" At last she understood his train of thought. "You have no way of knowing that's the change Lib planned to make."

"True, but I doubt she'd have asked Pete and Lorna to be witnesses if she'd planned to cut them out of her will. Regardless, they both have alibis for the night Miss Harland died."

"What about her shares in H.I.?" Pat asked, playing devil's advocate as much for her benefit as his.

"They remain in the family of the owners in perpetuity. But she could do what she liked with her own money."

"So?"

"So she and Miss Hetty had had a falling out—about what no one seems to know, but both Lorna and Pete concur that they weren't speaking. If Miss Harland had decided to cut your aunt out of her will, Miss Hetty had a lot to lose."

Pat's hold on her temper began to erode. "Adam, that's ridiculous. It's not as if this is the first time Lib and Hetty'd had arguments."

"Perhaps, but it was obviously a serious one this time."

"Not *that* serious," she countered, feeling the onset of panic. "Besides, Hetty doesn't need the money. Lib paid her enough so that it wouldn't impact on the amount she got from social security. She has her savings, and I send her money every month."

"Are you telling me she couldn't use that fifty thousand? I don't know anyone who couldn't."

"Suppose she was changing what she was leaving—"

"The cousins get nothing," he interrupted. "C.J. gets this house and grounds and whatever else was left. That's everybody."

"Why," Pat demanded, "do I get the impression that you think Hetty's the only one with a motive—one you've attributed to her purely on circumstantial evidence?"

Adam held up a hand. "She isn't the only suspect by any means, but—"

"Suspect?" The term jarred her. "Suspected of what? All you can prove so far is that someone moved Lib's body and then cleaned up. Just because you think she was murdered doesn't mean she was. Nothing yet says that she didn't drop those pills into the liqueur and drink it down of her own free will."

A frown of annoyance tugged his brows together. "Need I remind you that you're the one who maintained she wouldn't kill herself? Not that the reasons made much sense, but it happens that I agree with you. I don't think she did, either. What's the problem? Is her suicide suddenly a more acceptable theory?''

Head tilted to one side, she peered at him, eyes narrowed in thought. Suddenly she was repulsed by her attraction to him, certain that she'd been right to mistrust that open face. ''And I wonder why you rejected it from the first, even when there was no evidence to suggest anything else, why you've shot it down every step of the way—almost as if it's important that the verdict is anything but suicide.''

''What the hell is that supposed to mean?'' he asked, advancing on her.

She stood her ground, unconcerned about his menacing posture, but breathing shallowly to lessen the effect of his clean, woodsy scent, which threatened to derail her train of thought. ''It occurs to me one reason why suicide might be downright inconvenient...Lib's life insurance. The company wouldn't pay off if she took her own life. How much is it worth, Adam? A lot, right?''

''Two hundred and fifty thousand.''

''And who are her beneficiaries?''

He didn't respond.

''C.J. Harland, right? As you said, a nice piece of change. He could use it. The plant could use it. What'd he say, Adam? Investigate all you want, work it any way you like as long as it's not suicide?''

He reacted as if he'd been slapped, his pupils dilating with shock and anger.

''And there's poor Hetty,'' Pat continued, her deep voice resonating with sarcasm, ''the perfect answer to your quandary. And her niece with the Grand Canyon mouth, helping you build your case by telling you she and Lib were on the outs. The Harlands stick it to the Meltons again, is that it? You don't even have to worry about protests of innocence from her, because, hey folks, *she can't talk!*''

''Damn it, if you were a man...'' he said, fists clenched in anger.

''I'd be a man dealing with an errand boy.''

Pat knew immediately she'd crossed the line and held her breath, steeled for the possibility of a violent reaction.

She got it. Adam grabbed her, his hand like a steel band around her arm, the other holding the back of her head securely as his mouth came down on hers, hard, unrelenting, his tongue levering its way between her lips, breaching her clenched teeth, then raiding the space beyond, taking possession with authority. Pat struggled to pull away from him, but could not move.

Gradually the ferocity of his embrace began to subside, replaced by an ardor that overwhelmed them both. The hand on her upper arm traveled to her waist, pulling her closer, until there was not a sliver of daylight between them. Pat found herself meeting every thrust of his tongue with her own, her arms around his back, her nails grasping at the fabric of his shirt, her breath rapid, her pulse racing.

As abruptly as he'd grabbed her, he let her go, his eyes blazing down into hers. "That's to let you know you are *not* dealing with a *boy!*"

Furious that she'd been so easily seduced into yielding to and reciprocating his embrace, Pat's anger turned hard and cold. "So you're an errand man, big deal. C.J.'s flunky. I see now why you needed my help. Build a case against Hetty and who's going to question it? Her own niece was involved in the investigation. Well, I've got news for you, I'm off the team. I won't help the Harlands railroad Hetty the way they did me."

"I knew this wouldn't work out. I knew it," Adam said, visibly seething.

"Oh-hh, so it wasn't your idea? The fact that you went along with it tells me exactly whose idea it really was. Count me out, Chief Wyatt. Try to pin this on Hetty and I'll make a stink like you wouldn't believe. Now, if you'll excuse me, I have a funeral to attend."

Adam, ears ringing from the door Pat had slammed, looked around in frustration, longing for something, anything he could pick up and smash to smithereens. How could she have made him lose control that way? Why in heaven's name had he kissed her? He'd lost that battle. The sweet taste of her had made him almost forget what he'd meant to prove. She'd felt so damned good pressed against him.

The deal was off? Good! He wouldn't try to change her mind and he didn't care what Quint and C.J. or anyone else said. Storming from the wing, he took the steps two at a time, headed out of the house and almost ran over Troy Lee standing outside the front door.

"Take her back to town, so she can pick up her car," he growled, "then take over for Bo at the station."

Troy Lee followed him down the steps. "Right, Chief. Hey, you sure look funny. What's the matter?"

"Nothing." Adam strode toward the cruiser. "Start the car and get the air conditioner going. She'll be out soon."

"Say, you're mad, ain't ya? I've never seen you mad before. Patty say something that got to you?"

"I gave you an order, Troy Lee," he said, getting into the cruiser.

"She did, didn't she?" Troy chortled. "Man, you might as well throw in the towel. Any woman riles a cool old dude like you, she's got you. You're hers. Got your nose wide open. Who'd have thought it?"

Adam started the engine. "Officer Graham, do you want to stay on this police force?"

Troy tried mightily to contain his smile. "Yes, sir, Chief. Sir."

"Then don't push your luck. And keep your mouth shut while you're with Ms. Chase. Am I clear?"

"Yes, sir, I hear ya," he said, stepping back as Adam sped away.

Adam drove like an idiot until he reached the railroad tracks and had to sit, steaming, while the ten-thirty freight headed north. By the time it had passed, he had cooled down enough to analyze why he was so angry. One, she'd hit the nail on the head, at an angle, but still, she'd hit it. In acceding to C.J.'s and Quint's wishes, he probably did appear to be an errand boy, no matter what his reasons for going along. Two, given her experience years before and the way things were stacking up this time, it was only natural she'd draw a parallel with her past. Three, the whole time she was blowing off, the whole time he was kissing her, all he could think of was her comment about melting his fillings. Her anger had rouged her cheeks and had lit a blaze of passion in her eyes. For a split second he'd even pictured her with that same fire consuming her, under him, in his bed.

The caboose rattled by. Adam put the cruiser in gear and eased across the tracks. That smart ass Troy Lee was right. She had him. He wasn't sure how it had happened, but she had him. He ached for her. And she probably hated his guts.

Chapter 7

"Pat. You up?"

"Yesh." Pat, brushing her teeth, stuck her head out of the bathroom.

Lorna Forsythe stood in the bedroom door. "Mornin', honey. Chief Wyatt's here."

"What?" Pat stopped brushing. "You mean, downstairs?"

"Sure is. He was waiting outside when I came over from Mr. C.J.'s. He said you weren't expecting him, that he would wait. What are you wearing today? I'll get it out for you." She crossed to the closet with the characteristic wide-legged gait of the Forsythe family. It seemed exaggerated in Lorna, whose contours resembled that of the Pillsbury Doughboy. Her fine graying hair, coiled atop her head in an elaborate knot, and her pale, almost translucent complexion, did nothing to dispel the illusion.

Pat dispensed with the toothbrush. "The turquoise shirt-waist, I guess," she said. "I don't have a lot of choice." She'd planned on jeans, something casual, but that was before she knew she'd be seeing Adam. The turquoise was flattering, made her waist look even smaller than it was. She wanted him to see what he was missing. "If I don't do some laundry," she said to Lorna, "I won't have any choice at all."

"Let me do it. I'd be glad to." Lorna's round gray eyes pleaded with her. "It's hard being here with nothing to do. Hetty's getting better, is she?"

"By degrees. They're going to sit her up today."

"I'm so glad. She's the only reason Miss Lib kept going long as she did. But Mr. C.J. and Rena, they put her away in fine style, didn't they? A grand funeral." Lorna hovered, as if delaying the moment she'd have to leave.

Sensing it, Pat hot-curled her hair with the bathroom door open. She'd met the housekeeper for the first time the evening before, after returning from the hospital, and had been surprised to see her. She had assumed that, with Lib gone, Lorna's double duty, cooking for C.J.'s family while acting as housekeeper for the mansion, had come to an end. C.J., however, had asked her to continue while Pat was there. Truthfully, Pat was relieved, uneasy at being in the big house alone.

"Lorna, how long had Lib and Hetty been on the outs?"

"Oh, about a month or more." The housekeeper's face drooped with sadness. "They had their little tiffs before, but it was different this time. Hetty, she was fit to be tied over whatever. Miss Lib tried to make it up to her, but Hetty was having none of it, so Miss Lib just shut herself away, or went out a lot, working on her project."

"When did that start? After the argument?"

"No'm, before. See, Miss Lib started worrying about what would happen to the mansion after she was gone. Rena doesn't want it, says it spooks her. It does creak and moan like it's got arthritic joints. Mr. C.J. doesn't seem to have much feeling for the place, even though this is where he was raised. All he thinks about is how much it costs every time something needs fixing. So Miss Lib decides to see what she can do about making sure it doesn't get torn down."

"What'd she have in mind?" Pat delayed dressing, wanting to learn as much as she could before terminating the conversation.

"I don't know, but she was bound and determined to do something. Rooted around and found the drawings old

Ephraim Harland used, blueprints like. Then she got awfully sneaky about it. Anybody come into the room, she'd cover up her papers. Or she'd shut herself in the library and not come out for hours.''

"Well, that's where all the old Harland family documents are kept—at least, they used to be.''

She shrugged. "I never paid it much mind. Besides, she started locking the door, wouldn't let anybody in there, not even the people from the cleaning service.''

"That's odd.''

"Well, not meaning any disrespect, but she was getting odder by the day. She'd slip out the house without letting anybody know she was leaving or where she was going. I'd knock on the library door with her tea or afternoon snack. No answer. I go around to peek in from the garden side. She's gone. But whatever she was doing, she was sure excited about it. Lord, I'll miss her.'' Tears glistened in her eyes. "Well, I reckon I'd better get on downstairs. I'll tell the Chief you'll be with him directly.''

"Thanks, Lorna.''

"Shall I fix you a little breakfast?''

"Just coffee, please.''

She frowned in disapproval. "Hetty wouldn't like that. But if that's all you want . . .'' She left, shaking her head.

Pat dressed hurriedly, digesting the information she'd learned. Hetty wouldn't have objected to Lib's project. So what had they argued about? She'd planned to attack that question first thing. Now, with Adam appearing unexpectedly, it would have to wait. What could he want? She was mad as hell at him but that didn't stop her from wanting him any less.

Putting on her best gold hoop earrings, Pat began a slide into melancholia. Why couldn't she have met him somewhere else? She felt so comfortable with him most of the time, free to talk about anything, which was unusual for her, since off camera she was still a prisoner of her shyness. That, in combination with an unwillingness to trust, to open herself to rejection or betrayal, kept her behind bars she herself had erected. Adam had torn them down.

Adam Wyatt was the first man who'd appealed to her immediately on a variety of fronts: physically, intellectually, emotionally. She loved the look of him, his strength and sense of self, his presence. She had loved the feel of his arms around her, the sureness with which his mouth had taken possession of hers. Except for his loyalties to C.J. and Harland Grove, she'd have probably wrapped herself in a red ribbon and presented herself for the taking, another first for her. But those loyalties of his were insurmountable obstacles and the offshoot of one of them threatened the freedom of Hetty's remaining years. She couldn't let the fact that every cell screamed for him matter to her. She'd lived with other kinds of pain, she could live with this.

Adam waited at the bottom of the stairs, his face solemn, his amber eyes wary. Looking down at him, Pat felt her vital organs become jelly. He'd added the jacket to his summer uniform and carried his cap under his arm. The pale blue complemented his warm bronze skin. She longed to touch him, and shoved her hands in her skirt pockets. It was time for another Oscar-caliber performance. She had to mask her feelings for him.

"Good morning," he said. "Sorry to bust in so early, but we need to talk."

"About . . . ?" Pat labored to sound disinterested.

"Coffee's ready." Lorna beckoned from the kitchen door.

"Thanks, Lorna." Leaving him to follow or not, Pat crossed the foyer and entered the room that had been Hetty's domain years before. It was spacious, bright, in coral and wheat, with top-of-the-line appliances. Hetty must have enjoyed preparing meals here.

Lorna had set the table in the breakfast room, an alcove off the kitchen. "Y'all sit down, now, hear?" the housekeeper ordered, and bustled to get the coffeepot. She'd laid out delicate rose-colored porcelain, white linen napkins, and a plate of croissants. Pat sat down before Adam could get to the chair to hold it for her. He removed his jacket, draping it around the back of the seat opposite, a muscle twitching in his temple.

"Lorna, I didn't mean for you to go to any trouble," Pat said as her cup was filled.

She beamed at them. "Happy to do it. Rena sent the pastries. Now, y'all enjoy your breakfast. I'll be upstairs. If you need something just call me on the intercom there."

Pat was silent after the kitchen door closed, leaving it to Adam to begin the conversation, since she had no idea why he'd come. She watched his hands as he spooned sugar into his coffee. They were good hands, square, capable-looking, his fingers long, lean and agile. She longed to hold them, lace her fingers between his, feel them smooth her arm, her cheek, caress the skin at the back of her neck.

Perhaps he was trying to wait her out, but she'd downed half her cup before he finally spoke. "I want to clear the air," he began in a forthright manner. "I was wrong yesterday, Pat. I was mad as hell, but I had no right to get physical with you. I've never lost control like that before, never, and the fact that you're a damned attractive woman and I'm only human is no excuse. I'm here to apologize."

Pat hadn't expected this and he grew even taller in her eyes. "Apology accepted."

"Thank you. Now that that's out of the way, I'm also here to ask you to reconsider. I really could use your help."

"To construct a case against Hetty? You must be joking." Her eyes narrowed. "Or did C.J. twist your arm to get you to twist mine a little?"

A hint of red filtered into his face. "I grant you, asking you to work with me wasn't my idea, but for your information, it wasn't C.J.'s, either."

That was a surprise. "Then whose was it?"

"That's irrelevant. I admit, I didn't like it worth a damn at first, but yesterday proved your value. Your reaction to the condition of Miss Harland's bedroom and the things you were able to tell me about her shed a new light on what happened the night she died."

"Terrific, unless I helped focus that light on Hetty. I will not help you build a case against her, Adam."

Several seconds of silence elapsed before he said, "I'm going to be completely honest with you, Pat, and hope that will help change your mind. I can't totally eliminate Miss Hetty from the picture, but she's not as strong a suspect now."

Pat couldn't believe what she'd heard. "Why?"

"I found out what a hard-line teetotaler she is. According to one source, she chewed out Perry Franklin for taking over the liquor store, and I'd already learned from him that in the eleven years he's managed the place, Miss Hetty has never set foot in it. And—I'm coming clean here—the search of her house was a waste of time. We found—"

"Hold it," Pat interrupted. In trying to remember where she'd seen or heard Mr. Franklin's name before, she'd almost missed Adam's admission. "You searched Hetty's house? When?"

"The same day I brought C.J. to the hospital to see you. And before you ask, I had a search warrant. We hit C.J.'s and Lorna's that day, too. I didn't mention it because I didn't want to antagonize you. It was underhanded and I apologize. But the bottom line is that, considering your aunt's attitude about drinking, it's unlikely she'd supply Miss Harland with an alcoholic beverage for any purpose."

Was it possible, Pat wondered, that Lib's drinking had caused the rift between them? Playing for time, Pat refilled her cup, and without asking, his. No. Had Hetty known that Lib was drinking, she'd have given her notice on the spot, would have packed her belongings and headed for home.

"What I'm proposing," Adam broke into her train of thought, "is a truce. If Miss Harland committed suicide, help me prove it. Whatever the hell happened, help me prove it. You make a living by seeing to it that people honor their commitments. I'm asking you to honor yours."

The last thing Pat needed was to be hoisted with her own petard, especially by a man whose integrity had to be at least as malleable as her own. But perhaps he was right. She'd signed on because being a part of the team insured she could keep abreast of whatever information Adam and his men uncovered. If Hetty was no longer in the spotlight of his suspicion, it would be smart to make sure she stayed out of it, even if that meant compromising her integrity. God, Pat, she thought to herself. Her father had to be turning in his grave.

"All right," she said. "I'm in again. What do we do first?"

He exhaled gustily, as if some hurdle had just been cleared, and loosened the collar of his shirt. Pat averted her gaze to avoid staring at the smooth, strong column of his neck, the hollow above the juncture of his shoulderblades that begged to be kissed.

"I've talked to C.J.," he said, "but put off bothering Rena until she could get the funeral out of the way. So she's first. Then Miss Harland's garden club. They meet today. Perhaps they can give us a better feeling about her state of mind."

"Lorna says that the project Lib mentioned to me on the phone was a campaign to see that this house wouldn't be destroyed after she died. She probably never thought about it until she found out she didn't have long to live."

Adam nodded. "She had a couple of paperbacks squirreled under the bed about getting one's affairs in order, that kind of thing. Jim thinks she might have seen an out-of-town doctor about her condition. Somebody saw her getting off the train a couple of weeks ago." He reached around for his jacket. "We'd better get moving. Should we plan to run out to the hospital sometime today so you can visit Miss Hetty?"

"No." Pat took the cups to the sink. "Hetty still won't see me. She wakes up early and by eight at night, she's going down for the third time, so I'll run out there around nine. By then she'll be asleep, and my being there won't disturb her."

"Very clever," Adam said, with an admiring smile. "Pat, are we okay, you and me?"

Pat gazed into his thickly lashed eyes, felt her heart twist into a square knot, and lied like a champ. "We're just fine, Adam. Just fine."

They'd received the grand tour of the house, for Pat's benefit, and had been settled on Rena's immense white leather sectional couch with coffee and more pastries on bone china before Pat realized that as far as Rena was concerned, this was a social call.

"I'm glad you came so early," she said, casually elegant in a white silk jumpsuit and strappy sandals with heels high and pointed enough to be considered lethal weapons. "I've got a ten-thirty conference with the company that's designing Aunt Lib's headstone, and I go back to work tomorrow."

"You work?" Pat blurted in surprise.

"Didn't you know? I'm head of advertising and public relations at H.I."

"Rena, that's terrific. How do you manage with a house this size, three kids and a full-time job, too?"

"And the gourmet cooking club which I chair, and the hospital auxiliary and the Scouts, etc. It ain't easy." She guffawed, an echo of the horse laugh Pat remembered. "Seriously, if it weren't for Lorna cooking and a weekly housecleaning service, I couldn't do it. I'm sorry the kids aren't home to meet you. I promised they could go back to camp after the funeral. I figured with all the activities they'd be involved in, they wouldn't have time to brood over things. They were nuts about Aunt Lib."

"That was probably smart of you," Adam said, wresting the floor from her. She'd been talking nonstop since they'd arrived. "I put off bugging you as long as I could, Rena, but I'm still trying to trace the barbiturates your aunt took. We subpoenaed Heck Zimmerman's records to get a list of people who've had prescriptions for barbiturates filled at his pharmacy. As far as we can see, none have had even a remote connection with Miss Harland. If someone other than Heck is selling them, I've got to find out who it is and stop it now. So anything you can tell us about your aunt's last few days would be helpful."

Without warning, Rena burst into tears. "How could she have done this to us, to the children? What do I tell the kids? If I don't, somebody else will. There's no keeping secrets. Sooner or later, they'll find out she committed suicide."

Pat moved over to put an arm around her. "Come on, Rena, you'll think of the right thing to say. And kids are resilient. They'll bounce back."

"I guess. Oh, Lord, I'm a mess. Let me get some tissues." She left the room, a lithe figure with the grace of a model.

"Did you know her well when you were here?" Adam asked softly.

"Probably better than anyone else. We were pretty tight."

"Why don't I let you ask the questions, then? I hate to admit it, but I find her a bit intimidating."

Pat saw that he was serious. "Why?"

"Well, she's so damned gorgeous, for one thing."

"She is that," Pat conceded, with a mental wince from the bite of the green-eyed monster.

"Sorry." Rena swept back into the room, a wad of tissues in her hand. "Now, what can I tell you?"

"Did you see much of Lib, as a rule?" Pat asked.

She gazed from Pat to Adam and back, then said, "Oh, that's right. You're working with Adam. I'm glad. I keep telling him he could use the help of a good woman." She shot him a wicked grin and, to Pat's amusement, he actually blushed.

Pat poked her. "Quit it or you'll be late for your appointment. How often did you see Lib?"

She wrinkled her nose at Adam before answering. "I tried to check on her, either before work or during my lunch hour. She hadn't been looking well."

"Did she ever say anything about how she felt?"

"You remember how she was, Patty. She never complained, even when her arthritis was at its worst. I kept feeling, though, that whatever was bothering her was something new. Her skin had always been so clear—after all, she used Cammio every day—but her color had changed, become blotchy."

"She never saw a doctor?"

"I tried to get her to make an appointment with Doc Vernon. She kept saying she would, but she never did." Tears sprang into her eyes and she dabbed them away. "God, I'm tired of crying. Look, I hate to rush y'all, but I've got to change and leave for Charlotte. Why don't we finish this over dinner? Can the two of you come tomorrow night? Please?" she added when neither Pat nor Adam had a ready response. "Adam, we haven't had you here in ages, and Pat and I have to catch up on old times."

"All right with you?" he asked Pat.

It wasn't, but it might be the only way to find out more from her. "As long as it's after the hospital. Nine o'clock, maybe?"

"Nine-thirty, then. We'll eat fashionably late. Great." Rena led them to the door with the graciousness of an experienced hostess, making small talk all the way. "See you tomorrow, hear?" she said finally. "Patty, I'm so glad you're back."

Pat couldn't stand playing 'Let's Pretend' a moment longer. "Rena, why didn't you back me up with Chet Rowley that night?"

Her face crinkled in confusion. "Back you up? When? Chet Rowley's dead, didn't you know?"

"The night after the picnic our junior year. Chet Rowley called you—it had to be around midnight—to ask you—"

"Honey." Rena propped a hand on one lean hip. "Chet Rowley wouldn't call my house at midnight if someone paid him a million dollars. Daddy threatened to shoot him once, for making a pass at Ramona, although knowing her, she probably asked for it. I hate to say it about my own sister, but Ramona was a slut."

Adam, behind Pat, sounded as if he was choking.

"No kidding around, Rena," Pat said, "Chet Rowley didn't call that night to ask about the cameo?"

She seemed completely baffled. "What cameo?"

Her stomach churning, Pat backed off. "Never mind. I'll tell you about it later."

Still obviously confused, Rena took her hand and peered into her face. "Patty, are you all right?"

"I'm fine. See you tomorrow night."

"Well, all right. 'Bye, y'all." Her eyes troubled, she closed the door.

"That's three," Adam said as they walked to the cruiser. "You know what I think? I think that Rowley character never called anyone. I know C.J. pretty well, and when the subject came up in casual conversation, he was completely in the dark. You may have been holding a grudge against people who didn't know a thing about what happened that night."

"I don't believe that," Pat said, chin jutting stubbornly as she locked herself into the car. "You may know C.J., but I knew Margaret Harland. She'd have told anybody who'd listen."

"She might have told people in her circle, but it looks as if the kids you considered your friends didn't know and perhaps still don't. Doesn't that make you feel better?"

Pat had had enough of the subject. Her world was turning upside-down. "Drop it, Adam, for now. I can't...I don't..." Closing her eyes and throwing her head back, she gave up, not sure what she wanted to say. The possibility that she'd been wrong all these years had shaken her badly.

"Poor Pat. You look as if you could use a nice, friendly hug about now. I'd volunteer, but with my track record, I'm not sure how it would be received."

She opened her eyes. "Do me a favor, please. Risk it."

"That bad, huh?" He reached for her, pulling her close. Pat wrapped an arm around his midsection and buried her nose in the lapel of his uniform. Like him, it smelled fresh, spring-clean. He held her, his breath warm, slow and even, stirring the hair at her temple. He felt so good, so rock-solid, his taut, muscular body offering unyielding support. Pat imagined undoing the buttons of his shirt, running her hands over the broad expanse of his chest, his abdomen. She felt so at home. This, she realized, was contentment. This was where she belonged. Had she been a cat, she'd be purring.

But she wasn't and the man against whom she leaned, whose arms felt like home, was a man she'd be foolish to trust. He was an officer of the law in a town named Harland Grove. He was both friend and employee of C.J. Harland, who had a lot to lose if the coroner's verdict of suicide stood. If Adam had been knuckling under in asking her help, she had no guarantee he wouldn't be required to find a scapegoat to take the blame for Lib's death. Hetty was still too vulnerable. She couldn't afford to be misled by the false security of Adam's arms.

"Thanks," she said, sitting up straight. "I feel better."

He removed his arm, his eyes intent on her. "Honestly?" he asked, and tucked a stray tress behind her ear.

Ignoring the familiarity of the gesture, Pat crossed her heart. "Honestly. I'm ready to whip my weight in sweet little old ladies. Where do they meet?"

"On the other side of town." He stared at her, his eyes full of regret that the moment was over. "Guess we'd better go."

The members of the Pink Peony Garden Club were a perfect match for the petits fours they were serving, frosted in white, their bosoms well dusted, their colorful dresses riots of jonquils, violets and primroses. Adam hoped he didn't look as ridiculous as he felt, sitting on a tiny wicker chair while he tried to balance a dessert plate on one knee, a cup and saucer on the other. Pat, however, seemed perfectly at ease surrounded by all these little old ladies tittering and chirping like birds. He couldn't tell which pleased them more, that they had a genuine celebrity among them, or that the celebrity was one of their own.

Any illusion he'd had about conducting a run-of-the-mill interview was rapidly dispelled by the let's-just-chat atmosphere Pat created. It was easy to see why she was so successful at what she did. She had a chameleon's knack of making herself seem one of them, freeing their tongues in a way he couldn't have. And even though he'd been very clear on his purpose for attending this meeting, he saw now that rather than welcoming him as a lawman on the job, they viewed him as Pat's escort and therefore nonthreatening. That was fine with him, if he came away with something he could use.

"You really should let your hair grow, darlin'," one said— Annalee Gant, he thought. He'd long since lost track of who was who. They were names out of a different generation: Anna, Patience, Amanda, Beatrice. There were nine of them, five white, four black, yet as alike as peas in a pod and not one of them under seventy.

He'd held his peace while they'd oohed and aahed over Pat, inquired after Miss Hetty, followed by a detailed discussion of friends who'd suffered, survived, died from strokes of various severities. He'd eaten five petits fours, had sipped three cups of pink tea, whatever the hell that was. But it was a matter of some importance that he and Pat ask their questions so he could leave and do something about all the liquid he'd had so far.

He could have kissed Pat when, with no clue from him, she said, "We wanted to ask you about Lib. How did she seem during the last few meetings she attended?"

"Well, she wasn't here for the last three," Primrose Dress said. "We understood. What she was doing was much more important than sitting around yammerin' with us."

Pat picked up on that immediately. "She talked to you about her project?"

"Oh, yes. Harland Mansion really is a historical treasure. It's only right it should be declared a landmark. Ephraim Harland built that place to last."

"Not like these days," another chirped, her nose wrinkled with disdain. "I tell you, my dears, the ones today are held together with spit and toilet tissue."

"Sister!" Primrose rolled her eyes.

"What made her decide to do it?" Adam asked.

"We were discussing that at her wake," the eldest of them said. Adam searched for her name and finally remembered. Emmaline. "She'd been worried about how things had deteriorated, leaks, cracks in the foundation, things like that. Fix one problem and another would pop up."

"But she loved that old house," Primrose said mournfully. "She was born there, lived there all her life. It represented family, history, continuity. Rena's a dear child, but young folks have bulldozer fever. Lib was worried C.J. and Rena would tear it down."

"It was Hetty who suggested that if it were a historical landmark, no one could touch it," Amelia said. "That's all Lib needed to hear. Off she went to find out what she should do."

"Poor darlin'," Beatrice said. "Time ran out on her, but she was working on it to the end. Even went to Raleigh about it."

The other A, Amanda, Adam thought, frowned. "When?"

"Two or three weeks back, just after the last meeting she came to. I'd told her about our friend in the Historical Society in the Capitol, and she said she would definitely get in touch with him."

"She didn't go to Raleigh," Amanda protested. "She went to Washington."

"D.C.?" Pat said, her eyes alert and puzzled.

"That's right. My boy's the ticket agent. He told me. She didn't stay long, went one day, came back the next night."

"Did she finish whatever she had to do to have the mansion designated a historical landmark?"

"She hadn't when I saw her the Sunday before she died."

Adam looked at Pat, wondering what she made of this. She asked the son's name, then a few more questions before standing, and with a warmth he found utterly charming, thanked them, bade each one goodbye and was at the door before he'd successfully maneuvered past the two A's and the Primrose Dress.

Outside he helped her into the cruiser, mindful of nine pairs of eyes watching from Miss Emmaline's sunporch. Once in the car, however, he wasted no time. "Pat, my house is about two blocks away, and I'm sorry, but I've got to make a rest stop."

Pat gave him a distracted nod. "Fine. It's about time for my midday check on Hetty, if I could use your phone. Adam, there's no way Lib would have misunderstood what Miss Amanda said about going to the Capitol. If she went to Washington, rather than Raleigh, that's where she meant to go, but why? And why didn't she call me?"

"Maybe she didn't want you to know she was there. Miss Hetty must not have known she was going, either, or she'd have alerted you. But I don't remember seeing a ticket stub among the receipts in her desk. There was very little in there, stationery, address book, stamps, that's about it."

"I'll check the address book to see if she had any other D.C. correspondents. This is yours?" she said as he pulled in the driveway. "The Howards used to live here."

"That's who I bought it from. They moved after Ed was laid off from the plant." Adam cut the engine, trying to imagine the impression the small stucco house made on someone seeing it for the first time. It was much like Miss Hetty's, only with a reversed floorplan and a basement. It could use some flowers out front, he mused, maybe some ground cover. He hadn't realized how plain it was before.

Collecting odds and ends of Corey's from the living room as he led Pat to the kitchen phone, he at least had the satisfaction that there were no dishes in the sink. He'd left his son's possessions where they were because it made the house less lonely, and the fact that he was moving them now made him feel a little like a traitor. Tossing them on his son's bed on his way to the bathroom, he decided to call the camp tonight to see if he could catch the kid before bed check.

Mission accomplished, he returned to find Pat sitting at the table, her thoughts obviously elsewhere. His kitchen was all white with white appliances, simply because he'd been too lazy to select a color scheme. Pat was a brilliant jewel against the neutral canvas, the turquoise of her dress seeming a far more saturated color in contrast to her surroundings. With her hands folded in her lap, her eyes focused in some other dimension, she was like a painting, *Beauty in Contemplation* or something. God, Wyatt, he thought, you're getting downright sickening.

He sat down and watched her for a full minute, enjoying the play of sunlight across her bobbed hair, the pattern of her freckles, the red and yellow undertones of her skin. She was so still. Were it not for the rise and fall of her chest, she might be a statue.

"Pat." He touched her hand, pulling her out of her solitude. "Everything okay at the hospital?"

"Hmm?" She came to. "Yes. They've had her up, did another CAT. Dr. Vernon left a message for me to let them know which rehab center I've decided on. Depending on the results of the CAT, they want to move her, get her started on intensive therapy right away."

Adam got up and went to the back door, to hide his irritation with Jim. The least he could have done was let him know about this. Miss Hetty may well have tried to do a bit of cleaning after she'd found Miss Harland's body; it was the kind of thing an old friend might do to spare the other person embarrassment, even though it couldn't possibly matter. And he really was less inclined to think Miss Hetty had helped her friend off this mortal coil. Still, she wasn't clear of the woods yet, and he did not want her moved beyond his jurisdiction. "What are you going to do?" he asked.

Pat stood up. "I don't know. I guess I'd better check out this place near High Point. Dr. Vernon and everyone I've talked to keeps pushing it. Do you mind if I cut out on you this afternoon? I'd like to run up there and be back by dark."

His relief that she was considering some place in the state, at least, made him magnanimous. "Take as much time as you need. Would you like me to go with you?"

Unsmiling, she shook her head. "Thanks, but she's my responsibility. I'd like to do it alone." Her decision made, she became more interested in her surroundings, glancing around. "Your kitchen's nice. I like white kitchens. It makes them seem cleaner somehow."

"It also makes sure you keep it clean," he responded, pleased that it had passed muster with her. "Why don't I take you back to the mansion so you can get going?"

"I'd appreciate it. I have to stop at the bank on my way out of town, just in case they ask for a deposit or something."

"Don't forget C.J.'s offer," he reminded her.

She didn't respond until they were back in the car. "I haven't made up my mind about that yet," she said, a hard edge to her voice. "I'm not sure I want to accept his help. I'll see if it's needed and make a decision then."

Adam started to speak, but changed his mind. She still didn't believe that C.J. and, for that matter, Rena, had no knowledge of what had happened to her. Yanking the car into gear, he sped out of the driveway, annoyed with her, angry with himself. For a split second back there in the kitchen, he'd wondered what it would be like if she were there to share that table with him every morning, every evening. He'd wondered how it would feel to wake up with her next to him, to hear her footsteps in the house.

Fool. She still bore that grudge against the town. And as long as she did, she was a danger to him, his son, and everything he'd come to value. She was, damn it, a reporter. Her values would always be poles apart from his. Given the chance, she would bring the Grove to its knees. He wouldn't forget that again.

Pat rushed out of the bank, so intent on getting to the car that she was several yards past the graying, dark-skinned man before it registered that he had called her name. Spinning around, she looked back and remembered him from Lib's funeral, because she'd gotten the impression he'd wanted to talk to her. He hurried toward her now, then slowed, as if his rapid gait might attract attention.

"Miss Chase, I'm Perry Franklin."

Franklin, Pat thought. The manager of the liquor store.

"There's something I need to tell you," he said, panting slightly. He had the kind of bass baritone that probably carried, so pulling her closer to the curb, he lowered his voice. "Miss Hetty don't cotton to me much, but a man's got to make a living, and she's a good woman at heart, so I sort of overlook how she feels."

"She can be opinionated about some things," Pat agreed, hoping he'd get to the point soon.

"We hear there's something fishy about Miss Lib's dying and that the police think she might have had something to do with it. Don't nobody believe it, so don't you worry about that. What I wanted to say, Chief Wyatt, he come around asking questions, and I told him the truth. Miss Hetty, she's never been in my store. Miss Lib either. What I didn't tell him was that for the last few months, Miss Lib, she's had me meet her in the library and slip her a bottle of coffee liqueur."

Pat passed a hand across her brow, despairing that it had been going on for so long. "How'd you manage without Hetty or Lorna seeing you? Or did you go in the door from the garden?"

"Ma'am? Oh, I meant the public library. It's right across the street from my store and sometimes I run in there around lunchtime to read the paper. It was right pitiful the way she had to sneak and all, but she said she was having trouble sleeping and just needed something to help her relax. I knew right off she wouldn't want anyone to know she was taking a little nip at night, and Lord knows, Miss Hetty would have a hissy fit if she knew. I just hate that she found out."

"Oh, my Lord," Pat whispered, finally remembering where she'd seen his name. "Hetty wrote you a check, didn't she? How did she find out? Who told her?"

"My sister's boy, he goes to college, let the cat out of the bag," he said, his jaw working. "He didn't know. Miss Lib and me had an arrangement, see. She'd sit at a certain table in the library and I'd slip the bottle to her while we pretended to pass the time of day. She was supposed to mail the money for it, only the last couple of months nothing came and my nephew saw her tab in a book I keep in my office. He's been good about helping me clear up late accounts. He called the mansion to ask when she'd be paying and Miss Hetty answered. She told him she'd take care of it and she sent me a check. But Chief Wyatt, he didn't ask me about that, so I didn't tell him, and won't unless you say to.''

Pat was thoroughly shaken, and prayed it didn't show. "Thank you, Mr. Franklin. Let me think about it. When was the last time Lib bought a bottle from you?''

"A couple of days 'fore she died. I feel so bad, Miss Chase. The bottles weren't that big, less than a quart, but I figure she went on a binge and drank herself to death. The family may be embarrassed about it, but we ain't gonna stand by and let them blame Miss Hetty. They might have done dirt by you, but by the Jesus, we won't let them do it again.''

Pat blinked. She'd almost missed that. "You know what happened to me?''

"Oh, yes, ma'am,'' he said, his eyes glittering with anger.

"When did you find out?''

"Right when it happened. My brother and I used to clean the school at night. We were down the hall when they opened your locker. Saw the whole thing. I felt so bad for you. The Chases, they ain't thieves. Somebody just had it in for you.''

"How many people knew about it, Mr. Franklin?''

"That's kind of hard to say. Plenty did, though. It was all over town the next morning, even before they'd turned you loose.''

Then how could her friends not have heard, Pat asked herself?

"If we could have done something, we would have, Miss Chase. It's just that . . . well, you understand how things were back then. But they're different now, and if Mr. C.J. thinks us black folk are going to sit back and let Miss Hetty take the blame for something she didn't do, he's got another think comin', even if it messes up the deal with Mr. Tyler.''

"Tyler? What's he got to do with anything?'' Pat asked.

"Well, he took a liking to the Grove because everybody gets along and always has. No marches or sit-ins because we didn't need them. It never had anything to do with civil rights or equality, it just made good money sense. Everybody's young'uns went to the same school because it was cheaper for the Harlands than building separate ones. We lived on whichever side of town we could afford because the Harlands had to keep H.I. employees happy. Everybody's always understood that. We lived, worked and worshiped together and found out that, colored or white, wasn't all that much difference between us. But I'm here to tell you, little lady, if they pick on Miss Hetty, smear her name and try to hush it up like with you, this town's gonna be split right down the middle."

After three deep breaths, Pat could speak again. "Don't worry about it, Mr. Franklin. I'm doing my best to look after her. And thanks again for keeping that check to yourself."

"My nephew knows he'll be in a heap of trouble if he mentions it. No, ma'am, they ain't making a scrapegoat out of Miss Hetty."

Pat bit her tongue, so close to the edge that it was difficult not to burst into laughter at the malapropism. If she started, she wouldn't be able to stop. She'd lose it right here on Main Street.

He gave her a shy, conspiratorial smile, and walked away. Pat, her hand trembling, managed to get the key in the car door, but had to sit behind the wheel for several minutes before she trusted herself to drive. She could not deal with the confirmation that she'd been right all these years. That was for later. She had to focus on Hetty and how to protect her.

One mystery had been cleared up: she was sure Lib's drinking had been the problem with her and Hetty. The date on the check matched the time frame she'd first heard the anger in Hetty's voice when Lib was mentioned. But Hetty hadn't quit. She hadn't walked out on Lib. The question remained, what exactly had she done?

My fault. Killed her.

The memory that had been struggling toward the light finally emerged, frightening Pat more than anything Hetty had said in the hospital. When she'd been a teenager, Hetty had warned her she'd put up with a lot, but as long as Pat was a minor under her roof, drinking was out. Pat had been with her almost two years when Hetty caught her with beer on her breath.

She'd told Pat to wait in her room; she was going out and would be back shortly. She'd returned with two six-packs of beer she'd borrowed from the Grants, had sat her down and ordered her to start drinking. Pat, who'd had her very first taste of beer that day and had downed only a few swallows, detesting the taste, was at a distinct disadvantage. Hetty wasn't listening. She opened the first tall can and passed it to Pat. Two and a third beers later, Pat was in the bathroom, relieving her stomach of its contents. Even now, the smell of beer could make her queasy.

Had she goaded Lib into drinking more than she normally would, hoping it might make her sick enough so she'd stop? Goodness knows it worked with me, Pat thought. But with someone with a far higher tolerance? It was reaching, but it was the only explanation she could think of, in which case Hetty had indeed been instrumental in causing Lib's death. And if they already had one person on whom they could pin the blame, why should they bother to look for another?

Chapter 8

Pat got back into the Grove later than she'd anticipated. The rehabilitation center was everything she'd been told and more, bright and cheery with an upbeat staff for whom the impossible was a daily challenge they met with a smile. But after sitting outside in their gardens to think, Pat realized that it wouldn't do.

It was important that Adam not be able to locate Hetty once she left Harland Memorial. It was also important that he not realize immediately that she was out of state. That, Pat felt, would give her time to concentrate on the motive and the identity of the person who'd dosed Lib's coffee liqueur.

It had to be someone with access to the mansion, but since it, like most homes in the Grove, was never locked, everyone was suspect. Until that person was under arrest, however, Hetty had to be beyond Adam's reach. It would irreparably damage her already shaky relationship with him, but since there was no future for them anyway, it didn't matter.

Desperate for a phone she could use in private for as long as it took to arrange what she had in mind, Pat stopped at a Howard Johnson, rented a room, and dug out her phone card, address book, and local directories. By calling in a few favors in some instances, and in others, practically giving away her firstborn in the unlikely event she should ever have one, Pat checked out a couple of hours later with a private ambulance and medical helicopter waiting for her call.

The rehab center she'd visited would keep Hetty overnight, after which she'd be flown to a small, private hospital in western Maryland. Pat hated sending her aunt so far from home, but her hope was that Adam would assume Hetty was still a patient at the center outside High Point. If she, too, disappeared when Hetty was moved, he would realize instantly what she'd done and scour the east coast looking for them. She'd have to stay and do what she could to get Hetty off the hook.

At the mansion, Lorna's sturdy little Volkswagen Rabbit was parked in the driveway, a nice surprise, since Pat was certain she'd be gone by now. Lorna, hearing her come in, waddled out into the foyer, her arms folded across her chest, her expression as dark as an August thunderstorm. "Patty," she said by way of greeting.

"Hi. Why are you looking as if you could bite the head off a rattler?"

"Somebody complain to you about my cooking?" she demanded. "Mr. C.J. told you about the piecrusts, didn't he? All right, I allow as how my crusts never come out right and I end up using store-bought. But that's no reason for you to think the rest of my cooking's not up to snuff." She headed for the kitchen in high dudgeon.

Mystified, Pat went after her. "Lorna, you must be a dynamite cook or you wouldn't be working for C.J. What made you think I thought otherwise?"

"Why else would you have Mariana Foy dropping off lunch for you and Crystal Campbell bringing your dinner? That Foy woman thinks she's so hot because Rena invited her to join her gourmet cooking club. All they do is sit around, compare labor pains and swap recipes. And show off every chance they get." Yanking open the monster refrigerator, Lorna made a sweeping gesture. "Looka there."

It took a moment for Pat to locate the offending dishes—two plates heaped with food and neatly covered in plastic wrap. "Crystal and Mariana must be members of the Sunshine Club at Hetty's church. They've been bringing my meals from the day I arrived. I can't tell them not to, they'd be hurt. It's their way of doing something for Hetty."

"Oh." Lorna's jaw lost some of its pugnacious cant. "I thought . . . Well, what am I supposed to do with the dinner I fixed? I even got over here early because I knew you'd be starved after driving all the way to High Point."

"How'd you find out about that?"

"Rena called Chief Wyatt a while back, looking for you. She thought you might want to go shopping with her or something. Now here I am with all this food."

"I'll eat whatever you fixed, how's that?" Pat said. She'd had an early dinner at the motel, but she wanted to stay on the housekeeper's good side, no matter how many calories it cost her. "We'll put the others in the freezer."

Lorna brightened. "I'll set a place for you in the dining room. It's all ready."

"I won't eat unless you eat with me."

Lorna was pleased, despite her scowl of exasperation. She set a second place and they shared a companionable meal, during which Pat pumped her to get a sense of what the last few months had been like in the mansion. There really was reason, from Lorna's description, to think that the deterioration of Lib's mind had begun to outpace that of her body. Her memory had faltered. She missed lunch dates, meetings, appointments she had no memory of having made with friends. Rena, who normally drove her wherever she wanted to go, had finally given up the role of chauffeur. More often than not, she'd arrive, wait for Lib, only to discover that Lib wasn't where she was supposed to be, and in some cases, had never left home at all. C.J., taking over for Rena, had the same problems with her.

Lib had husbanded most of her energy to amass the documentation to prove the age of the mansion. What had begun as an idea to investigate had become a crusade, her behavior approaching the bizarre the longer she worked on the problem. Lorna wept as she recounted how paranoid Lib had become about anyone seeing what she was doing.

"Did she seem lucid when she wrote the codicil to her will?" Pat asked.

"If lucid means in her right mind, she was sharp as a tack that day or I wouldn't have signed my name as a witness. In fact, I never actually saw her any other way. But it's funny, Patty—about the will, I mean. She kept saying 'It's only right' under her breath. 'It's only right.' When I asked her what she meant, she held up the paper we'd just signed. 'This,' and something about family honor. Oh!" Her hand flew to her mouth, her eyes widening.

"What is it?"

"I just remembered. She said you would be proud of her. I plumb forgot that. I should tell Chief Wyatt. Then she put the sheet in a long brown envelope, but bad as she'd gotten about remembering things, she might have tossed it in the wastepaper basket five minutes later."

"I had no idea," Pat said, wounded that Hetty hadn't told her.

"I'll tell you, honey, it's just as well she went when she did. She was always terrified of becoming senile and winding up in a nursing home with strangers. Said she'd rather die first. She was a tad late doing it, but at least she was in her own house to the last. My, my. I've got to get home. Thanks for letting me break bread with you, Patty. I enjoyed it."

She cleared the table, loaded the dishwasher and left. The front door closed behind her and suddenly the house seemed twice the size of a second before. Noises Pat hadn't noticed before became crystal clear, creaks, raps, groans. Rena was right. The place did sound as if it was about to collapse.

The grandfather clock in the foyer chimed the half hour. Forty-five minutes before she'd leave for the hospital. Now was as good a time as any to see how far Lib had gotten in trying to save her beloved house. It would be the first time she'd been in the library since her return.

Pat approached the big double doors, her heart thudding so hard she felt as if her whole body was shaking. Hand on the knob, she turned it, then pushed. It was locked, thankfully.

The house groaned, somewhere something tapped. Pat grabbed her purse and fled. It wouldn't kill her to get to the hospital early.

* * *

She left Margaret Harland Memorial feeling better about Hetty than she had for days. The nursing staff reported definite improvement. All the new medical terms added to her vocabulary: aphasia, hemiplegia, thrombotic, nonhemmorrhagic, now sounded less frightening. Pat arranged for Hetty's transfer and for copies of her medical records so that she could be moved whenever they thought her ready. After peeking in and watching her sleeping form for several minutes, she started back to the Grove, wondering what Hetty's rosier prognosis boded for her if the worst happened and she was arrested, tried and found guilty of whatever. She couldn't imagine any judge so hard-hearted as to send her to jail, but...

Just as she passed the Welcome to Harland Grove sign, she abandoned the thought, suddenly aware of an unevenness about the feel of the car. Slowing, her senses probing the growing darkness around her, she swore. The ba-rump, ba-rump and higgledy-piggledy steering confirmed her suspicions. She had a flat.

"The end of a beautiful day," she grumbled, and got out. The car listed to starboard, nose down. No novice at changing tires, she sighed and opened the trunk, but two minutes later knew this would be one flat that would stay that way. There were flares, a work light, a spare, and a lug wrench, none worth a damn without a jack. Well, she wasn't going to sit in the dark waiting for a good samaritan to come along. She lit the flares, locked the car and set off down Ashburn Road, thanking her stars that she'd worn sandals instead of heels today.

The Grove had already settled down for the night. As tomorrow was a workday and the first shift at the plant reported at seven, porches were empty. The only interior lights were those glowing through bedroom windows.

She had turned into Lawton Street with perhaps a mile to go when a car rounded the corner from Wilson and sped toward her. Since she walked facing oncoming traffic and there were no sidewalks and streetlights this far out, she stepped over into the yard of the house she was passing, with kiss-kiss sounds for the dog on the porch. "It's okay, boy," she said softly as the headlights of the car swept past her. It skidded to a halt, brakes squealing, two houses beyond.

The door on the driver's side opened. "Pat? What in God's name are you doing way out here this time of night?" Adam called.

Blinded by his low beams, Pat hadn't seen the chase lights on the roof of the car. She retraced her steps. "I had a flat and there was no jack in the trunk."

"Where's the car?"

"Back on Ashburn. It'll be all right. I left flares burning."

"Get in," he said, sliding back behind the wheel. "What idiot would even turn the key in the ignition without a jack in the trunk? That's not like C.J. or Rena, either."

"No harm done." Pat closed and locked her door, peering at him as she secured her seat belt. He sounded angry. "I'll call the gas station and have them send someone to change the tire."

He glared into the darkness, his fingers tapping against the steering wheel. "I'd do it, but I don't have time. Damn it!"

"Adam, what's wrong?"

"It's Corey. I called the camp, just to...I don't know, I just wanted to hear his voice. The manager told me the boys were clearing a campsite today and hit a nest of yellow jackets. Several of them got Corey."

"Oh, Adam." Pat shuddered, remembering her one experience with an angry wasp. "Is he allergic to insect stings?"

"Yes, but they knew that and had the epinephrine ready. They swear he's okay, but I just need to see for myself."

"Of course. Look, I don't mind walking back to the mansion. It's perfectly safe out here. That's one thing about the Grove that hasn't changed."

"Maybe so, but..." Whatever the thought, it went unfinished. He turned to look at her. "Pat, come with me. It's not that far, about an hour this time of night. I won't be staying long."

"Adam—" She wasn't sure it was a good idea.

"Come on, it's a nice ride. And I'd like you to meet Corey."

Pat weighed her options. She could hike back to the mansion, lock herself in the guest wing and listen to the house complain the rest of the night, or go with Adam, spend two or

three hours, and get back late enough that nothing would keep
her awake. Not that she hadn't already twisted and turned the
night before with visions of Adam, and the way he had kissed
her. Pat, she told herself, you'd better grab what little pleasant
time you can get with this man before the bomb drops. "All
right, but I'll wait in the car while you see him. He needs his
father now, not a stranger."

"Why don't we make that decision when we get there?" he
said, pulling away. He reached for the mike. "In the meantime, I'll radio Wes at the station and have him call the garage
about the flat. We can pick up the Caddy on our way back." He
smiled. "I'm glad you're coming."

Oh, brother, Pat thought. If he did that too often, she'd be
no more good. He had a smile that could dissolve rocks. It
wasn't too late. She could still change her mind. One surrepti-
tious glance at him from the corners of her eyes and every
ounce of willpower dissolved. Not regretting her decision for a
minute, she sat back to enjoy the ride.

"How'd things go at High Point?" Adam asked once they
were on the highway.

She told the truth. "I was impressed. I see why everyone
recommends it. I think Hetty would like it."

"Would she have to be there for the duration—until she's
ready to come home, I mean?"

"We'll see," Pat said, unwilling to dissemble any more than
she had to. "By the way, I had an interesting talk with Lorna.
She told me a lot about Lib I hadn't heard before."

"For instance . . ."

Pat outlined Lorna's picture of Lib's deterioration, Adam
listening with concentration.

"You sound as if you have problems believing it," he said.

Pat turned sideways, wondering whether she was that trans-
parent or whether he was that tuned in to her. It was an unsettling possibility. "Hetty was concerned because Lib was losing
weight and had little appetite, but she never said anything about
the kind of mental confusion Lorna mentioned. And Lib
sounded fine on the phone when we spoke that last Sunday."

The few times I ran into her she seemed okay to me," Adam said.

"And Lorna remembered something. The day she and Pete witnessed the codicil, Lib kept saying 'It's only right,' and something about the family honor."

"She told me that."

"But she forgot to tell you that Lib said I would be proud of her. Perhaps we need to concentrate on the codicil again and what she was leaving to her family."

Adam maneuvered around a monster semi before responding. "She could only do so much when it comes to that."

"I don't understand."

"Miss Harland could do what she liked with any money and personal property, but she had no choice about her shares of Harland Industries. They stay in the family. It's set up so that the Harlands retain the whole kit and kaboodle. They can sell the whole business if they want to, but none of this owning fifty-one percent with outsiders holding the other forty-nine. Before the codicil, C.J. inherited them. The most she could do was spread it around, say to his kids or to the cousins. Which, of course, brings up an interesting question."

"What?"

He took his time about answering, as if he had to think about it. "Pat, this is confidential," he said finally. "H.I.'s up for sale."

"What!" Pat was stunned. There was something blasphemous about the whole idea. She listened as Adam explained how desperate the situation had become, and Asa Tyler's promise to retain all the employees if he purchased the business. "Then all the relatives would have to agree to the sale, right? If Lib decided to leave her shares to, say, Rena, and for whatever reason, she voted against selling, everything would come to the proverbial grinding halt, right?"

Adam nodded, and shot her an admiring glance.

"Which drops one hell of a motive in C.J.'s lap, right?"

"Yes," he said, with obvious reluctance.

"How does Rena feel about having to sell?"

"I'm not sure. She's gung-ho H.I., throws her heart and soul into the job, and she's always backed C.J.'s decisions. Trying to block the sale would be a departure for her."

It put an interesting slant on the whole case. Pat felt a short-lived surge of sympathy for Adam. He was obviously uncomfortable with his good friend occupying the hot seat. All the more reason for her to be sure Hetty didn't take the fall alone.

"What kind of leeway did Lib have with the mansion?" she asked.

"Same kind of deal. Only a Harland—by blood, mind you—can own and live in it."

"So she couldn't have had it declared a historical landmark."

"I'm not sure. It's C.J.'s now, but I've asked Mr. Stokes to check whether property with that designation has to be signed over to the state."

With all the new information to digest and file in various mental categories, Pat was silent for several miles, trying to figure out how Lib's codicil could have contributed to her death. Her focus kept drifting to the strength of Adam's profile, the flex of the muscles in his forearm. And his hands. Those long fingers. Wrestling with her concentration, she forced herself back to the subject.

The question was to whom Lib had assigned her shares of H.I. and whether they would have gone along with its sale to Asa Tyler. But no, Pat decided, it wasn't the only question. A new one had surfaced since her conversation with Perry Franklin, and it dealt with the man beside her.

"Adam, after the coroner declared Lib's death a suicide, why didn't you leave it alone?"

For a moment he didn't answer. His response, when it came, gave her more insight into his character than she'd had so far. "I'm a cop, Pat. That means dedicating yourself, mind, soul and body, to certain principles."

"Justice?"

"I've always thought of it in terms of seeing that the people who prey on others aren't allowed to get away with it. It sounds corny, but I'm looking out for the good guys and going after the bad. That's what cops do, and I'm a cop."

"Why?" Pat asked, her curiosity getting the best of her. "Of all the careers you could have chosen, why this one?"

He shrugged. "It's the only thing I ever wanted to do. My dad was a cop. His dad was a cop, one of the first black patrolmen on a municipal police force. I can remember sitting on my granddad's lap, fascinated by the way his badge gleamed in the light. He and Dad were my heroes. To my sisters, too."

"You have sisters?" Pat asked, pleased at finding out more about him.

"Three sisters. They're on the force, too."

"Wow. That's marvelous."

He turned to look at her, one brow raised. "I'm surprised to hear that from you. I thought you didn't think much of us boys in blue."

He was right, but then, so was she. "You have to admit, my first experience with them—what I thought were police, anyway—wasn't exactly a positive one. And you're the first one I've known personally. How did your mother survive with all her loved ones choosing such a dangerous occupation?"

He glanced at her speculatively. "You're the first person who's ever thought about it from her point of view. It wasn't easy, but she believed in what we were doing. Still does."

Pat reflected on Mrs. Wyatt's long days and nights of waiting and doubted she could survive them. Of course, she wasn't in love with a cop. *Or are you?* a small voice asked. She looked at the strong jaw, his self-assurance, manifest in the confident manner in which he carried himself, and admitted to herself that she was drawn by far more than his physical attractiveness. The inner man was every bit as attractive.

"How do you keep from becoming cynical, Adam, and hard?"

He took a deep breath. "You really don't. God, Pat, the things I've seen people do to one another. You have to keep reminding yourself that somebody has to make sure that the good folks can live out their lives in peace. When someone interferes with that, you have to see that they pay for it so it doesn't happen again."

The road had become more difficult, requiring his complete attention, so Pat let conversation lapse. There was a certain parallel in what they'd chosen to do with their lives, and their attitudes about the need to protect and defend, the primary difference being in the danger accompanying his. He was no less dedicated, in fact, probably more so, since he put his life on the line to do his job.

It was time to stop deluding herself. In choosing to pursue the possibility that Lib had been murdered instead of taking the easy road that would have left any number of cages unrattled, Adam had put the lie to any doubts she could have about the kind of man he was. His personal code of ethics overrode his loyalty for the place he'd come to love, the community, which he credited with his son's emotional well-being. It was time to stop doubting his integrity. It was also time to stop fooling herself. She was falling in love with Adam Wyatt.

"Here we are," he said, turning onto a road more suited for walking than vehicular traffic. Narrow and rutted, it was barely wide enough for one car. Trees hugged the shoulders of the road, their limbs slapping at the chase lights atop the car.

After a mile of assault by potholes and branches, they reached a large one-story building of rough-hewn timber. A floodlight above the entrance illuminated a sign: Camp Redfern—Administration. Aside from one light in a window toward the end, it was dark.

Adam parked and got out. "Coming?" he asked.

"No, I'll wait here." Pat was determined not to intrude on his meeting with his son. "Take your time."

He opened her door and leaned down to look at her. "I'd rather not leave the motor and air conditioner running."

"I'll open the window."

"I wouldn't, if I were you. The wildlife visit at night. The deer probably wouldn't bother you, but I can't vouch for the bears."

Pat scrambled out and followed him onto the porch.

Before he'd had a chance to knock, the door was opened by a stocky pajama-clad man with hair the color of a ripe tomato. "Hi, Mr. Wyatt. You made good time. Uh...sorry," he said, seeing Pat as they crossed the threshold into a dimly lighted foyer. "Didn't know you'd have a lady with you."

Adam pulled her to his side. "Pat, this is Bob Fenster, the camp administrator. Bob, meet Pat Chase."

He shook her hand. "A pleasure. I don't usually greet visitors in pajamas, but . . . Excuse me while I get a robe."

"Please, don't bother," Pat said.

"Thanks." He grinned. "Tell you the truth, ma'am, I don't even have one. Corey's in the infirmary down there at the end of the hall. Shall I wake Mrs. Raines? She's the nurse on call tonight."

"Why don't I wait until I've seen him and judge from there."

"Your choice. She said she'd be glad to talk to you. I'll be up if you want to talk to me again. Nice meeting you, ma'am."

"You, too," Pat said. A deacon's bench sat beside the door, a perfectly good place to wait. "Adam, why don't I—"

"Chicken," he said, and nudged her toward the light at the end of the building.

Camp Redfern's infirmary housed eight beds, only one of which was occupied. A lamp obviously made in someone's woodworking shop served as a night-light for the sole patient. With a firm grip on her arm, Adam walked softly to the bed nearest the door. "Corey?" The lump under the sheet changed shape. "Corey, wake up. It's Dad."

"Dad?" The lump shifted and the sheet was lowered to expose the child. "Daddy! When'd you get here?" Pushing free of the covers, he rose on his knees, arms extended for a hug. Adam embraced him with vigor, lifting him completely off the bed, and kissed him before putting him down. "Dad, guess what?" the boy said, looking at Pat with open curiosity. "I got stung, four whole times. Hi. Who're you?"

Pat had had a good deal of trouble coming to grips with her feelings for Adam. She had no such difficulty with his child. With her first clear look at him she was in love.

He was very much like his father, his skin a little darker, perhaps influenced by summer camp sun, his eyes even lighter than his father's, more hazel than amber. But he'd inherited Adam's dark hair and brows, the shape of his face, his smile. He wore a T-shirt, pajama bottoms and several circles of a white substance on his arm and one foot.

"Hi. I'm Pat Chase. Pleased to meet you." She stuck out a hand, which he took with an expression that revealed his appreciation of the gesture.

"Pleased to meet you, Miss Chase." He focused on her with the same intensity his father occasionally showed, smiled again, and turned to plump his pillow. He spread the sheet across his legs and patted the bed. "Would you like to sit down?"

"It takes a nine-year-old to remind me of my manners," Adam grumbled, and grabbed chairs from between other beds. "Okay, buddy, what happened?"

"We were clearing a place to build a fire and Chris Hong hit a yellow jacket's nest. Man, were they mad! They flew all over the place, buzzing and stinging. I ran, but they got me anyhow."

"Did your face blow up like last time?"

"No, sir. I got a little dizzy, but that's all, and Larry—he's our group leader—he had the kit with him and gave me a shot. I could have done it myself," he added with diffidence, "but I let him."

"Must have hurt a lot," Adam said. Pat could tell he was fishing. "Did you cry?"

"Maybe a little." Corey looked embarrassed.

"A little?" Pat joined the conversation for the first time. "You're good, Corey. I got stung by a wasp once, one little wasp, and you could hear me yelling in the next county."

He giggled. "I wasn't *that* bad. And I'm okay now, Dad, honest. Can I stay?"

"I didn't come to take you home. I was just checking on you, that's all. Of course, if you want to go, no problem. I miss you."

"I miss you, too," he said, even more at ease now, "but I'd like to stay. This place is cool. I'm learning all sorts of neat stuff. And I'm making you something. A surprise. Guess what color."

They played the game for several minutes, Pat completely charmed by the rapport between them, Adam's willingness to indulge his son by coming up with crayon colors, and Corey's delighted reaction and ready wit. Adam had described him accurately. He seemed emotionally grounded and bright, with a nine-year-old's silly streak. And Adam was so good with him. The longer Pat watched them, the lower her spirits sank. She was facing her moment of truth. Adam Wyatt, the man sitting on the other side of the bed, was the man she wanted as lover, husband, father of her children, and all three categories were out of the question.

After a time, Adam cried uncle and said he would wait to see what his surprise was going to be. The game over, Corey turned to Pat. "You're visiting Miss Hetty?"

If he'd wanted to surprise them, he had. "Matt and C.J. told you, right?" Adam said.

"Nope." He giggled. "I knew who you were soon's I saw you," he told Pat, "even though you used a different name. Miss Dora watches your show every Wednesday and sometimes she'll give me a snack if I watch with her."

"Miss Dora?"

"She keeps an eye on him after school," Adam said. "You're one up on me, son. I didn't recognize her."

"Well, you're always on duty Wednesday nights. What's it like being on TV?" he asked Pat.

"Hectic. A lot of work."

He nodded wisely. "I bet. My mom had a chance to work on TV but she liked writing for the newspaper better."

Pat looked at Adam, whose face had tightened noticeably. "Your mom was a reporter?"

"Uh-huh. She got shot."

Pat gasped. "Corey, how awful. I'm so sorry."

He shrugged. "It's all right. That was a long time ago. I was just a little kid."

"You're a big kid now," Adam said, rising abruptly, "but you still need your sleep. We'd better get back to the Grove. You sure you'll be okay?"

"I'm sure. Besides, tomorrow's chili day. The cook makes the best chili."

"'Nuff said. Scoot down." Adam pulled the covers over him, and pecked him on the forehead. "Get some sleep. I'll talk to you this weekend."

"Okay. It was nice meeting you, Miss Chase. Tell Miss Hetty I said hi."

Pat hesitated, unsure of what to say. Adam stepped into the breach.

"Miss Hetty's in the hospital, Corey."

The boy's eyes widened, concern darkening his features. "Is she gonna die?"

"No," Pat said. "She'll be fine."

"Good." He settled down. "Maybe I'll make her a card. I don't like it when people die."

Adam leaned over to kiss him again. "No one does, son. Take it easy, hear?"

"Yes, sir. 'Night. 'Night, Miss Chase."

"Good-night, Corey. Be cool."

He grinned, his humor restored. "Yes, ma'am."

Pat waited on the porch of the big log building while Adam conferred with the nurse and Bob Fenster, her feelings decidedly mixed. The circumstances surrounding the death of Adam's wife had been far more tragic than she could have imagined, and she resented having to learn them from the son instead of the father. That the late Mrs. Wyatt had also been a reporter wasn't as important in the scheme of things, but she found it curious that Adam hadn't mentioned it. She wasn't sure why but that omission bothered her, too.

"He's a charming kid," Pat said when they were on the road again and had maneuvered back down the torturous route from the camp to the highway.

"Corey's okay," Adam responded with quiet pride. "No angel, but a good kid."

"The two of you seem to have a terrific relationship."

"We do. I try not to take it for granted. Kids grow up so fast. I don't want to wake up one day and realize he's eighteen and about to leave home. I want to enjoy him."

Pat had auditioned several different approaches to the subject of his wife. None had passed. She decided to attack it head-on.

"Tell me about your wife," she said abruptly. "I'm not sure you ever mentioned her name."

She saw his jaw tense. "Ginny. I met her in college, married her after she graduated. She was smarter than I am by half, beautiful, and driven."

"She must have been quite a woman," Pat ventured. "Wife, mother and reporter, too."

"She was good at her job, not as good as a wife, and a dismal failure as a mother," Adam said, a brittleness about him. "She knew what she wanted and went after it with a frightening single-mindedness. She was determined to be a reporter on a major newspaper, her one goal in life to scoop everyone else. More often than not, she did. That left little time for me and almost none for Corey."

"Then I'm surprised," Pat said, treading lightly, "that the two of you decided to have a family at all."

"Corey wasn't planned, if that's what you mean. And at no point did I expect her to give up working, even after he was born. I knew her job was important to her, that she wouldn't be happy staying home with him. I guess I did expect her to accept fewer assignments, but she went in the opposite direction. In the end, she became the kind of reporter I detest."

Pat was increasingly uneasy. She'd assumed that Adam, like his son, had recovered from the loss of his wife. It sounded to her as if the father still had a ways to go. "What kind of reporter are you referring to?" she asked.

"First cousins of sharks. A tragedy happens and they smell blood from the other side of the city. They show up circling around the poor victims and their families, shoving their lights and microphones and notepads into the faces of people in shock or the cop trying to do his job. All that matters is getting the Story—with a capital S—and if that means stomping all over a crime scene or badgering victims or witnesses, too bad. Whatever tolerance I had for the media, I lost in the first couple of years on the force. By the time I'd worked homicide six months, I couldn't stand the sight of them."

"That couldn't have helped your marriage very much," Pat said, surprised by his vehemence.

"It didn't. The character traits that had attracted me to her to begin with were the very ones that drove us apart. I'd liked the fact that she knew what she wanted. She was independent, a feminist, and since I had sisters, I was all for that. But Ginny...I don't know. She felt that because she was black and a woman, she had to work twice as hard to get where she wanted to go."

"She was right," Pat said, finding herself in the odd position of coming to his wife's defense.

"Yes, only Ginny took it to the extreme. She had to get there first, no matter what. That's what got her killed."

"How did it happen?"

"She'd just started working for the *New York Post*. She was supposed to be off by six to pick up Corey from the neighbor, who kept him until one of us got home. Only when Ginny came up out of the subway, the sirens were screaming onto the block. A man two buildings over had barricaded himself in his apartment to keep from being evicted and was taking potshots at anything that moved."

"When was this?" Pat asked, a vague memory of the incident stirring.

"Three years ago. Corey was playing out front with the neighbor's kids and, naturally, went flying toward the police cars to see what the fuss was about. Ginny did, too, only instead of grabbing Corey and getting him out of harm's way, she ran right by him, rushing to be the first reporter on the scene before the police could set up a roadblock. Meanwhile, this madman is shooting out windshields, threatening to shoot anyone who came close, and the cops are trying to get people off the block. Corey thought she hadn't seen him and went running after her."

"Oh, God," Pat said, envisioning the scene.

"She's arguing with the beat cop that she knows the man and can talk to him, and he's about to arrest her for not following orders, when Corey squeezes between them. The cop picks him up and she uses the opportunity to run hell-for-leather toward the steps of the apartment building the guy's in, waving her press credentials at him. He shot her."

"And Corey saw it."

"Yes. That's what traumatized him, why I had to get him away from that whole environment. That's why the Grove was such a godsend."

"I see." Pat longed to kiss the pain from his face, to smooth the tension from his hand clutching the steering wheel so tightly that even in the dim light from the dashboard, she could see the tendons standing out. But she didn't dare touch him. She wasn't sure she'd be able to control herself.

There were other reasons not to start something she'd be hard-pressed to stop. Adam's dedication to duty threatened Hetty's future and she was willing to bend her oft-touted integrity to see that it didn't happen. And there was still the Grove between them. Even if the town didn't survive, he would probably stay, and she couldn't blame him for that. It was where his son was happiest, and Corey Wyatt was understandably the most important person in the world to Adam.

"I'm sorry about your wife," she said, "and I'm glad things have worked out for you and Corey. I—" Her sentence ended in a screech as without warning, Adam hit the brakes and simultaneously snapped his right arm straight out to the side, pressing her back against the seat. An enormous stag, caught in the cruiser's high beams, stood dead center of the road.

Adam's choices, Pat saw in a split second of recognition, were limited. He could hit the stag and wreck the cruiser, or take his chances by going off the road. He chose the latter, whipping the steering wheel to the right. The cruiser skidded along the soft shoulder, crashed through the rough foliage beyond, and airborne, sailed out into darkness.

Chapter 9

The cruiser landed with a molar-jarring thud, slewing crazily amid waist-high weeds damp with night moisture. Pat was tossed about, her body straining against the confining embrace of the seat belt and Adam's outstretched arm. Adam struggled to gain control of the skid and was very nearly out of it when the back of the car slammed against something with such violence that the rear passenger window shattered, the sound ripping through the night. The car rocked in place, and was finally still.

"God!" Adam exclaimed, breathing audibly. "Pat, are you all right?" He released his seat belt with a snap, then hers, and slid an arm around her shoulders, his voice hoarse with concern. "Are you hurt?"

"Not as far as I can tell," she responded breathlessly. Belatedly, she began to shake. "Maybe a few bumps and bruises. How about you?"

Instead of answering, he wrapped his other arm around her and held her tightly, his lips against her ear. Pat was grateful for the embrace, needing to hold onto him, to be held by him, and assumed that what he needed was time to let his adrenaline settle down. For as long as it took, she would leach from him whatever strength and sense of calm she could.

After a while he released her, stroking her cheek as he let her go. "I'd better see how much damage I did." Grabbing a flashlight from underneath the seat, he got out and disappeared into the darkness behind the car. Pat concentrated on stopping her shakes.

Centuries later, he returned. "Can't move around too much. The right rear's lodged against a tree," he said getting back inside the car. "The impact drove the fender and bumper into the tire, probably bent the axle. God, Pat, I'm sorry, but I couldn't chance hitting a stag that big. We'd probably be in a lot worse shape if I had."

Pat knew of more than one instance where such a collision had proven fatal to the occupants of a car. "You were marvelous. I'm glad you were driving. What do we do now?"

"Well, we're about ten miles from the camp. Hold this a minute," he said, handing her the flashlight. He opened the glove compartment, dug out a map, spreading it out between them. "Unless I'm completely turned around, we're in luck. Are you up to walking?"

"How far?"

He made a guessing face. "Three miles?"

"To where?"

"Wally Quinton's cabin. I've been there a couple of times with him. I'll have to break in, but I doubt he'll hold it against me."

"I'm game," she said, scratching vigorously at a spot on her upper arm. "If we stay here, the bugs will eat us alive."

"Let's go then. Unlock your door and wait for me." He got out again and worked his way around the front to her side. Opening her door, he slid one arm around her back, the other under her legs.

"Adam, I can walk," she protested.

"It's better this way. Trust me." Lifting her out, he remained still a moment, getting his balance. Looking over his shoulder, Pat stared down into nothing. The car had come to a stop a foot or so from the edge of a chasm. Gasping with horror, she squeezed her eyes shut and tightened her grip around his neck as he inched his way around the front of the car, then climbed the embankment and put her down on the shoulder of the road. Even with solid ground under her feet, Pat couldn't let him go. He held her, murmuring in her ear, until she could release him.

"Right back," he said, and went down to cut the lights and lock the cruiser. Rejoining her, he looked at her intently. "Okay now?"

Pat nodded. "Sorry for going octopus on you. I got a good look at that drop we could have made and it spooked me."

"Lady, you've got good sense. Let's go."

All things considered, it wasn't that hard a trek. Adam held her hand, aiming the flashlight at their feet, and a bright moon bathed the countryside with a white glaze. Between the two sources of illumination, the walk began to take on the air of a romantic moonlight stroll. Still shaken by the accident, Pat expunged from her thoughts the fact that Adam was not and would never be her guy. What could it hurt to just enjoy the here and now for once?

She was hungry to find out as much about him as she could, and with little prompting, Adam talked about his childhood as a member of a loving family and the usual struggle to make ends meet, all four children taking on after-school jobs to supplement meager allowances. She found herself envying his years of stability, living in one place, seeing the same faces every day in his neighborhood, his school.

Being the son of a policeman, he'd had his share of fights, but in spite of that, he had no complaints and she began to understand the forces that had gone into making him who he was. They arrived at their destination without Pat realizing that she'd walked three miles. In fact, she was sorry it was over. It had been so nice keeping the real world at bay for a while.

The Grove's mayor was a believer in roughing it. The cabin, a small two-room edifice to which Adam gained entry with ease, had few amenities: a small refrigerator, a two-burner hot plate and, to Pat's relief, indoor plumbing. The furniture in the larger room, what there was of it, was bargain-basement modern and had seen hard use: two vinyl-cushioned couches of different vintages, a small dinette table with three battered chairs. Fraying rag rugs covered the floor. But to Pat, the cabin's screened-in front porch, complete with hammock, and the enormous fireplace outweighed the paucity of other frills.

"No phone?" Pat asked with dismay.

"'Fraid not. Quint didn't even have electricity until last summer. I'd hike to the nearest gas station to call for help, but it probably closes at eleven."

Pat's watch glowed midnight. She hadn't realized it was that late. It was time to ask the question uppermost on her mind. "Where do we sleep?"

In the smaller room was one double bed and stacked bunk beds. A closet held bedclothes and towels. "I think these fit the double bed," Adam said, passing her a set of linen and a pillow. "I'll take one of the couches."

Pat glanced back into the living room, wishing she had the nerve to suggest that they share the bedroom—or a bed. "They don't look very comfortable."

"They're sleep sofas, and actually, not too bad. It's where I slept before. The bathroom's small but there is a shower, if you'd like to use it. Meanwhile, I'll open the windows."

"A shower sounds like pure heaven. I'll keep it short and try not to use all the hot water."

He handed her a bath sheet, his lips twitching. "There won't be any, unless you want to wait until morning. The water heater's turned off."

"Oh, God," Pat groaned. "I repeat, I'll keep it short."

True to her word, she was in and out of the shower in record time, with the bra and panties she'd washed as best she could using the Cammio scented soap she'd found in the stall. But instead of leaving, she stood in front of the crazed mirror of the medicine cabinet and held a silent dialogue with her image. Beyond the bathroom door was a man who made her body growl with hunger. How would she survive the night with him in one bed and herself in another?

You're a mature, consenting adult, she told the face in the mirror. You *want* this man more desperately than you've ever wanted anyone or anything. So you won't be spending the rest of your life together, probably won't have any semblance of a relationship beyond the purely physical. So what? What's the big deal?

The big deal, her reflection responded, is that you're a sissy when it comes to pain. Go to bed with that man knowing that tonight can't possibly be enough for you, that you'll live the rest of your life in agony for the few moments of passion you had and will never have again? Uh-uh. Besides, he told you flat out that as much as he'd like to make love to you, he won't touch you. If you throw yourself at him, he's going to turn you down. That's pain of another type, the pain of rejection. Any way you look at it, you lose. So quit hiding in here and go on to bed—alone.

Her argument won and lost, Pat turned off the light. With her half-slip pulled up as far as it could reasonably go and wrapped in the damp bath sheet, so large that it trailed on the floor, she left the bathroom.

Adam, barefoot and shirtless, had opened the couch and was tucking in the sheets. "Your bed's made." The sight of his muscular chest and shoulders sent a spear of anguish through Pat's slender frame. Spotting her underwear in her hand, he jerked his head toward the front porch. "Why don't you hang them over the railing?"

"Good idea." She draped them on the end of the porch opposite the hammock. Returning to the living room, she faked a yawn. "I've had it. I'm turning in."

He gave her a tired smile. "You've had a long day, thanks to me. I woke you up this morning, so I won't keep you up any longer... Good night, Pat. By the way...the bedroom door has a lock on it."

She stopped and swiveled toward him, feeling a pinch of hope. "Is there any reason for me to use it?"

"No, I just thought you'd like to know."

Hope died. "Thanks. I trust you," she said, and as she turned to go into the bedroom, stepped on the hem of the towel. It came off, dropping to the floor. She stooped to retrieve it, bumping against the door sill. "Ouch!"

Adam got to his feet. "Did you hurt yourself?"

"Not really." She re-draped the towel. "Probably just hit a bruise. I'm a little sore here and there."

"Let me see." He crossed to pull her back to the sofa bed, picked up one of the lamps and held it above her head. "Holy... *Look* at you."

Pat glanced down. The point of her right shoulder had begun to darken where she'd been slammed against the car door. "It looks worse than it is. I bruise easily. It's not that bad, honestly."

"The hell it isn't. Don't move." He disappeared into the bathroom and returned with a tube of ointment. "It's only first-aid cream, but it's better than nothing." Overriding her protests, he smoothed it on with a gentle hand, watching her carefully for any sign of discomfort. Pat willed herself to remain perfectly still while her skin gloried in his touch. "There, that's better. Anywhere else?"

"No," she lied. She had to get away from him. "It should be fine in—"

"What is that?" Holding the lamp directly in front of her, he frowned. An angry red stripe began at her right collarbone and angled down under the half-slip, to disappear in the valley between her breasts. "From the seat belt?"

"I guess so. I'm not complaining. Without it, and your arm—by the way, thank you for doing that—I'd probably have gone through the windshield."

"That's about the only good it did." Smearing more of the first-aid cream on his fingers, he spread it gently along the length of the abrasion, hesitating when he reached the top of her half-slip. Then, unexpectedly, he hooked both little fingers under the lace-trimmed elastic, lowering the garment to her waist. Pat froze, uncertain how to react. Poker-faced, he continued his ministrations, covering the reddened streak between her breasts and below, to the point where it faded just above her slip. Her breathing quickened and she bit her lip to avoid moaning from the sheer ecstasy of his touch.

"Thank you," she said, barely above a whisper.

Without a word, he replaced the cap on the tube, set it aside, then turned to look her squarely in the face. Pat held her breath. She felt more uncovered than if she wore nothing at all, yet resisted the urge to pull up the half-slip, her eyes locked with his, determined to wait out whatever was happening.

He reached for his wallet on the lamp table, fished in a pocket and removed a small square package. A condom. "It's not too late to lock that door, Pat," he said finally.

The choice was hers. She waffled, but only for a second, reminded that they had flirted with death tonight. The sudden realization that she could have died never knowing what it was like to cradle his weight between her thighs, to feel his power as he moved into her, put matters in perspective. She took the package from him, unhurriedly ripped it open, then set it aside to smooth a finger along his top lip. "Adam, it was too late exactly one minute after I met you."

He regarded her somberly. "As long as that. I beat you by about fifty seconds." With one arm supporting her, he lowered her until she laid on her back. Leaning over her, he kissed the hollow above the uninjured collarbone. "No strings, Pat," he said, his voice muffled. "Just let me have tonight."

He understood. Touched that he was asking no more of her, and saddened that after this night there would probably be no more of him, she lifted his face from her neck and looked into eyes that shouted his raw need of her. Raising her arms to him, she pulled him down to her and offered her lips as her first gift of the night. He took them as if they were precious jewels, easily damaged, with gentle pressure, then nipped at her bottom lip.

From there he brushed her face and neck with tender kisses, his hands smoothing the skin of her back and slender waist. His touch at first was calming, soothing, then gradually changed character, waking every inch of surface under his fingers, bringing her skin to life until each cell screamed for his attention.

Adam came back to her mouth, took possession with authority, to which Pat yielded willingly. Cradling the nape of her neck with one hand while he visited the delicate lining of her lips, the other hand strayed lazily around to her front. Her body tensed, waiting, her back arching toward him. When he cupped her breast, a finger sliding across its peak, she gasped, welcoming it, demanding more. Adam complied, his hand teasing, stroking, setting little fires that spread, burrowed deep, trailed the tunnel of her spine, aimed straight for the dark triangle between her thighs.

Abandoning her mouth again, he nibbled at the hollow of her neck, then with gentle lips followed the path of the abrasion left by the seat belt into the valley between her breasts. Slowly, maddeningly, he set a path toward each dark tip, taking his time, drawing out the moment he would reach his goal. Pat was paralyzed with anticipation, not daring to move. When she felt the warmth of his breath, then the heat of his mouth, encircle the waiting peak, she heard a moan—his. The sound, the admission, ignited her.

Until now she'd lain passively, accepting his kisses, his touches. She had let him bring her alive, awaken urges that had lain dormant until the moment she'd turned in the hospital lounge to see him standing there. She had wanted him from that moment. Never had she reacted to anyone as she had to Adam Wyatt, gripped by outright lust from the very first. What she felt now, however, had nothing and everything to do with lust.

It went beyond an itch to be scratched, curiosity to be satisfied. She wanted more, much more, an intimacy that went deeper than skin on skin. She wanted the whole man, his body, his spirit, but what she demanded of him, he had a right to expect from her. She could only get as much as she was willing to give. She had to show him what this meant to her, what he meant to her, even if it was their one and only union. That she would be baring her soul, stripping herself to her core, was a risk she had to take.

Her breathing rapid, labored, Pat gradually shed any inhibitions she had left, peeling them away layer by layer. She let her hands speak for her, playing across the broad expanse of his chest and back, the muscular plane of his abdomen. She let her silent mouth speak for her, converse via kiss for kiss, nip for nip. He responded by easing the half-slip from her, drawing it down over her legs and laying it aside. In the light of the mayor's tacky little lamp, he gazed at her body with the appreciation of an aesthete before fine art.

When she touched the buckle of his belt, he stood up to loosen it. Slowly he lowered his slacks and briefs and stepped out of them. Pat's eyes feasted, took their fill. He was beauti-

ful, masculine perfection, from the broad slope of his swimmer's shoulders to the slim hips, the dark vee of curly hair that
began at his navel and marked the trail to surround the proud,
bronze symbol of his manhood. Adam nude filled Pat with a
burst of avarice that demanded satisfaction.

Unable to forget that this night might never come again, she
wanted to make this man a part of her, etch a permanent imprint of him in each and every sense. She wanted the smell of
him in her nostrils, the taste of him on the back of her tongue,
the sight of this autumn-brown Adonis on a screen in her mind,
the sound of his moan in her ears. She fixed on the rigid excla-
mation of his desire for her, and enamored with her power over
it, smoothed, squeezed, stroked, encircled it, ecstatic at its vel-
vety strength, watched it quiver, swell and lengthen even more.

"Pat, darling, stop," he moaned.

It was just as well. In administering to him, she herself was
nearing flame-out. She picked up the condom, removed it, and
with loving fingers, sheathed him.

Bending again, he began to graze the length of her body, his
lips adding fuel to flame, exploring secret places, nudging her
toward whimpering abandon. Her center began to yearn for the
immediate feel and pressure of him, but Adam seemed determined to see that she shared the same plane of rapture he occupied and played her slowly, leisurely, with the expertise of a
master guitarist. When she could take no more of his hands, his
mouth, she pulled him to her, her hand grasping velvet and
steel, guiding him to the seat of her hunger. Adam hesitated
above her, his gaze locked with hers. If he had any doubt that
she was ready, she tried to let him see it in her eyes, to feel it in
the silken dampness between her thighs, in the arch of her back,
the pressure of her grasp on his hips.

He moved into her, slowly, smoothly, as if going home, a
place he knew well, a place meant especially for him and him
alone. It showed in his face, in the pace of his breathing, in the
staccato throb of his pulse under her hand, and Pat, assured
now that she'd reached his heart as he had hers, peeled away the
final layer. Thrusting gently once to meet him in a gesture of
welcome, she became quiescent, as did he, to listen for the primal beat that would guide their movements.

When it began, ever so softly from some remote corner deep in each of them, they responded in sync, slowly, hypnotically, helpless to ignore its gradual increase in tempo and volume. It began to build and they moved to its rhythm, Pat clutching Adam in a fierce grasp and clasp, her body aflame, searing him, becoming part of him, a willing participant in the dance. Faster and faster, the drum drove them, to the edge of control, teasing them, maintaining a steadily escalating, pulsating beat, then increasing again until it was the complete master of them both and hurled them over the edge.

They made the leap as one, soaring above the abyss on a thermal of their own making, Pat screaming his name again and again until the heat faded and, with the drum's beat receding in their ears, they drifted back to the plane of their normal existence. Except that Pat knew, accepting and returning a kiss acknowledging the special nature of the journey they'd shared, that her existence would never be the same again. This was the man to whom she belonged in a way that surpassed his mere possession of her. And she would have to learn to live without him. Too exhausted to handle the emotions that realization brought, she drifted off to sleep in his arms.

When she awoke again, the bed was empty, the sheets where Adam had lain, cold but permeated with the scent of his cologne and their lovemaking. The memory of it washed over her, and her stomach fluttered under her hand. He had been so gentle, so giving. She'd totally lost her heart. It was now Adam's, and he'd never know it. But she would. There could never be another man in her life, and she accepted that. Tears sprang into her eyes and she let them flow, crying into her pillow, allowing herself this small indulgence. She might as well get it out of her system and be done with it. When she'd exhausted the supply, she wiped her eyes and turned over, ready to face whatever.

Outside the trees glistened like emeralds, the rays of the morning sun reflected in the dewdrops decorating the leaves. Six-forty. She sat up, stretched, and hiccuped in unexpected pain. Everything hurt, shoulders, elbows, back. An examination of her body revealed the severity of the jostling she'd suffered during the rough ride down the embankment. The bruises and abrasions were clearly visible now, turning interesting colors under the warm sienna of her skin. It looked as if she'd be wearing long sleeves for a while.

Leaving the bed, she wrapped herself in the sheet and opened the door. The welcome aroma of coffee filled the outer room; an ancient percolator occupied a burner on the hot plate. There was no sign of Adam, but a note propped against the mug he'd left out for her explained his absence.

Good morning, sleepyhead!

   Gas station opens at six. Have gone for tow truck and phone. Relax, have a hot shower and a cup of java. Back a.s.a.p.

   Today's my day off. Had planned to work, but have changed my mind if... Any chance of your spending it with me? Again, no strings. Just trying to make our one night last as long as I can. I'll understand if you say no.

                                                                A.

Spend the day with him? Pat laughed aloud. "Yes. Oh, yes." She hurried to shower and dress.

A little after seven, a battered, rust-infested pickup in dire need of a new muffler literally roared into the yard. Pat, lazing in the hammock with the last of her coffee, sat up too fast and almost fell out. Adam hopped down, pointedly avoiding the deteriorating running board. "Your chariot awaits, m'lady," he said, taking the steps two at a time.

"Where'd you get that?" Pat asked, eyeing it with trepidation.

"Bought it off the station owner for seventy-five dollars."

Pat shook her head. "I've got news for you, buddy. You was robbed."

"I can sell it for parts—I hope." On the porch again, he joined her in the hammock. "How do you feel?"

"Battered, bruised, glorious. How about you?"

"I'll show you." He looked at her and she watched the amber eyes begin to smolder. For a split second Pat thought of all they had to do today, but the desire in his face erased all considerations. They would be back in the real world soon enough. She snuggled against him, unbuttoned his shirt, searched and found the diminutive peaks on his chest. She watched, fascinated, as the telltale activity began at the juncture of his thighs, and he squirmed in the prison of his slacks.

Pat dealt with his belt buckle, lowered the zipper and once again went searching under the fabric until she found her prize. The feel of him inflamed her passion again and for the first, and she hoped later, the last time in her life, Pat made love in a hammock.

After they'd shared a shower and were dressed again, Adam asked, "What did you decide? About today."

"Adam, I'd love to spend it with you, but there's so much to do. With Hetty so close to being released, I have to nail down arrangements for moving her. Also, I'd like to gather up all the historical material on the mansion to give to Rena tonight. Perhaps she'd be willing to follow through on it, since she knew that's what Lib wanted."

"Then I might as well go on to work. But that was not how I had hoped to spend the day." He embraced her, his lips brushing across hers, his fingers deftly undoing buttons until her dress was open to her belt. As much as she wanted to remain exactly as they were, with his hands driving her to distraction, she trapped them under the silky fabric.

"Adam, please. I'm nervous about being away from a phone. I'd feel a lot better if we went back to town, so I could check in with the hospital, just in case."

"You're right," he said and, sighing, began fastening the buttons again. "How are the bruises?"

"Not bad. Oh, thanks for the coffee."

"It was the least I could do after what I put you through last night."

Pat caressed the back of his neck. "Granted, I wouldn't want to go through the first part again, but the last part wasn't bad at all. Neither was this morning."

His chuckle, deep and warm, made her pulse jump. "You can say that again. Thank God I don't have any fillings. Do you always make a man feel as if the top of his head is spinning off?"

She moved away from him. "If you're fishing, Adam, there haven't been that many. In fact, embarrassingly few. What happened with you..." She stopped, still slightly amazed at the events of the early morning hours.

"Regretting it?" he asked, his tone light. His eyes, however, were deadly serious.

"No. I'll never forget it, either."

"That sounds as if last night and today is all there'll ever be for us."

She stood up, needing to put some distance between them. "One, I can't handle casual sex, Adam. It's too intense an experience for me. Two, I live in Washington, D.C. You live in the Grove. A long distance relationship would be futile, since neither one of us plans to move. It makes more sense to end this now."

He came to her, propped his arms on her shoulders. "You're right on all counts, Pat, but that doesn't mean I'm not going to try to change your mind. If we can just get past this case, have it over and done with..."

"Adam, please..."

He persisted. "Your animosity toward the Grove is poisoning you, Pat Chase, and I plan to work on the antidote. I want to rekindle the love you used to have for it. If I can do that I'll have won half the battle."

"By...?"

"By proving you wrong. By showing you that the Grove didn't turn its back on you, that they couldn't come to your defense because practically no one knew what was happening to you."

"Then you've already lost the war." Pat cradled his face between her hands and kissed him lightly. "I talked to someone yesterday who was at the school when they had me open the locker. According to him, by the time I was released the next morning, it was all over town."

Adam frowned. "Who was that?"

"Mr. Franklin. I ran into him outside the bank, and he stopped me to ask about Hetty."

"But how'd the subject come up?"

Unprepared for that question, Pat opted for the truth. "He said word is that there's something suspicious about Lib's death, and they don't intend to sit back and see Hetty take the blame for it. The Harlands had gotten away with it last time, but it wouldn't happen again."

"They who, Pat?" Adam asked, drilling her with his gaze. "Does anyone really think I'd be a part of a plan to treat Miss Hetty—or anyone for that matter—unjustly? The truth, Pat. Even if there's never anything else between us, at least let there be truth."

He hadn't intended it, but what he'd done was to deliver a swift kick in her conscience. So far she hadn't out-and-out lied to him about Hetty, she'd simply lied by omission. Now, without meaning to, she'd stumbled into the unenviable position of exposing him to the kind of hurt she'd experienced at discovering that she was considered an outsider. She tried to buffer her response. "Perhaps they feel you may have no choice, Adam."

"We've been through this before," he said, towering above her, magnificent in his anger. "I'm my own man. I thought I'd lived there long enough for everyone to know that."

The victim of a perverse twist of irony, Pat found herself defending the same people she'd been condemning. "They're speaking out of almost two centuries of experience as indentured servants, in one guise or another, of the Harland family. And being your own man and having no choice aren't mutually exclusive. If you'd had your druthers, you wouldn't have asked me to work with you. You admit it was not your idea, so obviously someone put the squeeze on you. They've probably seen it happen before any number of times, so don't be too hard on them."

"Have you left any of your belongings inside?" he asked abruptly. She shook her head and, his face taut, a muscle in his jaw pulsing, he went into the cabin. Pat heard him slamming windows closed, then the front door. "Let's go," he said, and headed back to the real world.

The ride to the Grove was hell. If the pickup had ever had shock absorbers, they no longer worked. Evidently the challenge of avoiding bumps and potholes that could toss them to the ceiling of the cab helped Adam regain his temper. Perhaps as confirmation of the end of their hiatus, he began discussing the case, outlining the assignments he and his three co-workers, armed with search warrants if needed, had tackled on and off since Lib's death: checking the local pharmacy and liquor store, and those in communities closest to the Grove to track down the source of the barbiturates and the liqueur, trying to track Lib's movements in the days prior to her death, especially the mysterious trip to Washington, D.C., establishing alibis, all the foot-slogging, mind-numbing minutiae that were part of an investigation of any kind. They had accumulated a mine of information, none of which, as far as they could tell, contained the mother lode.

"Adam," Pat interrupted the recital, impelled by a sudden thought, "Lib used to hide things in the most bizarre places because C.J.'s mother had a habit of poking through Lib's personal belongings whenever she could get away with it. I remember a few of her hidey-holes. I should check them for her codicil."

"We tore that place apart," Adam said, "and we're professionals at it. But help yourself. By the way, the search of your aunt's house was strictly a formality. I saw her leave the day Miss Harland died, and the next day. She was empty-handed both times, not even a purse. That's another reason she moved down on the list of suspects."

Pat breathed a sigh of relief. She, too, had searched the house, and hadn't found anything. When they'd exhausted that subject, however, she found herself on a hot seat of a different sort.

"It occurs to me," Adam said, "how little I know about the things that matter to you. Your job, for instance. How long do you see yourself staying with it? I guess I'm asking if you enjoy it that much."

She considered it an odd question. "It doesn't pay to say how long you'll do anything in television, because it's rarely up to you. The ratings determine that. At this point I feel that what I'm doing makes a difference. And yes, I enjoy it that much."

"Is it what you want to do the rest of your life? What kind of dreams do you have?"

There was no way to reveal her dreams, since they were full of him and the impossible. "That's difficult for me to answer."

"Do you see marriage in your future?" he persisted. "Children?"

"I used to," she admitted. "I don't anymore."

"Why the hell not?"

Because it was Adam Wyatt or nobody, she thought. "Just a feeling. I don't mind. I'm basically a loner anyway."

"Loners get married and have kids." He sounded almost angry. "You enjoy chasing down the story that much?"

Stung that he'd reduced her career to that level, Pat spoke from the heart. "The story is not a two-column article, Adam. It's people. I grant you that going after a rental agency with a history of cheating tenants out of their security deposits isn't as noble a calling as protecting the peace. But when that money means the difference between buying groceries or going hungry, or perhaps becoming homeless because the money's needed to pay a security deposit somewhere else, it becomes just as important as what you do. That I enjoy. Why'd you ask?"

"Just curious," he said, his eyes flat and hard.

Pat, sensing his withdrawal, felt something shrivel inside her and began concocting an anesthetic to numb the pain. Then, a thought occurred to her. "Adam, are you lonely?"

He took a deep breath, shrugged. "What's the point in lying? Yes. Don't get me wrong, I wouldn't trade Harland Grove for anything. I don't have to worry about Corey running home from school past the dealers and streetwalkers. He can play in the yard without ducking bullets. But I miss the mental challenge I used to wrestle with every day. I miss the kind of camaraderie that develops between partners riding in a blue and white, or tackling cases together."

"And female companionship?" Pat prompted, openly curious.

He nodded. "That, too. Pat, if I came up to D.C. now and then, would I be complicating your life if I asked to see you? On your terms, of course."

Pat couldn't quite believe what she was hearing. "You'd really come? Just to see me?"

His lips stretched in a slow, provocative smile. "Don't you think you're worth it?"

"I know I am. I'm just surprised to find that you do."

Without warning, Adam edged onto the shoulder and stopped, slamming the truck into neutral and stomping on the emergency brake. Pulling her into his arms, he kissed her with such depth of feeling that Pat's heart cried out with grief at the magnitude of her loss.

"I just needed proof that I hadn't dreamed what happened between us," he said when he released her. "And wanted to remind you what you'll be missing."

Pat edged back over to her side of the seat. It was move or bawl like a baby.

When they reached the Grove, Adam's first stop was at the station, where Bo and Troy Lee ragged him unmercifully, howling with laughter at the mode of transportation to which their chief had been reduced. Once the hilarity had died down, he and Pat went to separate phones. Adam had a message that Corey had called, and with a frown of concern dialed the camp. Pat called the hospital and was told that she should arrange for the ambulance to pick up Hetty at noon the next day. Since Rena's car, complete with a new tire, was parked outside, she decided to return to the mansion and contact the ambulance service from there. She needed complete privacy.

Adam's call was a short one, his bemused expression as he replaced the phone assuring Pat that there was no problem with his son. He caught her out in the foyer as she was leaving. "You've made another conquest. Parents visit on weekends. I've been given orders not to come unless you're with me."

Pat was pleased beyond words, but hesitated. "I'd love to go, Adam, but do you think it's wise?"

The sparkle dimmed in his eyes. "Pat, not that it changes anything, but I'm going to tell you something so you'll have no doubt where I'm coming from. I'm in love with you, and I fight for what I love."

Pat's breath stopped, along with her heart. "Oh, God, Adam." It was crazy, she thought. According to the calendar, she hadn't known the man two weeks. But she'd realized the night before that she wasn't just responding to the insistent call of lust. She loved him. She might never live with him or feel his weight pressing against her again; unfortunately, love rarely cared about little things like that. "I love you, too, but…" She didn't have the emotional stamina to finish the sentence.

His eyes filled with sadness. "Life's a bitch, ain't it? I'll see you in a while. And don't forget, we have dinner with C.J. and Rena tonight." Backing through the double doors, he went to work.

When she'd recovered enough of her composure to drive, Pat made a detour to stop at Hetty's to see how the roofers were progressing. Mr. Evans had said it probably wouldn't require more than two or three days, unless he ran into problems that weren't obvious from his initial inspection. Not that she wasn't comfortable at the mansion, but it was haunted by too many memories, quite aside from being the noisiest place she'd ever stayed in.

The news was good. If the weather held, they would be finished by the next day, the morning following at the latest.

"That was one hell of a leak," Mr. Evans informed her. "You might want to take a look at the things in that corner of the attic. The water did a lot of damage up there, and termites are taking care of the rest. Miss Hetty'll probably have to throw some things away. Doesn't look like anybody's been up there in a coon's age."

Pat was willing to believe it. She'd forgotten Hetty had an attic; the access to it was hidden by a false ceiling in the hall closet. According to family lore, a previous Melton hadn't trusted banks and had put in the sliding panel to hide every penny he'd owned. Pat snorted to herself. Not all the Meltons had been smart.

After calling an exterminator to inspect the damage, she pulled the ladder from the toolshed. Mr. Evans agreed to show him the area of concern once he arrived. All she had to do was clear the way so he could get up there from within the house.

Working quickly, she moved Hetty's winter wardrobe from the closet, worked the panel to one side and lowered the steps, which dropped with a stiffness that spoke of years in the raised position. It would be smart to make sure the light hadn't been shorted out. Pat climbed the steps and, sweeping mazes of spider webs aside, found the string. The dim, low-watt bulb came to life immediately, casting the space in a hazy gloom. She left it on and started back down when she saw the ghost of something else she'd put out of her mind all these years. The tapestry-weight backpack she'd made in Home Ec, propped against an old steamer trunk.

Going back up far enough to reach it, she grabbed it, sneezed at the dust she'd disturbed in the process, and came down again, heading for the back porch to shake off the residue of fifteen years of sitting. There was none. Perhaps it had been protected by something, but picturing the scene supplied no clue as to what it might have been.

Pat sat at the picnic table, eased the drawstring open and slid out the contents. A world literature textbook, a three-ring binder and a pale blue folder. It couldn't be. Here was the past again, the title page typed on the sturdy old Underwood Hetty had rented for her. *The Meltons. The Story of a Family.* Nine pages of carefully worded text. It was an omen. She'd told Adam she would finish it. Well, now she had no excuse.

Putting it aside, she unsnapped the flap of the outer pocket, hoping she hadn't left a lunch in it. It would be fossilized by now. With cautious fingers, she raised the flap. No lunch. A big padded envelope wedged in, the sides folded so it would fit. Puzzled, she pried it out, goring herself on one of the staples used to seal it. It was addressed to Hetty by her own hand. That was definitely Hetty's writing.

Pat dredged through her memory bank. Was it something she was supposed to have mailed for her? The single stamp, probably not enough postage even fifteen years ago, was uncanceled. What could . . . ? The question evaporated as she flipped back to the previous thought. That was not a fifteen-year-old stamp. She had a book of them in her purse right now.

Her hands trembling, she yanked the envelope open and looked in. Fabric? "Oh, no," she whispered. Carefully, to avoid snagging the pale pink material on a staple, she removed it, saw that it was wrapped around something else. Then, she unfolded it, using two fingers. A gown, lace-trimmed, one strap stained brown and another brown stripe below the waist. The bounty it had cushioned, a bottle of coffee liqueur, 25.4 ounces, two-thirds empty. Café Carib: 53 proof. And a shot glass, an "E" etched in Old English script on one side, a tissue stuffed in it.

Pat removed the tissue and realized it was not empty. There was no need to unfold it. Clearly visible through the thin white paper were the capsules: one green, one yellow. The murder weapons. They were real, incriminating, lethal. Perhaps she'd been fooling herself all this time. Perhaps Hetty hadn't been confused, hadn't been speaking figuratively. She might have meant exactly what she'd said, that she'd killed Lib Harland.

Chapter 10

"Patty?" Sarah Ransom's voice boomed her name. The front screen slammed. "Where are you?"

Oh, God, Pat thought. All thumbs, she crammed things back into the front pocket, but there wasn't time to get rid of the backpack itself. With no place to hide it, she shoved it under the picnic table as far out of sight as she could. "On the porch, Miss Sarah," she called, then saw that she'd forgotten the padded envelope. All she could do was turn it facedown.

"It's my day to bring your lunch." The house vibrated under her heavy-footed gait. "Good thing I saw Rena's car or I'd have taken this to the mansion." She appeared in the back door, filling its frame. "Mercy, child, you're pale as a ghost! Something happen to Hetty?"

"No, she's fine, honestly. I'm just tired." She took the plate. "This looks marvelous. And I'm starved. I haven't eaten since last night."

With the familiarity of someone who knew her neighbor's house as well as she knew her own, Sarah went back into the kitchen and returned with flatware and napkins. "Eat, child. The world looks a sight better when your stomach's full." To

Pat's dismay, she picked up a rocking chair and moved it over to keep her company. "I hear Hetty's 'bout ready to go."

"Tomorrow." Hoping that if she ate something, her neighbor would leave, Pat removed the plastic wrap and tasted the shrimp salad. "It's as good as it looks."

"Oughta be, considering how much them little bitty things cost. I want to ask you something. How come Hetty won't see anybody? That's not like her."

Pat heaved a genuinely heartfelt sigh. "She's been so low, Miss Sarah. She doesn't seem to care whether she lives or dies."

Sarah's jowls sagged. "I was hoping that after a time, she'd rest easier in her mind. Eat now, baby. The problem is, with her being laid up, she's got nothing to do but fertilize that guilty conscience of hers. I tried to tell her that being riled up at Miss Lib wouldn't do neither one of them any good. Damn sure wasn't going to change anything."

"Change what, Miss Sarah?" Pat asked, dumbfounded to learn that the answer to her question might have been right next door all the time. "Why was she mad at Lib?"

"She wasn't really mad, just upset. After all these years, for Miss Lib to start nipping at the bottle again . . ."

This confirmed what Pat had surmised after her conversation with Perry Franklin. "I was shocked when I heard Lib used to have a drinking problem."

Sarah's raucous laughter floated out across the yard. "Child, that woman could put away some liquor, just like her brother."

"C.J.'s father was an alcoholic?"

"His father's brother, J.D. Jeff Davis Harland, his name was. Sometimes that weakness just runs in the family. Anyhow, Miss Lib, she stopped years ago, probably because her daddy threatened to disown her, like he did Mr. J.D. Wouldn't even allow him to be buried in the family vault. So when Hetty found out Miss Lib had started up again, she 'bout died. Tried to talk her into stopping, 'specially since she was already so peaked. Said Miss Lib claimed she was only taking a little at night to help her sleep."

"Did Hetty know why Lib hadn't been feeling well?" Pat asked carefully. "Other than her arthritis, I mean?" She wasn't sure whether Lib's cancer was common knowledge.

"If she did, she didn't say. Hetty wasn't much for spreading Miss Lib's business. Only reason she talked to me about it was because it worried her so. Hetty took it so personal, like Miss Lib was drinking to spite her. She was bound and determined to get her to stop or else. Just turned out to be or else. Miss Lib took one little nip too many. As if getting rid of the empty bottle would fool anybody."

"Well, she did a good job of that," Pat said. "Adam checked with the trash collectors. They never saw any liquor bottles in her garbage cans."

"Miss Lib? Probably stashed them somewhere in the house. I wasn't talking about her. I meant Hetty." She tipped her head toward the padded envelope.

Pat dropped her fork. "You knew Hetty took the last bottle?"

"Well, yes." Her expression bordered on the sheepish. "To tell you the truth, she gave it to me."

"She *what?* When?"

"The morning Miss Lib died. I was driving by, see, on my way to the Granger's house— I watch their babies a'morning. I see Hetty out at Miss Lib's mailbox, trying to cram in that big envelope there, so I slowed down and asked her if she wanted me to drop it off at the post office. She said yes and gave it to me. She hurries back up to the mansion."

"What time was this?"

"Must have been around seven-thirty. The thing is, Patty, I plumb forgot I had the thing until the next morning when I got out to the car, and there it is. I look at it and by God, it's addressed to her own self. So I just bring it over here. For one thing, it didn't have enough postage, so I figured she might as well save the one stamp she had on it. I swear, I thought she was going to faint. She thanked me, but that thing bothered me. I know Hetty—we played together as little nippers. She was up to something. I come over later to ask her why she would mail a package to herself, and knew soon's I saw her that something was wrong. She was talking out of her head and making no sense at all. So I had my son drive her to the hospital and I called Mr. C.J."

"Thank you for acting so quickly, Miss Sarah," Pat said. "You may have saved her life. But how did you figure out what was in the package?"

"Well, I heard this and that, and put it all together. It's the kind of foolishness Hetty would do for her friend."

"Then why haven't you told Adam?"

Sarah heaved herself to her feet and smoothed her dress over her Valkyrian figure. "Maybe," she said, meeting Pat's gaze, "because he didn't ask. Best he don't. I'd hate to lie to him—he's such a nice child—but for Hetty? I'd lie like a stain-resistant rug. Well, I'd best be getting back. You finish that shrimp, hear? Let me know if you need me for anything else. Anything, Patty. We ain't gonna let you down this time." She left by the back steps and marched toward her house without a backward look.

Incredulous, Pat stared after her, her gratitude swelling like a lump in her throat. So she, too, knew about the fifteen-year-old skeleton in her closet. Somehow, it didn't matter for the moment. That Sarah Ransom, as solid a citizen as one could meet, was willing to conceal evidence and keep silent about Hetty's idiotic act, did matter. Not only was she touched by the woman's unquestioning loyalty, it made her furious that Hetty had placed her neighbor in such a position. In that moment, Pat reached the limits of her patience. Snatching the backpack from under the table, she grabbed her purse, the envelope and car keys and lit out for the hospital.

Adam shut himself into the room used for interviews, interrogations, conferences and naps, and sprawled on the beat-up couch that came in handy during long, uneventful night shifts. That described practically all of them, save the odd Friday and Saturday night. Hands behind his head, he stared at the ceiling. He had to make a decision.

Either he had to turn the case loose, let the suicide verdict stand, or turn everything over to the county cops. He wasn't getting anywhere and he had to admit that he wasn't half trying. If he'd handled a case in New York as half-assed as he had this one, he'd have been off the force long since. But he'd fouled up, broken the first law of police work. He'd become emotionally involved.

Even on those occasions when Pat had aggravated the hell out of him, he'd still been attracted to her. And last night . . . Just thinking about the smooth velvet feel of her against him, around him, caused immediate discomfort in his nether regions. He couldn't ever remember a woman, neither during his oat-sowing days nor his years with Ginny, who'd so completely surrendered herself to him—a do-with-me-what-you-will with an entirely different feel to it. She gave herself to him, hid nothing from him, retained no shields to mask what she was feeling physically or emotionally. Letting it all hang out was a trite expression, but that's exactly what she'd done. She was completely naked to him. If she had told him before last night that she couldn't be casual about making love, he would probably have taken it lightly. He had no doubt about what she meant now.

You only gave as she did if you were in love. And unless you were an unmitigated bastard with your ego and little else between your legs, you didn't take that unique gift from a woman like Pat unless you loved her. And he did. Dear God, he did. But if he stayed on this case much longer, he would lose her with no hope of ever getting her back. Because Miss Hetty had risen to the top of the list again. He'd tried discounting her long enough.

Granted, her motive was murky, but if she was as angry at Miss Harland as Lorna, Pete, and even Rena had mentioned in passing that first day, she might have been angry enough to kill. That frail old lady could have dragged Miss Harland out of the bathroom fairly easily, which would account for the vacuuming to erase the marks in the carpet. Getting the body up on the bed would have been hard work, but if she'd been determined enough, she could have managed it. So far he had no evidence that she'd done anything at all. Now he was concerned that he might be so blinded by love that he couldn't see it or anything else clearly, even if it was right under his nose.

If he couldn't do his job, he needed to give it to someone who could. It might be better if the county boys found whatever evidence there was against Miss Hetty anyway. Perhaps if he was out of the picture, no matter what happened, there might be a chance for himself and Pat. It would be the first time he'd ever willingly ducked his responsibility. He would give it one more day, just one. If he hadn't gotten anywhere by the end of his shift tomorrow, he would let it go.

"Chief?" Bo tapped at the door.

Adam sighed. "What is it, son? Come on in."

Bo satisfied himself by sticking his head around the door. "Miss Lorna just called from the mansion. She says you told her to let you know if mail came for Miss Lib. She got a couple of things today. She wants to know if she should bring it in."

Energized at having a legitimate excuse to visit the mansion, Adam sat up. "Tell her no. I'm going to run home to shower and shave, and then I'll be there."

"What's the matter, Chief? Don't you think Pat would appreciate Eau de Sweat?"

Adam threw a cushion at him, but hit the closed door. Smiling to himself, he left the station humming.

An R.N. Pat hadn't seen before was on duty when she stopped at the nurses' station. "I'm Miss Melton's niece," she said by way of introduction. "How is she?"

The nurse gave her a plastic smile. "Doing well today. We've got her sitting up while her bed's being made."

"No," Pat said. "I mean, how is she really? If she's to be transferred tomorrow, she's obviously in no danger. She can withstand the excitement?"

"Certainly, or we wouldn't be releasing her."

"Fine. Thank you very much."

"You're welcome, I'm sure." Clipboard in hand, the nurse left the station and went into a patient's room.

Pat, after waiting to be certain the woman wouldn't pop right back out again, hurried down B wing to Hetty's room. Ignoring the No Visitors sign, she swept in, startling the aide making the bed. Hetty, looking wizened and even tinier than usual, sat in a wheelchair by the window. Her eyes flew to the backpack in Pat's hand.

An expression of annoyance pulled the aide's face into a disapproving frown. "You can't come in here. Didn't you see the sign?"

"I saw it. Leave us, please. I have to talk to my aunt."

The aide straightened, hands on her hips. "Look, miss, this patient isn't supposed to have—"

"Honey," Pat said, "get out."

"You can't—"

"Out." Opening the door, she held it for her.

Hetty, leaning as far as the safety strap around her waist would allow, touched the aide's arm and nodded feebly.

"Well, if it's all right with you . . ." With one final glare for Pat, she left the room.

Pat dumped her purse on the dresser and sat down on the unmade bed, facing Hetty. "Now you listen to me, old woman," she began, to get her attention. "You'll be leaving here tomorrow, going by ambulance to the Ridgely Rehabilitation Hospital outside High Point. You'll be there overnight. The next morning you'll be flown by helicopter to a rehab center in western Maryland."

Hetty frowned, her eyes puzzled.

"No one except me will know where you'll be, especially Adam, because I figure sooner or later, he's going to be looking for you. I'm not going to tell him where you are, which means I may be arrested for harboring a fugitive."

Hetty's mouth opened. She emitted a strangled sound.

"I don't have any qualms about what I'm doing, I will protect you with my last breath. But by God, Hetty, if I'm to flush the honor of our family down the toilet, and alienate the man I've come to love, I *damn well want to know why!* Do you hear me?"

Clearly flabbergasted at Pat's outburst, Hetty nodded.

"Since I found this—" Pat picked up the backpack and slammed it down on the bed "—there are certain things I can safely assume. The question is why you removed them. Did you know Lib was dying? That she had cancer of the liver?"

There was no doubt this was news to Hetty. She shook her head, her face pained.

"That eliminates a mercy killing as your motive." Hetty squawked, her eyes widening. "And since she had a previous drinking problem," Pat continued, "pulling that stunt where you'd encourage her to drink enough to make her sick or so hung over that she'd give it up wouldn't have worked. Hetty, I can't believe I'm asking you this—did you kill Lib simply because she'd started drinking again?"

Hetty literally gaped at her, shook her head violently, and kept shaking it.

"Okay, okay. And if you didn't know she was terminally ill, it follows that there'd be no reason for you to think you were helping her commit suicide, either. *Ouch!*"

Hetty had reached out with her left hand and had pinched Pat on the thigh with surprising strength. She placed that hand over Pat's mouth—"Shut up and listen" in any language. Then she pointed to herself and shook her head.

"Hetty, you *didn't* kill Lib?"

The indignation on her face would have served, but her head swung from side to side. No, no, no.

Pat wanted to shake her until her teeth rattled, but managed to control her temper. "Hetty, if you didn't kill Lib, why in God's name did you tell me you did?"

Hetty seemed at a loss, then rubbed her thumb against her fingers.

Pat thought for a moment, trying to interpret the gesture. "I balanced your checkbook and saw a check you'd written to Perry Franklin. Did you feel Lib's death was partly your fault because you'd paid that liquor bill?" A nod of relief. "Oh, Hetty. All right, what about the pills? Did you get those for her?"

Hetty looked blank. For the first time, Pat wondered if her aunt had even noticed the tissue wedged in the shot glass.

"Darling, listen carefully. Lib died from mixing alcohol and barbiturates." Hetty gasped and sat up as straight as she could. "The pills had been dissolved in the coffee liqueur she'd been drinking, enough to kill a horse. Do you think Lib did that herself, that she committed suicide?"

If there were degrees of astonishment, Hetty swooped through them all. Her answer? No, no, no! She pulled her mouth into a wide smile, batted her eyes, then deliberately limp-wristed, she flapped one hand in a remarkably convincing impression of Lib at her happiest.

"Even though she was sick?" Pat asked.

Yes. She tapped her temple, made an okay circle with her thumb and middle finger. Translation: there was nothing wrong with Lib's mind.

"Are you sure? I understand she'd gotten very forgetful."

No way. Lib was fine.

Something was definitely fishy, Pat mused. "Adam Wyatt thinks someone murdered Lib. Hetty, why, *why*, did you move her and change her gown? Why did you take the bottle? Were you trying to hide the fact that she'd been drinking?"

Slow tears rolled from one eye and slid down her cheek. She nodded.

"For pete's sake, Hetty, you could have had a stroke and died right there in the bathroom with her. When I think of you dragging her back into the bedroom, lifting her into bed. Hetty, please *stop* that."

Hetty had pinched her again, this time on top of a bruise. She tilted her head to one side, closed her eyes and pressed a hand against her cheek.

"Lib was in the bed when you found her?"

A vigorous nod.

Pat sat back, shifted gears, revised her thinking. There was no reason for anyone to clean the bathroom, wipe away all fingerprints and vacuum the rug unless that person was trying to eliminate any trace that they'd been there. That ruled out Lorna and members of the family; it would be natural for their prints to be in Lib's suite. Who was left? And there was still the question of motive.

"Hetty, Lib changed her will. Pete and Lorna signed as witnesses, and Lib told Lorna I would be proud of her for what she'd done. Adam hasn't been able to find the new will yet. Was the change she made reason enough to kill her and destroy all trace of the document?"

Pat could see the wheels turning in Hetty's mind, but in the end she shrugged one shoulder. Perhaps she hadn't known about the codicil.

"What about that secret project she was working on that everybody in the world knew about, to have the mansion declared a historical landmark?"

Hetty waved her to silence, and through trial, error and sign language, corrected Pat's reading of the situation. The crusade to save the mansion and the secret project were two different things.

"Did you know what she was up to?"

No. She zipped her lip. Lib wouldn't tell her.

Disappointed, Pat gave up on that line of thought. Getting on her knees in front of the wheelchair, she took Hetty's hands, her heart contracting at the complete absence of strength in her right one. "Okay. Now, let's clear the air. I hadn't planned to make the trip tomorrow, but I'll go with you if you like."

Hetty shook her head and pointed to the floor. She didn't want to leave at all.

"Dr. Vernon thinks a rehabilitation center will get you up and going a lot faster than staying here. I hate to think of you up in Maryland alone, but I've got to hide you from Adam."

No. She almost mouthed the word.

Pat sighed. She didn't want to force her. "Then would you mind being up at High Point? That way I could at least come and visit. You've got to go somewhere, Hetty. If Miss Sarah saw you out at the mailbox an hour and a half earlier than you told Adam you'd gotten there, someone else on the street may have seen you, too. If he ever realizes you lied to him," she said, ignoring Hetty's pained expression, "you'll be number one on his list of suspects again. What you did made you look guilty, Hetty. It'll probably be easier to find the person who did kill Lib than try to convince him that you didn't."

Hetty leaned her forehead against her hand, her face forlorn.

"I'm working with him on the case, so that's in our favor. But I need you out of the way, and you know how I mean that. And I don't want you in handcuffs based on circumstantial evidence."

Hetty made a face, clearly still unhappy about it, but finally nodded.

"Okay. Want me to ride up with you?"

No. Hetty pointed at the backpack.

"Stay here and find out who killed Lib?"

An emphatic yes.

Pat stood up and hugged her. "I'll do the best I can. Hetty, please, don't ever push me away again. You're all I have."

Hetty hugged her awkwardly with her good arm, then nudged her away and tilted her head toward the door.

"Okay, darling. Adam and I are having dinner at C.J.'s tonight, so I won't be back until tomorrow. I'll come early so I can spend all morning with you before you go." After a good loud kiss on the cheek, an old routine that had lasted through the years, Pat retrieved the backpack and her purse, and left.

"Oh, damn." The monster, the seventy-five dollar pickup, sat in the driveway in front of the mansion. Pat snatched up the backpack and crammed it under the driver's seat. When it was completely out of sight, she scrambled from behind the wheel and walked slowly into the mansion, trying to quiet her jangling nerves.

She'd spent the trip from the hospital debating the wisdom of giving the contents of Hetty's package to Adam and telling him everything. If there were prints on the glass surfaces, she could well be handing him the key. Except Hetty's prints had to be there, too. As much as she'd like to share what she had, she didn't dare.

Adam, looking refreshed and newly scrubbed, sat at the telephone table in the foyer, studying the contents of a white envelope. In civvies again, he wore a bright yellow polo shirt over khaki slacks. The clean lines of his body reminded her of that body sans clothes and she felt a familiar warmth ripple down her spine.

"Hi," he said, getting to his feet. He kissed her lightly, his lips welcoming her back. "Where've you been?"

The warmth became heat and Pat wriggled out of his arms. She couldn't allow herself to be distracted. "At the hospital. I got fed up with Hetty's ban on visitors, especially since she's leaving tomorrow, and decided to have it out with her. It was chancy, but it worked. I'm no longer persona non grata."

"Good. I know that's a load off your mind. You even look different. How'd you manage to get through to her?" He stroked her cheek.

"I had her at a disadvantage. I talked—all she could do was listen. I think she was so frustrated at not being able to tell me how impudent I was being that she'll get down to business now and really work at her speech therapy."

"That's great, Pat. I'm relieved for both of you." His eyes were suffused with open hunger.

"Then that's three of us. What are you doing here?"

He waved the envelope at her. "A credit card bill. It came today. Miss Harland charged the whole trip to D.C., tickets, hotels, restaurants. Look at this." He sat down on the steps and patted the space beside him. She hesitated. "Hands off, I promise," he said softly.

God, how she would miss his voice, that New York accent. Giving up, she joined him. He smelled of soap, and water still glistened in his hair.

"See?" He held the bill so she could see it. "She went up to D.C. one morning and was back the next night, telling everyone she was going to see an old schoolmate in Danville. She stayed at the Willard. That's near the White House, isn't it?"

Pat was surprised. "You know the District that well?"

"I've been there a time or three. Look at the names of the restaurants. Two in Washington, and... Where the hell is Crystal City?"

"Northern Virginia. I don't know it all that well. A lot of offices, government buildings, shopping. Adam, I've got an office full of people who thrive on puzzles like this. Why don't I put one of them to work on it? With a good description of Lib, they can check with the hotel doormen to see if any of them remembers putting her into a cab."

"That's a dynamite idea." Adam beamed his approval of her suggestion. "Give it a try."

Pat dug out her long distance phone card, and passed the assignment on to Iliana Ortiz, a dark beauty who fancied herself the next Mata Hari and had no qualms about using her womanly wiles to worm information out of a source. Iliana wouldn't just pick up a phone, she'd go to the hotel. When she returned to the office, flipping her waist-length hair off her shoulders, she'd be in possession of everything she'd wanted to know and about twice as much that she didn't.

"I've got to freshen up," Pat said when she'd completed the call.

"Want your back scrubbed?" Adam asked, and nibbled her ear.

Sparklers erupted under his lips. "Adam, please."

He moved away, grinning. "Sorry. The offer still stands, though."

"No, thanks. I'd like to tackle Lib's suite for hiding places. I bet the codicil's stashed up there somewhere. And all the historical material, too. Unless it's in the library. But the door's locked."

"That's another thing for us to look for upstairs. Lorna says Miss Harland had the locks changed and kept the keys herself. She seems to have become really paranoid."

Yet Hetty had said the opposite. The divergent opinions, it seemed to Pat, were important. But she'd thought too long. Adam backed her against the railing, penning her against it with his body. He was aroused; she could feel it.

They were alone in the house. There was no reason they couldn't... Pat wrestled with her libido and won. She wanted him as much as he wanted her, but that bundle of dynamite she'd left in the car had reordered her priorities. "Adam, please. Let's work first, play later."

Giving up, he backed away, hands in the air. "You're right, and don't think I won't hold you to it, especially the playing."

"Give me twenty minutes," Pat said, and ran upstairs to duck in and out of a cold shower to douse the flame Adam had ignited. If she stayed in the Grove much longer, she mused, pulling on jeans and a T-shirt, she'd be the cleanest woman in the state.

Adam waited for her at the doors to Lib's suite. "You realize that the only reason I'm going through this exercise is to spend more time with you. Bo and I went over this room, twice."

"Why?" she asked, following him into the bedroom.

"The first time we reviewed the issue of the rugs and pillow-case. At that point we didn't know the cause of death. The second time we knew what was missing—the bottle. It wasn't in the house."

"Indulge me, anyhow," Pat said, her conscience shaking its head at her deceit. "Lib needed a devious mind to outwit Margaret. For instance, did you check the headboard of her bed? I know it doesn't look like it, but I bet it opens. And she was always altering things. Check inside the hems of draperies, sheets, anything on the bed. Behind the faceplates of wall switches and phone jacks, inside the posts of the four-poster. Light bulbs may not be light bulbs at all. That was Lib."

Adam eyed her with skepticism. "None of those places sounds big enough to hide a liquor bottle. A codicil, maybe. It won't hurt to look. Maybe we'll get lucky and find the key to the library."

It was the only thing they did find. They picked through the odds and ends, costume jewelry, a stash of dollar bills, all hidden in the places Pat had predicted, but did not find the codicil. Pat was struck by the dearth of paper. That, for Lib, was unusual.

Downstairs, waiting as Adam unlocked the door of the library, the dread she'd experienced before returned. It had been her favorite room in the house. She could still remember the smell of old books, leather bookbindings, lemon-oiled tables.

Adam pushed the door open and stepped aside for her. Pat didn't move. Understanding, he took her hand, lacing his fingers through hers. "We'll go in together." His strength flowed through Pat and she entered the room.

Shelves, books neatly aligned on them, climbed from floor to a rococo ceiling, a rail for the ladder sweeping around three sides of the room, interrupted only by the doors that opened onto the garden. The fireplace was almost tall enough for Pat to step into without stooping, and the faint aroma of charred wood still remained; evidently Lib had not aired out the library since winter.

The furnishings were unchanged, leather-upholstered easy chairs, each with its own side table and reading lamp, one long mahogany table, a massive desk between the doors to the outside. The glass-topped case containing Harland family memorabilia, minus Ephraim's daughter's cameo, still held center stage. Something else was missing from it, as well, something that eluded Pat. It pinged at her, like a deteriorating tooth.

The room itself was very neat, which was surprising. According to Lorna, it had been several months since Lib had allowed the weekly cleaning service access in the library. If she'd been locking herself in here to work every day, the place should have looked as if a hurricane had come through. There were no loose papers, no drawings of the mansion, none of the historical material Pat had expected to find, neither in the desk nor the drawer in the table.

"Where could she have put it?" Pat asked. "Lorna said she'd dug up bills for the wood used to build the house, receipts, contracts, even. I don't get it."

Adam looked around, eyes narrowed. "They aren't on the premises. Someone's removed them. Why? Pat, I wonder if the motive for Miss Harland's murder has been staring us in the face all along, if something she discovered about this house got her killed."

"But what? There's nothing secret about it. It's been featured in magazines any number of times, blueprints and all. There are probably copies of them in here somewhere. If not, the public library would have them. They have a small section dedicated to the Grove and to the Harland family."

Adam circled the room, wearing a troubled expression. "Rena and C.J. may have them, too. I'll ask tonight. What's in this anyhow?" he asked, stopping in front of the display case.

Pat commandeered one of the easy chairs, letting him look for himself while she considered the information Hetty had tried to relay: the document search and the secret projects were two different things. Perhaps in the process of coordinating material about the mansion, Lib had stumbled onto some information that launched her in a different direction. There was nothing to say that either theory, hers or Adam's, was wrong. But neither was there anything to say they were right. It was such a muddle, all of it.

Pat closed her eyes to think. What she really needed to do was write everything down, fall back on her usual outlines and lists. She hadn't removed the lid of her laptop since her days of waiting outside Intensive Care, when she'd organized her Seattle notes for Milt. She missed the structure her life had had before she'd hit the Grove, missed the—

"Pat. Wake up."

Pat opened her eyes. The housekeeper stood over her. "Lorna. Hi. Where's Adam?"

"He went home to change and asked me to wake you at seven-thirty."

"Seven-thirty!" Her watch confirmed the time. She had slept over three hours. "He should have awakened me. I've got to run out to... Oh, I forgot. I'm not going to the hospital tonight."

"He told me you weren't. He said he'll pick you up at nine."

Stretching, Pat stood up. Almost two hours before she'd see him again. Pat, you're a lost cause, she told herself. You're counting the minutes like a teenager in love for the first time. Well, she was. The two previous relationships had been nothing like this. She couldn't even think straight. She had better, however, get that backpack out of the car.

"Thanks, Lorna. You don't have to stay. Adam and I are having dinner at C.J.'s."

"Who do you think's fixing it for you? I'm on my way over there now. Anything you need before I go?"

"Not a thing," Pat said, going with her to the front door. "And thanks for taking care of my laundry. I really appreciate it."

Lorna looked pleased. "Like I said, it gave me something to do. I'll see you in a while."

"I'll walk out with you," Pat said. "I left something in the car." She stepped outside onto the veranda and gasped. The pickup was still there. The Cadillac was gone.

"Where's Rena's car?" she asked, her voice unnaturally high.

"Oh, Chief Wyatt took it. He couldn't get the truck started, and since he's coming back to pick you up anyway... You thought somebody had stolen it?"

Pat nodded, feeling the blood leave her cheeks. There was nothing she could do but pray that Adam would have no need to look under the seat.

"I can't believe she'd do that." C.J. was the color of library paste. "Hell, Patty, you were practically family! How could she believe you'd steal that damned cameo?"

"I hope I haven't taken the gloss off a terrific dinner," Adam said, "but I thought it was past time we got it out."

Rena moved from her seat next to C.J. and sat down beside Pat. "Honest to God, Patty, we didn't know a thing about it. Any one of us could have told Miss Margaret the only thing you had when you came out of that house was Aunt Lib's hat. We both had on next to nothing—bikinis, wasn't it? There's no place you could have hidden anything without it showing."

"And all these years you thought we'd sold you down the river?" C.J. shook his head. "That hurts almost as much as knowing what you went through. No wonder we never heard from you."

Pat was too emotionally drained to respond. She hadn't wanted to bring it up, but Adam had forced the issue by coming right out and asking them. And he'd assessed the situation correctly. Neither of them had known. She was sure they were telling the truth. C.J. had always been a lousy liar, turning blood red when he even tried. Rena's reaction had convinced her, as well. It was obvious she was appalled and disgusted, but had to bite her tongue. Margaret Harland was, after all, her husband's mother.

"There's been a conspiracy of silence for years," Adam said. "The adult community of the time found out, but for whatever reason never discussed it with any of you."

"That's why you asked about Chet Rowley calling my house." Rena's lips configured in an angry slash. "That bastard. Treating you like a common criminal. I'm glad he's dead. He was nothing but dirt, he and his brother."

"Calm down, Reen. Pat." C.J. cleared his throat. "I don't know what to say. I won't insult you by asking you to forgive my mother. If I were you, I don't think I'd be able to. I just wish we could figure out who had it in for you, because sure as hell, somebody set you up.''

"That's ridiculous," Rena snapped at him. "Everybody liked Patty. How do you think she got elected Miss H.G. High? She never talked about anybody, never stomped on anyone's feelings. Whoever took the thing must have panicked and figured they'd better get rid of it. The locks on the lockers weren't worth two cents, all you had to do to open a door was hit it just right. Remember, Patty?''

"I'd forgotten that," Pat said. "I owe you two an apology. I should have known . . .''

"And Aunt Lib knew?" Rena asked. "As much as she adored you, I'm surprised she didn't explode from holding it in.''

"Well, that's that," Adam said, rising. "We'll say good-night, but before we go, I wanted to ask you whether you plan to follow through on having the mansion designated a historical landmark.''

"Huh?" C.J. seemed to have trouble shifting gears. "Oh, that wacky idea of Aunt Lib's." He rumpled his hair, à la Stan Laurel. "I don't know, Adam. It would be nice to commemorate it in her memory, but it would take a small fortune to fix it up so's it would pass inspection. I guess I wish the problem would just go away. I've got enough to worry about. So the answer is, I don't know.''

"Do you have the blueprints and other material Lib had found?" Pat asked. "I just wondered how much needed to be done on it.''

"We don't have it," Rena said. "It's probably in the library.''

Adam let that pass. "What do you think should happen to the mansion, Rena?''

She shrugged, a gesture of helplessness. "I haven't made up my mind. I would never want to live in it again, I'll tell you that.''

"I didn't realize you had," Adam said.

"Only six months, but it felt like six years. It was right after Miss Margaret died and we were having this house renovated. Plaster dust all over the place, so we moved in with Aunt Lib until they were finished here. The mansion's too big. I tried re-decorating downstairs to make it feel cosier, but nothing seemed to work. And that basement, all those tiny rooms. No thanks. I think I'd like to see it used as a museum or an art gallery—the town doesn't have either one.''

An alternate suggestion popped into Pat's mind. ''What about letting the public library use it, Rena? It's twice as big as the building they're in.''

C.J. sat up. ''That's a thought. I won't be able to make a decision one way or the other until we know what Tyler's going to do, but I'll certainly keep that in mind. Not to change the subject, but how's the investigation going? Any line on how Aunt Lib got her hands on those barbiturates?''

''C.J., please.'' Rena's features twisted with pain. ''I thought we agreed not to talk about that tonight.''

''Sorry, I forgot. Say, Adam, before you leave, there's something I want to show you.'' Getting up, he deposited his snifter on the bar. ''Let's leave the girls for a minute.''

''Sure. Lead the way.''

''Men and their toys,'' Rena said, chuckling as they left. ''C.J. just bought something else for his computer.'' She poured a teaspoon of cognac into her snifter and gave Pat a coy smile. ''Just between us girls, as my idiot husband insists on calling us, what do you think of Adam? Isn't he the greatest?''

Pat searched for a response that wouldn't give too much away. ''He's very nice.''

''Nice! That's the best you can do? He's had the women in town standing on their heads from the day he arrived. He's a widower, you know. A real tragedy, the way he lost his wife. C.J. says it left him with an attitude about reporters, though. Of course, you aren't exactly a reporter.'' She waggled her eyebrows meaningfully.

Suddenly Adam's barbed questions and remarks about the work she did made sense. Uncomfortable at trying to hide her feeling for him, Pat changed the subject. ''Rena, can I ask you just one question about Lib?''

''What?'' The question was posed with a cautious overtone.

''Had Lib's mind begun to fail?''

Rena sighed. "It happened so fast. I wangled a promise that we'd go out for lunch together every Wednesday just to get her out of that damned library. I stopped to pick her up. No Aunt Lib. She'd gone out somewhere without letting anyone know where she was going. Or she'd ask me to take her shopping, or to pick her up somewhere. I'd show up and either she'd forgotten she wanted to go or what she'd been going for, or she wasn't where she told me she'd be. I finally gave up."

"I'm just surprised Hetty never mentioned it," Pat said.

"Honey, those two were thick as thieves until right there at the end. Miss Hetty was fiercely protective of her, covered for her whenever she could. But I have to be honest, Patty. I'll always feel a little responsible for what happened."

"Why?"

"Because Aunt Lib was forever saying that if she began to lose her faculties, she didn't want to live. I should have seen it coming. If I hadn't been so wrapped up with things at H.I., I might have been able to prevent it."

"How, Rena?" Pat saw no reason for her, like Hetty, to spend the rest of her life feeling guilty about Lib's death when neither could have stopped it. But if C.J. hadn't yet told her it wasn't suicide—if he knew, at all—she wouldn't find out from Pat Chase.

She changed the subject again by asking about Rena's children. That led to a half hour of looking at pictures of genuinely ugly newborns who fortunately appeared to be taking on a more cherubic resemblance to their parents. She could truthfully say they were good-looking kids, now.

Adam returned. "Rena, C.J.'s looking for the magazine articles about the mansion and can't seem to find them."

"If he can't, he moved them. Honestly, he drives me crazy!" She left the living room in a huff.

Adam sat down beside Pat and pulled her back against him. "I've brought C.J. up to date on what we've learned so far," he murmured in her ear. "But I didn't mention that the mansion may be the key to everything. If there's any possibility that C.J.... I'd hate to think he'd snuff that old lady, but he grew up in that house. If anyone is aware of what there is to hide about it, he is. No point in letting him know we're thinking along those lines."

"Adam, we should check Harland family history," Pat said. "Maybe what we're dealing with is a literal skeleton in their closet."

He looked thoughtful. "Anything's possible." Repositioning her, he began to massage her shoulders. "Are you feeling any better about C.J. and Rena now that you know they didn't leave you in the lurch?"

"Yes," Pat said, trying to concentrate despite the magic his hands were working. "Davie isn't around anymore, but I need to talk to Celia. If she says the same thing, I'll feel even better."

"Will it change your attitude about the town as a whole?"

Pat held up a hand to silence him. "Let me deal with one thing at a time. The best I can say is that it's not quite as hard being here."

"Oh, God, Pat." Adam pulled her back against him, holding her close, his lips against her neck. "Give the place a chance," he pleaded softly. "Give me a chance."

"A chance to what, Adam?" Pat asked, lost in the crisp, masculine scent of his cologne, the feel of his arms around her. The *click click* of Rena's high heels warned of her return. Rattled, Pat stood up just as both Harlands entered the room.

"Here they are." Rena held a leather-bound scrapbook, a small stack of magazines on top of it. "The newspaper articles are in the album. The most recent magazine is at least eight or nine years old, but this is all of them."

"We'll take good care of them," Pat promised. "Thanks for everything, Rena, C.J. I enjoyed the evening, and the meal was spectacular. Lorna outdid herself."

Rena gave her a pleased smile. "My gourmet group deserves part of the credit. The chicken Kiev recipe was Mariana Foy's, the asparagus amandine was Denise Taylor's, and Yolande O'Connor made the orange custard herself."

"Bill O'Connor's wife?" Adam asked. "I thought she was still in the hospital."

"She's out and back to work at the plant," C.J. responded. "She did it to herself, took an antihistamine, which reacted with some other medication she's on. She's fine now, giving anyone who'll listen a blow-by-blow of what happened." He chuckled. "Which takes care of your next meeting of the gourmet gals, Reen. Reen says they spend more time talking about what ails them than they do about recipes. And Yolande's got everybody beat this time."

Rena rolled her eyes. "I think I'll call in sick and let Peg chair the meeting."

"Still, it was nice of her to make the dessert," Pat said. "I'll call and thank her. Now we really are leaving."

Rena, towering over Pat in her spike heels, hugged her, magazines and all. "I'm just so glad we had a chance to talk. You're the only best friend I've ever had. I don't know if we'll ever be able to make it up to you, but we're sure going to try."

Adam removed the burden from Pat's arms. "I've got a sensitive stomach, so if you two are about to get sickening, I'll wait out in the car."

"I'll go with you," C.J. said. They left the room, indulgent smiles on their faces.

"They're so damned smug." Rena looped an arm through Pat's and walked her to the door. "But I meant everything I said. If there's anything we can do to repair the damage . . ."

"Forget it, Reen." Pat used the pet name for the first time. "It means a lot to find out you didn't know. Let's do lunch, as the saying goes."

Rena gave her a slightly watery smile. "Wednesdays are open. Just leave a message at the plant."

Stepping out onto the stoop, Pat saw the two men, heads bent in conversation in front of the car. Both doors stood open. Her anxiety about the hidden backpack mushroomed. "I'll call," she said, and hurried down the steps.

C.J. intercepted her route toward the passenger side, sweeping her off her feet in a bear hug. "Haven't done this in fifteen years," he said, grinning. "Come to think of it, I almost flunked my European history final because you weren't here to drill me." He put her down. "I really, really missed you. She was the closest thing to a sister I ever had," he said to Adam. "Now there's something else to lay at my mother's door. I'll never forgive her for what she did to you, and for what she made you think we'd done to you."

"But you didn't and that's what counts," Pat said. "Now," she added in a conspiratorial tone, "there are no kids in that house. Get in there and make love to your wife."

"Yes, ma'am!" He turned, ogled Rena, then raced toward the front steps. Rena shrieked, darted inside and tried to shut him out, but he leaned against the door and it opened. When it closed behind him, it cut off the sound of Rena's girlish squeals.

Adam shook his head in amazement. "First time I've seen them like that. You bring out the gorilla in men." He opened the back door and placed the magazines on the seat. "My place or yours?"

"Not yours," she said firmly, getting in. She wasn't all that comfortable with the idea of their making love in the mansion, either, and wondered what had happened to her resolve to end their physical relationship. Her answer was the furnace generating heat in secret passages not visible to the eye.

Adam started the engine, then groped under the seat.

"What are you doing?" Pat asked in as normal a tone as she could.

"There's something under here. I keep kicking it." He pulled out the backpack. "Must be Rena's. I'll leave it on—"

"No, that's mine. Here, I'll take it."

He handed it to her and, with her heart knocking against her ribs, she dropped it onto the floor behind them, determined to take it back to Hetty's attic until she could decide what to do about it. Leaving it in the car had been risky and foolish.

When they reached the mansion, he got out and closed the door. "You aren't sore about me bringing up the past tonight, are you?" he asked, reaching in to unlock the back door.

"I was when you did it," she responded truthfully, climbing out, "but I'm all right now. And a little relieved, I guess."

He smiled, and unlocked the back door to retrieve the magazines and scrapbook. "Then some of the air's been cleared. Now if I can just change your mind about—" He broke off. "What is that?" He was focused on the floor behind her.

Pat's mouth went dry. "What is what?"

He opened the back door. The overhead light came on, and he squatted, looking in.

Pat turned slowly, bile rising in her throat. The shot glass had rolled out from under the flap of the front pocket of the bookbag. She couldn't even claim the glass was hers. The monogrammed E was in plain sight. There was nothing she could say.

Adam dug into his pocket and brought out a handkerchief. Folding it over the shot glass, he picked it up carefully, examined it, and dropped it into his shirt pocket. He reached in and pulled the backpack toward him. Opening its main compartment, he removed the padded envelope and the nine pages of typed manuscript, glancing at the cover before laying it on the seat.

With great care, he pulled the flap of the front pocket free, and peered in, then using thumb and forefinger, eased the gown out. The bottle followed as if loath to stay behind, rolling to a stop, label up.

Pat felt nothing, having shut down all feeling in anticipation of whatever was to come. "You left something," she said woodenly and, opening the rear door on her side, leaned in to fish inside the pocket, remove the tissue containing the capsules, and place it on top of the gown.

Adam looked across the width of the car at her, his face rigid, his eyes cold brown marble. Fury arced around him like a force field. "I should have known you were too good to be true. I *trusted* you. *Damn* you, Pat Chase."

Chapter 11

"'Get in," he commanded, wrapping the gown around the liqueur bottle and the tissue. He slid them into the larger compartment of the backpack, and after a glance at the padded envelope, added it and the stapled pages, and stood up.

Pat stood, too, closed the back door, but didn't move.

He glared at her across the roof. *"Get in the damned car.'* After a second, she complied. He put Pat's bag in the trunk, got back behind the wheel, and backed out of the driveway. On the way to the station, he forced himself to count to ten, then added another couple of hundred for good measure. He hadn't been this close to exploding in years, not, in fact, since the traffic accident that had made him decide to try for homicide. That anger had burned so fiercely, so intensely that he'd had to back away from the job for a while, talk to the department's therapist, hang out a Gone Fishing sign.

There were nights it still invaded his dreams, three toddlers in the back seat of a mangled station wagon, robbed of life courtesy of a nail in one of its tires. That had convinced him that he couldn't handle the meaningless death arbitrarily selected by fate. It made him feel helpless, impotent, and his ego couldn't take it. There would be far more satisfaction going after the culprit who took human life with malice afore-thought, or out of uncontrolled passion. He'd used that anger constructively. He wasn't sure he was capable of it this time. The woman he loved, the woman he'd convinced himself to trust against every ounce of his better judgment, had used him, abused his trust and the oath she'd taken. What was he going to do about it?

"Out," he said when he'd parked in front of the court-house. Pat left the car and stood waiting until he'd removed the backpack, raised the windows and locked the doors. Taking her arm in a firm grip, he walked her into the station proper, not releasing her until they were through the door.

Wes Kennedy nodded in front of the communications con-sole, chin on his chest, the ceiling lights reflecting off the bald spot in his thinning blond hair.

"Wes."

He was awake immediately, his face flaming red. "Evening, Chief. Everything's quiet."

"Glad to hear it. I'm trading watches with you. Go home. Maybe you can catch the end of the Atlanta game."

Wes gave him a wide-eyed stare. "Uh . . . yes, sir, Chief. I wasn't all the way asleep, honest."

"I know you weren't. Every cop in the world learns to nap with one eye open. Scram."

"Yes, sir." He grabbed his cap, glanced at Pat, then away. "See you tomorrow?"

"Right. Regards to Ophelia."

"I'll tell her, sure will, Chief. 'Night, now. 'Night, Miss Chase."

"Good night, Mr. Kennedy."

He fairly flew out of the door.

Adam took Pat's arm again, steered her through the gate to a chair on the near side of his desk. "Sit."

She turned to face him, pale, but erect, her shoulders squared. "I'm not a dog, Adam."

"I beg your pardon. Sit, *please*." Damn her, why didn't she have the decency to even fake remorse? How could she be so lovely and so deceitful at the same time? How would he ever evict the memory of the fire she'd lit in his gut last night? Would he ever stop wanting her?

He grabbed an ink pad, pulled a print sheet from supplies. Taking her right hand, he inked each finger and pressed it in the appropriate square on the sheet, repeating the process with her left. "The bathroom's that way," he said, jerking his thumb toward the rear of the room.

"I remember." Head high, she went in, leaving the door ajar, and washed her hands.

While she was gone, he parked his anger. It was getting in his way. He removed the shot glass, bottle, gown and tissue, and after a careful visual examination of them, dusted the bottle and glass for prints. Pat came out and returned to the chair she had left. She crossed her legs, the fitted skirt of her white sheath riding up a ladylike inch. Knowing what was under that sheath, he found the pose distracting.

Adam picked up the phone and slammed it down on her side of the desk. "First call High Point and tell them they can let someone else use Miss Hetty's bed. She won't be needing it. And you might want to contact a lawyer. Walt Callaway, perhaps? We'll spring for the toll."

She gazed up at him, her expression bordering on insolent. "I get to make two calls? How magnanimous. Unfortunately, I can't take advantage of your generosity. I don't have the numbers with me—they're in my other purse. And I don't have Walt's number at all."

To Adam's disgust, he was relieved that she didn't know Callaway's number by heart, and not because he was concerned about the publicity that would always follow in Callaway's wake. He didn't care about that anymore. In fact, he wasn't sure he cared about anything anymore. Wyatt, he told himself, get hold of yourself. She *used* you, man. There are plenty others out there who won't. You don't need her.

Liar, a little voice whispered.

"Adam, I know I have no right to ask," she said, "but please let Hetty go to Ridgely. If she doesn't start the kind of intensive therapy they have planned for her, she may never regain the use of her arm and leg. And let's face it, even if you arrest her tomorrow, you're not going to put her in jail. You're not the kind of man who'd do that.''

"My first obligation," Adam said, steaming because she was right, "is to Harland Grove as a whole—"

"To which Hetty presents no danger. Deposit her back there in a cell and you'll split this town right down the middle. I'm not saying there'd be rioting in the streets, but I guarantee you precisely the kind of trouble that'll send Asa Tyler scurrying elsewhere to relocate his factory. Let her go on up to High Point, Adam. Please."

He was stuck and he knew it. "I'll think about it." He gestured toward the items on his desk. "I assume your prints will be on these?"

"I hate to disappoint you, but the only thing I touched was the gown."

"Smart move. How long have you had them? Where were they? You don't have to answer, of course."

She fixed him with a steady gaze. "Have you intentionally not read me my rights?"

She was pushing him too far. He knew he should deal with the Miranda statement, knew he should arrest her this minute. But he couldn't bring himself to do either, at least not yet. Ignoring her question, he nudged the shot glass with the end of a pencil and examined the quality of the prints he had raised. There appeared to be only two. One, he assumed, would be Miss Harland's, the other, Miss Hetty's.

"Are you going to answer my questions or not?" he asked. "How long have you had these?"

Pat placed her purse on the desk, folded her hands in her lap. "I found them today," she said, "in the attic."

He shook his head. "That won't wash, Pat. Bo and I went through every damned room in that attic, through every piece of furniture. The basement, too. This stuff wasn't there."

"Not the mansion's attic. Hetty's."

That brought him up short. "She had an attic? How do you get to it?"

Her explanation—the Melton who'd set up his own private bank—made him feel immensely better. He thought he and Bo had dropped the ball, but it was understandable why they'd missed it. Besides, his house, much like Miss Hetty's, had no attic. With the stairs so well camouflaged, it never occurred to him that hers might.

"What were you doing up there?" he asked, wondering if she'd suspected it might have been there all along.

"Making sure the exterminator could get to the corner Mr. Evans says should be checked for termite damage. The only reason the bag caught my eye was because I made it in Home Ec during my last year in high school. So I took it down with me and found those in it."

"Is that why you went to the hospital?"

She nodded, her mocha face showing strain for the first time, as she brushed her bangs to one side. "I was fed up with not being able to see Hetty. And after stumbling onto those, I had to find out why she'd taken them."

"How'd you figure you could do that if she couldn't talk?"

"By framing questions she could answer yes or no to. There are probably things I missed asking, but I found out the basics. May I stand?" She was offensively polite.

"Are you cuffed to the chair? Stand on your head if you like. Just don't mistake the latitude I've given you for anything other than common courtesy, which is more than you deserve."

She moved to the window and looked out into the darkness. Playing for time, Adam decided, to figure out the next snow job. "I realize how incriminating those things are," she said, turning around, "but they won't make your case for you. At best, all you have against Hetty is circumstantial evi—"

"Circumstantial?" Adam bellowed, his rear coming up off the cushion. After a deep breath, he turned down the volume. "Maybe it hasn't occurred to you, but based on the suppositions we made, these aren't the mechanisms of suicide, they are the murder weapons. Your aunt removed them, and I have to congratulate her, hid them well. Why would she do that if she hadn't used them to kill Miss Harland?"

She perched on the windowsill, crossed her legs at the ankle, the sheer hose she wore driving him crazy. "She said she was trying to hide the fact that Lib had started drinking again—but probably for entirely different reasons than I first thought."

"Oh? Let's hear this fairy tale.."

She flushed, but didn't rise to the bait. "Lib had a brother, J.D., who was an alcoholic. Her father kicked J.D. out of the house and the family vault, wouldn't allow him to be buried there because he was still a two-fisted drinker."

"Ah," Adam said, anticipating the direction in which she was headed.

"Lib was also in his doghouse because of her drinking problem, but she did stop. Things relating to family were important to Lib, she was proud of what they'd accomplished. I bet Hetty thought that getting rid of the bottle and glass would protect Lib's place in the family vault. That's how much she loved her."

"But you don't know any of that for sure," Adam said, taking a seat at the desk.

"No," Pat admitted. "I didn't think of that until I'd left the hospital. She did manage to relay that she was trying to hide the fact that Lib was drinking."

"In other words, Miss Hetty didn't kill her."

"No, she didn't."

"Of course, she didn't." Adam leaned back in his chair, resting his feet on the desk top. "As if either of you would admit it if she had."

Pat's eyes narrowed with anger. "Need I remind you that she's innocent until proven guilty?"

He sat up straight, the front legs of the chair hitting the floor with a thud. "Need I remind you that she may or may not be guilty of murder, but both of you are guilty of tampering with evidence, withholding evidence and obstructing justice in a felony murder? Or does Miss Hetty maintain that Miss Harland committed suicide?"

"She rejected that idea as vociferously as she could, given her limitations. Even after I told her Lib had been dying, it didn't change her opinion. She said Lib had been excited, happy."

"I swear," Adam exclaimed in exasperation, "for a woman who can't talk, Miss Hetty sure told you one hell of a lot."

"Yes, she did. It was hard work, but she did. Are you interested in hearing the rest of the story or not?"

"Go right ahead." God, she was so gorgeous, so proud. "There's nothing I enjoy more than a good, imaginative yarn," he said.

Her cheeks reddened, her temper erupting. "Then I won't waste my breath. Let's get this over with. Book me right now, and let me call my lawyer so he can arrange bail. Then I'll get busy proving the rest of what Hetty told me, perhaps even work out who killed Lib while you sit here and sulk."

"Don't push me, Pat," he warned.

"You have every right to be upset with me," she acknowledged, "but there's a killer out there somewhere, and you're so damn thin-skinned, I'm not sure you're objective enough to accept the truth if you heard it anyway."

"Oh, I'm objective all right. Last night, I wasn't. This morning, I wasn't. But you can bet your sweet little tush I am tonight." That hurt her. He saw the pain slice through her and watched her deal with it. A part of him was glad he'd drawn blood, retribution for having been used, fooled by her. Another part brought out the brass knuckles. He was in for a self-inflicted butt kicking.

"Try me. Spin your tale," he drawled, tossing the double entendre. She could field it any way she liked.

What she did was erase all expression from her face, all emotion from her eyes. He might wound her again, but she would never let him see it. Or perhaps he'd cut so deeply that she no longer gave a damn about him, in which case he had canceled out his ability to hurt her. Whichever, the person who confronted him now was someone he hadn't met: ice princess, indifferent, impermeable.

"Hetty got to the mansion at her usual time—seven o'clock, and yes, she lied to you. She found Lib in bed, and was shocked when I told her that Lib had actually died in the bathroom."

"You had no right to tell her that. It was privileged information."

"You figure she's going to tell anyone else?" Pat asked, sarcasm oozing from her voice. "She assumed Lib had died in her sleep. Her gown and the pillowcases were stained with the liqueur, and to cover up her drinking, Hetty changed them. I don't know what she did with the pillowcases—perhaps she stashed them outside where she could pick them up later. Then Lorna showed up. The rest you know.''

"You didn't mention the capsules.''

"When I opened the backpack, the tissue with the capsules was crammed in the shot glass. Hetty never actually saw them. She didn't know anything about the barbiturates until I told her the cause of Lib's death. That's really when she opened up.''

"For God's sake! Is there anything you didn't tell her?'' She flushed, this time, he thought, with embarrassment, then resumed her mask. "I'm curious, Pat. What were you planning to do with these?''

"Does it matter?'' she asked.

"It might.''

"That's too bad, because I can't tell you.''

His temperature began to climb again. "Can't or won't?''

"Does it matter?'' she asked again in exactly the same tone as before. It was like listening to a tape loop.

Adam exploded. "Damn it, Pat, don't play with me! You don't seem to—''

The telephone rang, interrupting his tirade. He snatched it to his ear in frustration and barked "Harland Grove Police.'' The musical cadence of the voice at the other end jarred him back to professional civility. "She's here,'' he said, handing the phone to Pat, and moving to the next desk to pick up the extension.

Pat waited until he was on. "Hello.''

"Hi, *chica*. Who's the angry man who answered the phone?''

"The angry chief of police who, for your information, is also on the line. So keep it clean.''

"Oh, shoot. All right. I got most of the information you wanted. You ready?''

Adam pulled a scratch pad toward him and nodded to Pat.

"Ready,'' she said.

"Your little old lady friend was evidently a real charmer. That's the only reason I managed to track her movements. She was so thrilled to be in D.C., she talked to any and everybody. To make a long story short—I've got a late date—Miss Harland went to two places. The Archives first, where she dug into family backgrounds and . . . *and*—" Iliana leaned on the word "—all the records dealing with the slaves her family owned. She tracked births, deaths, sales from 1800 to Emancipation. Ahem, ahem. You got some relatives of the Caucasian persuasion you haven't been admitting to, *chica?*"

"None I'm aware of," Pat said, clearly puzzled.

"If you say so. The next day she went to the patent office. I didn't have as much luck finding out what she wanted there. Big place. I'm going back tomorrow to the restaurant where she had lunch—just in case. If she talked as much to the waitress there as she did the waiter at the Willard restaurant, we'll know to the letter what she was doing at Patent. But does any of that help?"

"I don't know yet. It needs some mulling."

"So mull, already. How's Tia Hetty?"

"Getting better slowly."

"*Bueno.* Tell her we're thinking about her and just waiting for her next batch of oatmeal raisin cookies."

"I'll do that." Pat smiled for the first time since they'd left the mansion. "She'll be touched. Thanks, Iliana. I owe you one."

"No, you don't. The hunk I met at the Willard canceled the debt. Hurry home. We miss you."

"Ditto, kiddo. Take care." She deposited the phone, frowning, baffled.

Adam's expression was a twin of hers. "Why would Miss Harland need to look up her ancestors, or anyone else's for that matter? This is the only place I've ever lived where people can rattle off the names of their ancestors practically to the time they got off the boat, whether they paid for their passage or arrived in chains."

"Kids here grow up learning their family begats along with the alphabet," Pat said. "And as far as I know, at no point do the limbs of the Harland family tree entwine with any of the black population. What could she . . ." Her eyes lost focus, the frown deepening. Adam watched, fascinated by the facility she had for completely tuning out when she needed to concentrate. "That's what was missing," she said softly.

"From where?"

"The glass case in the library. There were two or three census reports listing the slaves on the Harland plantation. They aren't there, and everything else in the case has been rearranged so that the gap isn't so glaring. Someone must have swiped them, otherwise Lib wouldn't need to visit the Archives."

"Wait a minute." Adam returned to his desk, sitting on the edge of it this time. "Let's see what we've got. Miss Harland begins searching for documents to prove the age of the mansion. In the process she discovers something about... about what? The mansion? How did she make the jump from the house to the slave population? I don't see a connection."

"Some of them built the mansion, but everybody knows that, and the plans of the house are no secret. But since that's where Lib began, perhaps we'd better... Correction. Perhaps *you* should start with the mansion." She yawned, a genuine jaw-stretcher that caught her off guard. "Sorry. Adam, can we get the booking process over and done with? I'm so tired that I might not even mind sleeping in a jail cell tonight. Oh." Opening her purse, she stuck her fingers in a zippered pocket and removed the badge he'd given her. She laid it on the desk. "You'll want this."

Adam stared at it, picked it up and slipped it into his shirt pocket. He should never have caved in to Quint and C.J. in the first place. How could he have expected her to feel any loyalty to a piece of tin and a position for which she held such little regard?

Get off it, Wyatt, his little voice said. That's not what's got your chitterlings in a turmoil. You feel used, betrayed. Time to look at what she did with a little objectivity.

Not wanting to give the appearance of indecision, Adam sat down at the computer, logged on and opened the data base, requesting an arrest report form. Name. He typed in Honor— that was a laugh—Patrice Melton Chase. Address. He was sitting across from the woman he loved and didn't even know her address or date of birth. And it didn't matter. He still loved her. He'd never completely trust her again, but what difference did that make? She wouldn't be around to trust.

"Pat, after you'd talked to Miss Hetty, why didn't you just drop these things in the trash at the hospital?"

She examined her hands, the long, slender fingers that had had him gasping for breath the night before. "I considered it. But I couldn't do it. I wasn't putting you off, Adam. I wish I could tell you what I'd planned to do with them, but I can't because I don't know."

"You must have had something in mind," he persisted, unwilling to let it go.

"I think I hoped we could find out who'd killed Lib without needing the bottle as evidence. If there was a danger the person wouldn't be convicted without it, I'd have seen that you got it."

"How?"

"Sent it to you, I guess. Understand, Adam, my primary goal from the time I realized how things were stacking up, has been to protect Hetty."

"Even if she was guilty?"

She gazed at a spot in some other dimension. "Probably. If she was, there's only one reason she'd do it, and that's if Lib was dying and her quality of life was intolerable, which wasn't the case. Lib might have been terminally ill, but she was still up and running. Besides, Hetty hadn't known about the cancer."

Pat's body language, intonation, facial expression was an indication of the change in their relationship. She was all business, as if discussing next week's special with her staff. Adam was relieved. This was about the only way he could deal with her.

"But I'm confused about her mental state," she said. "Allegedly, her mind had begun to fail. Yet Hetty has never mentioned it and vehemently denies Lib was having problems. She certainly seemed to get around D.C. and Virginia as if she had all her faculties. Something's fishy somewhere, but after talking to Hetty today, I felt strongly that Lib had not committed suicide and that Hetty had had nothing to do with her death, either. Given my experience in this town, I wasn't willing to chance she'd wind up in the same position I was in fifteen years ago."

Adam was fed up with her continual harking back to the past. "She's one of the people I've taken a vow to protect, Pat."

"One of many. For me there's no many, only one."

He gave up. She seemed to clutch that fifteen-year-old abuse to her breast, allowing it to color her whole existence. She seemed to need it. And as long as she did, he wouldn't be able to reach her.

He tossed the keys to the Cadillac on the desk. "Go on back to the mansion. And take the badge with you. If you're going to the hospital tomorrow morning, I'd like to be there. I need Miss Hetty's statement, and I'll be bringing a video camera to record it."

"You want me to keep the badge? Why? You still trust me?"

"Not totally, no. But I still need your help."

She looked at the badge and shook her head. "You can have my help without it. I'll see you tomorrow morning. And thank you, Adam."

He posted himself at the window, watching until the Caddy's taillights had disappeared in the darkness. He picked up the badge, put it in his pocket. It's just as well she wouldn't keep it. Her ethics were too flexible. But what she'd pulled on him hadn't changed the bottom line: he still loved her. He still wanted her.

The rising wind filtered through Pat's sleep in the guise of a whistling teakettle that hovered atop camera number one, forcing her to speak louder and louder in order to be heard above its persistent squeal. When a distant banging started, however, Pat came awake and sat up, trying to identify the source of the sound. Outside somewhere. A loose shutter? She looked at her travel clock. It was three-forty in the morning.

She turned over, but after fifteen minutes of bang, bang, bang, knew that the only way she'd get any rest would be to do whatever was necessary to halt that racket. In robe and sandals, she crossed to Lib's wing and looked out back from the bedroom window. She could just make it out, the door of the outbuilding just beyond the fish pond. It had served any number of purposes over the years, had been razed or blown down and rebuilt. Pete used the end closest to the house to store his gardening tools. It was the door of this section causing all the clamor. Pat glanced at the sky. At least it wasn't raining—yet. But the wind whipped past, hinting at the storm to come. If she was going to do anything, she'd best do it soon.

All the keys dangled from hooks beside the upright freezer near the pantry. Pat located the key to the solarium door at the rear of the house, the exit closest to the path leading to the shed. Head bent against the wind, she pelted down the bricked walkway past the pond. The shed door flapped like the cover of a book, slapping against the clapboard siding, the padlock dangling from the hasp. Pete had forgotten to lock it.

Grumbling, Pat closed the door and secured it. She'd have to add this one to the list of security measures she took before bed, although with luck she'd have only one more night to worry about it. She'd lived in metropolitan areas too long to be able to sleep in a house with unlocked doors. She had locked all of Hetty's when she was there and had done the same here, including the door to the basement just off the pantry. With the shed door taken care of, she hurried back to the house.

Now she was wide awake. With a vague memory of a dream about a kettle of some sort, she heated some water and went in search of Lib's store of herb teas, eventually settling down at the kitchen table with the magazines Rena had loaned her. The house groaned and cracked. She almost welcomed the sounds. After a fashion, they were company. She flipped through the publications idly, unable to concentrate. The day had been so draining.

She'd torn it with Adam. After the night they'd spent at the cabin, it had appeared that she might at least have been able to see him, if he was serious about coming up to D.C. occasionally. She never fooled herself that there could ever be any more between them. He had obligations and so did she. And even though she felt infinitely better knowing her friends had not let her down, she was no more inclined to live in the Grove now than she'd been before.

That no longer mattered, either. In withholding the evidence, she had hit him where it mattered most—professionally. There would be no recovery from the effects of that blow.

She had lost Adam forever, but at least she had a free Hetty for a little while longer.

The tea was tepid; she hadn't even touched it. She poured it in the sink, gathered the magazines, feeling they'd be safer in the library than on the kitchen table. As soon as she opened the library door, the smell from the fireplace hit her. Those ashes had to go. It was amazing that the odor was still so pungent, in fact, a good bit stronger than it had been this afternoon.

Turning on the ceiling lights, Pat dropped the magazines on the display case and crossed to the fireplace. Earlier there'd been the corpse of a log and attendant debris. Now, however, there was more, the charred remains of several piles of paper strewn from one side of the massive grate to the other, curled, shriveled, singed. They hadn't been there long; the odor was too fresh. There was no identifying what they had been. Only the ragged edges of one or two had escaped the flames. From the looks of them they'd been torn from a book.

Backing to the desk between the garden doors, Pat picked up the phone and called the station. Adam answered immediately.

"Adam, this is Pat. I'm in the library. Someone's been burning paper in the fireplace, recently from the smell of it."

The house creaked. A window rattled.

"Lorna?" Adam said.

"When she left C.J.'s, she said she was on her way home. But even if she came back here, what would she be burning? It looks like pages torn from a book."

"I'll come by in the morning. There's probably—"

Suddenly the room went black. Pat let out a squawk.

"What was that?" Adam asked.

"Me. The lights just went off. In the foyer, too. Maybe the wind blew down a power line or something."

Instantly, Adam sounded more alert. "It's not blowing that hard. Check and see if lights are out in houses in the neighborhood."

"Adam," Pat said with strained patience, "it's four o'clock in the morning. I wouldn't expect to see any lights anywhere. Let me see if the floods went out." Afraid to relinquish the phone lest she lose it in the dark, she held it in one hand and groped for the cord to open the draperies. "They're out, too."

"Sounds like the circuit breaker might have tripped."

"Terrific," Pat grumbled. "I haven't the slightest idea where it is. I'll just have to feel my way back upstairs and—"

It didn't occur to her until it happened a second time that the creak she'd heard before had sounded surprisingly nearby. She removed the phone from her ear. There it was again, softer this time. And again. Goose bumps exploded from her arms.

"Pat, you still there?"

"Adam," she whispered, "someone's in the house!"

Chapter 12

"Are you sure?" Tension and doubt in equal measure coarsened his voice.

"Yes. Oh, God. How'd they get in? I locked all the doors!"

"You're in the library?" She could hear the change in his tone. The doubt was gone.

"Yes."

"Can you get out the doors to the garden?"

"No! I'd need a key to open them. All the keys are in the kitchen and I wouldn't know which was which in the dark."

"All right. I'll break in, but I don't want to shoot you by mistake. Stay in the library so I'll know where you are. Pat?"

"Yes, I heard you."

"Hang on. I'm six minutes away, tops."

The line went dead. Pat felt as if she'd lost all connection to the outside world. Darkness was total, except for the rectangle of less intense black showing through the drape she had opened.

The minutes stretched like rubber bands, each tick of the grandfather clock in the foyer clearly audible through the open door. Her heart thudded with such force she wondered if it might crack a rib.

She'd never been afraid of the dark, even as a child, but now it took on an oppressive nature. Pat glued her eyes to the space between the open draperies, only to have that small relief succumb to the optical trick one's eyes played when staring at something in the dark. It seemed to shrink into the blackness surrounding it, and only blinking every few seconds in order for her eyes to refocus allowed her to maintain her link with what little relief the less intense darkness outside afforded her.

The quiet, stealthy sounds of movement continued, maddening because it was difficult to determine their location. Her sense of smell began playing tricks on her; suddenly she detected an odor she associated with basements: close, earthy. Finally, on the edge of screaming panic, Pat crept toward the other garden door and felt for the cord. If she had two rectangles of night, perhaps it wouldn't be so bad.

The cord wasn't where she thought it should be. She moved carefully to the side of the door farthest from the desk, extended her arm to find the cord and screamed as her hand made contact with fabric, muscle, a shoulder. Reflexively, she recoiled, scrambling backward, her breath a shrill whistle in her throat. A hand clutched at her, finding purchase at the neck of the knee-length T-shirt she'd slept in. The fabric tore as she tried to pull away, and the hand grazed her breast. That contact tripped Pat's personal circuit breakers. Reduced to a raw primal fear, she went berserk, became a windmill of flailing legs and arms, hitting out, kicking, with no thought or strategy involved, self-defense at its most base level.

Perhaps unprepared for the ferocity of her reaction, the intruder released her nightshirt. Off-balance, Pat fell to one side, her thrashing feet catching her assailant behind the knee, pulling the dark figure forward to fall with her. They crashed into the display case and it toppled under them, its contents clattering against the glass lid. Pat's head struck an upturned leg, stunning her. Rainbows arced behind her eyes and she felt herself losing her grasp on consciousness. She fought it as valiantly as she'd struggled against her invisible assailant, but in the end lost the skirmish.

When she came to and her ears stopped ringing, sounds were muffled. The surface beneath her was hard, cold. She was no longer in the library, and someone seemed to be very busy, moving around her, rattling papers, but she couldn't see anything. Her eyes were open, but her vision seemed obstructed. After a second, she realized that fabric covered her head and was pulled tight around her upper arms, pinning them to her side. As the effects of the blow began to subside, Pat remained still, fighting a new battle, against nausea. She could not get sick now, not wrapped up like a mummy. Exerting mind over matter, she tried deep breathing, no easy task under the circumstances, searched for her center, found it and relaxed as calm washed over her.

With the calm came the realization that at least her legs were free. And she'd heard no sound for several minutes. Ears probing the silence, she listened for breathing other than her own. Nothing. She sat up, and slowly, ignoring the thud in her head, knelt, then finally got to her feet. Something smelled funny. Rubbing her shoulders against what felt like a shelf, she managed to loosen the fabric around her enough to raise her arms until it was gathered around her neck and she could snatch it off. Total blackness of a sort she could never have imagined. And there was smoke in the air. Something was burning.

Somewhere above her, there was a crash, wood splintering, glass shattering. "Pat! Pat!"

"Adam!" Pat screamed. "I'm here!"

"Here where?"

"I don't know. There's no light. Something's burning, Adam. I don't see any fire, but I can smell it."

"Okay. Cover your nose and mouth if you can, and keep close to the floor. The sound of your voice seems to be coming from the basement, under the library. I'll get down there one way or another."

His footsteps receded to some other part of the house, then after a short interval, returned, hurrying.

"Pat?"

She coughed, the only response she could manage. Smoke scraped her lungs. Removing her robe, she pressed it to her face with one hand and searched for a corner with the other. The room seemed to be lined with shelves, rough boards from the feel of them. A wine cellar? Eventually the shelves abutted an adjoining wall. Crouching, she huddled under her robe, and prayed.

Overhead, the sounds were confusing. Pounding, tapping, swearing. What was Adam doing? It seemed to last forever.

"Pat?" Adam sounded frantic. "How's the smoke?"

She lifted the robe. "About the same," she called hoarsely.

"Look, darling, there's got to be a hidden latch or something to open a door or panel, but I can't find it. There are probably stairs and a latch on your side, too. You'll have to find it on your own."

Pat figured she had little choice. The smoke seemed no worse, but it was like breathing razor blades. Her lungs couldn't take much more. She had to save herself. Getting to her feet, the robe pressed against her face, she followed the shelving along one wall, turned a corner, more shelves, thin hardback books on them. At the end of that set, her toe bumped against something projecting into the space. Groping blindly, she followed its contours. Steps! She measured their width, felt for a railing, and began to climb, her legs as heavy as lead weights. The stairs made a right angle. Here the air seemed a little clearer, less acrid. When there were no more steps, she patted the walls, found herself in a three-sided enclosure.

"Adam, I'm at the top."

"You're wonderful." The naked relief in his voice clutched at her heart. He was so close. Obviously only a wall separated them. "I can't tell you what to search for, but there's got to be something on your side that'll let you out."

Pat draped the robe over her shoulder and wrapped it loosely around the lower part of her face. Sliding her palms along the walls, she felt for a knob, handle, anything, fighting despair at the impossibility of finding the mechanism. There was nothing on the first wall of the enclosure, nothing on the second. In the end she didn't find anything because there was nothing to find. The third wall moved outward as soon as she touched it. She fell through the opening into Adam's arms.

"God, Pat." He swooped her off her feet, and with the amber beam of a flashlight arcing across the room, carried her to one of the easy chairs and put her down. "Stay right here. I've got to see what's burning."

She nodded, preoccupied with wiping her eyes and trying to clear her lungs. The clear air was heavenly. Now that she was free of her smoky prison, she realized she had one whale of a headache, one she intended to enjoy. It was the greatest headache she'd ever had, given the alternative.

She wasn't sure how long Adam was gone, but when he finally reappeared, he knelt in front of her, using the sleeve of her robe to wipe her face. "How are you?"

"Fine, now." She coughed, sat up straight. "What about the fire?"

"Evidently it never really caught. There's a mountain of paper smoldering in the middle of the floor. Lots of smoke, no fire—not that it couldn't have done you in. Pat, what happened after I hung up?"

"I was waiting for you right here when I bumped into whoever was in the house. He grabbed me and we scuffled and knocked over the display case. I guess I must have hit my head when I fell. The next thing I know I was down there." She shuddered. "He put a bag or something over my head and left me."

"There's a curtain missing from the door I kicked in, so that's probably what he used. He didn't leave by the front door. The deadbolt was still thrown." Adam probed her scalp in the dark. "No dampness, but you've got a goose egg back there. Look, darling, we have to make sure that bastard's not still in the house. To do that I've got to find the circuit breaker so we'll have some light. Sit tight. I'll be right back."

Pat longed to curl up and give in to the shakes; the memory of her wrestling match with the intruder was just beginning to affect her, but she'd had all she could take of being alone in this blackout. "I'm going with you."

"No. If he's still in the house, I don't want you between him and me."

"I'm coming," she said, slipping into her robe again.

"Pat, I don't have time—"

"You're right, and you're wasting it."

She could feel his glare in the darkness. "Why is it that the only women I seem to give a damn about are always hard-headed?"

"Just lucky, I guess."

"Give me strength," he muttered. He grabbed her hand and led her around the upended display case. "Jesus, I can't believe how dark it is in here. This place is pure bat bliss."

"Bat bliss?" Pat, trotting beside him toward the kitchen, began to giggle. "Bat bliss?" Laughter bubbled in her sore throat and she clamped a hand over her mouth. It didn't help. She began to laugh in earnest, aware that she was reacting all out of proportion to the humor of his analogy.

"Come on, it wasn't that funny," he said softly, tracking the beam of his flashlight around the perimeter of the kitchen. It wasn't quite as dark here.

Pat doubled over, both hands covering her mouth. She shook with laughter, groaned with the pain of containing it.

"Hey." Adam spun around, held her shoulders and shook her roughly.

"I'm s-sorry," she rasped, between gales of stifled laughter. "I c-can't seem to h-help it." Shaking uncontrollably, she steeled herself for the inevitable slap.

Evidently Adam had his own method of dealing with hysteria. One hand pulled her head back and his lips covered her open mouth, silencing her with lightning flicks of his tongue against the silken tissue of her lower lip. Heat slithered down her spine as she melted against him. Fingers splayed against his back, she tried to pull him even closer, to burrow through him, her hands sliding down to his lean, hard derriere.

He broke off the kiss immediately. "Pat, stop that or I'll take you right here on the kitchen table. We may not be alone, remember? Are you all right, now?"

"I'm not laughing, if that's what you mean," she said, stepping away from him. She felt like a starving woman who'd just been teased with a single grape.

"Let's check the pantry for the circuit breaker." Even in the near darkness, he looked so solid, competent to deal with the situation, so metaphysically masculine. He was all business again, moving silently ahead of her past the open basement door.

"Adam." She touched his back. "I locked that before I went to bed."

"You're sure?"

"Why do you always ask me that?" she demanded in annoyance.

"Okay, okay. Now we know which way he went. How many exits are there from the basement?"

"Two. One at the end of each wing. The rooms under the wings are okay, but the ones under the middle of the house are the size of cells, and the layout is crazy. I've only been down there once. It's like a rabbit warren. I got so turned around in them, it took me a half an hour to find my way out. I haven't been back since."

"One of the magazines says it's a maze," Adam said, shining the flashlight into an ebony abyss. "I'll tell you about it later. The circuit breaker's probably near the bottom of the stairs. Stay close and watch your step." He started down slowly, the amber beam pointed at his feet.

When he reached the bottom, he waited until she'd joined him before searching the area near the base of the stairs. The circuit breaker was behind them on the wall. Its door stood open.

"Bonanza," Adam said softly, moving to it. He flipped the master. "Stay right here and don't argue." He took the steps two at a time, and at the top, found the light switch for the basement, and came back down. Pat breathed easily again. She doubted she'd ever be completely comfortable in total darkness again.

Dogging his footsteps, she directed him toward the basement doors to the outside. Both had deadbolts that required a

key to unlock them. As they retraced their route, Pat stopped
him. There was the scurrying sound she had come to know so
well. "Adam, I hear something."

"Damn it! The s.o.b. doubled back on us!" He took off at
a run toward the steps leading up to the kitchen, Pat laboring
to keep up with him, her lungs still stinging from the smoke. He
pelted up the stairs, a feat she could not imitate. Climbing them
slowly, she stopped at the top to lock the door behind her and
catch her breath. By the time she left the kitchen for the foyer,
Adam was standing in the door of the library. "The front
door's still locked, so he must have gone out through the garden. The question is, how'd he get inside in the first place?"

"Well . . ." Pat described her experience with the shed door
"I was only out there a minute, if that long."

Adam made no attempt to hide his exasperation with her. "If
he was in the right place at the right time, a minute would be
long enough, except how could he know that noise would bug
you to the point you'd come out to take care of it? Uh-uh. I
think our boy has a key. That narrows it down to C.J. and
Pete." He looked pained.

"Lorna has a key," she reminded him. "The cleaning service probably has one, too. And anyone could walk in, take a
key off the hook and it would never be missed. There are several keys to each door."

"Terrific. I've got a few calls to make before I take another
look at that room downstairs."

Pat steeled herself to go with him to her basement prison. She
would rather have waited until morning, but she planned to
stick to Adam like a second skin.

While he used the phone, she dragged one of the easy chairs
to the doors he had destroyed to get in, and propped it against
them. Getting the glass up would take more effort than she had
energy to tackle. But for all the wrestling she'd done with the
intruder, the library was, on the whole, undamaged except for
the display case on its side, the glass unbroken. The wood on
the bottom side had split; other than that it appeared to have
survived with no scars.

"Well," Adam said, his calls completed, "C.J. answered the phone. There's no way he could have gotten home that fast."

"What did you tell him?"

"Nothing. I hung up. I don't want him rushing over here until we've had a chance to find out what's in that room. I rousted Bo. He's going to patrol the area, in case our boy's on foot in the neighborhood. How do you feel, Pat?"

Rather than lie, she went into his arms, grabbed him and wouldn't let go. "I thought I was going to die," she said, her voice shaking. "I thought I'd never see you again, that you'd never know how much I love you, in spite of everything."

"We were thinking along the same lines," he said, and his lips found hers in a soft, gentle kiss. "When this is over, isn't there something we could do to get rid of all the crap keeping us apart?"

Pat gazed up at him and slowly moved out of his arms. "You mean, isn't there something *I* can do, don't you? Like quitting my job and moving to the Grove? Give up everything I've worked so hard for. Give up making a difference. What would you say if I asked that of you?"

Adam held her gaze for a long moment. "I'd say no."

"Then how could you ask that of me?"

"When you put it that way, I guess I couldn't. So perhaps you were right this morning. We're postponing the inevitable and making love last night simply made matters worse, letting us know what we'll be giving up."

"I'd rather know than wonder the rest of my life." Pat belted her robe and squared her shoulders, determined not to cry. Nothing had been more difficult than being wrenched from the Grove fifteen years ago. Then, she had left Hetty—and her pride. This time she would be walking away from Adam—and love.... "Let's go look at that room and call it a night."

The library lights were on when they entered, and Pat immediately saw how simple access to the hidden room had been. The eight foot wide ceiling-to-floor section of bookcase next to the fireplace pivoted. All you had to know was where to push. Flashlight aimed, Adam preceded her down the steps. The air in the lower room was heavy, but clearer than before.

Pat marveled at how scaled down the space was, about fourteen feet squared; it had seemed enormous in the dark. Curiously, there appeared to be no access to the rest of the basement. As the library above it, three walls were lined with the rough boards she'd felt in the dark, most crammed with what appeared to be ledgers, assorted notebooks, old-fashioned hatboxes piled high with paper. On one, a row of empty liqueur bottles, all Lib's dead soldiers.

The fourth wall was bare of shelves but covered with scribbles, as if a child had gotten loose with a crayon. The only furnishings were a small table and chair, and several battery-operated lamps. Adam switched them on. In the middle of the floor was a mountain of charred books and more paper.

"What's this room for?" Pat asked.

"One of the magazines alluded to the answer. Ephraim Harland was worried about the rumors of war and the possibility that Yankees might invade the house. Don't forget, the middle section of the mansion was built first. He chopped the basement into a maze of tiny rooms with doors in each wall, except for this one space. His family could hide here and would never be found."

"What if the house was afire?" Pat asked, remembering her earlier predicament.

"I'm guessing that unshelved wall acts as a hidden door that pivots so his wife and daughter could get out if they had to, and of course, they'd know how to get through the maze. But the Yankess could wander through the maze for hours and never find this room."

"But if the intruder knew this room was here, why didn't he know how to get out?"

"He did," Adam said, shoving a toe through the pile of papers. "He went through the maze, intending to leave through the pantry door to the kitchen. You fouled things up for him by locking that door and blocking his access to the first floor. Fortunately, he'd made certain he could get back in here, just in case. With the only other route back through the library where you were, he cut all the lights, hoping he could slip past you. Darkness was the only protection he had."

"Don't remind me." Pat shivered, feeling a resurgence of her earlier hysteria. "Doesn't that narrow it down to C.J.? He grew up in this house. Maybe he had his car outside. If he'd driven, he might have been able to make it home by the time you called."

"I'd have passed him leaving, but Bo will check to see if the hood of his car is warm, just in case. And C.J. might know this room exists but not know where it is or how to get to it. I don't think Miss Harland knew until she began researching the house and had the actual plans of the layout in her hands. Those times Lorna thought she'd ducked out through the library, she was down here. If Miss Harland didn't know before, why would C.J.?"

It seemed to Pat that each time C.J. seemed the most likely culprit, Adam found some way to wiggle his friend off the hook. She removed a book from a shelf, flipped through it. It appeared to be a ledger.

As if reading her mind, Adam said, "If it makes you feel any better, I'm taking nothing for granted. Someone must be desperate to have pulled this stunt tonight. We're dealing with arson and attempted murder now. We've made someone very nervous. The reason has to be right here."

Pat decided not to fix on the attempted murder, unprepared to digest the fact that she was to have been the victim. "I hate to beat a dead horse, but asking C.J. and Rena for the magazines had to tip them off that we'd become interested in the house."

"Lorna knew, too," he pointed out. "And the people I've spoken with to find out what was required to have the house declared a historical landmark. But you're right. C.J. and Rena move into the spotlight, depending on what we find here. Are you sure you're up to this?"

"It depends on how much you want to do," Pat confessed, fatigue weighing heavily now. "I've looked through a few on this shelf. They're all ledgers dating back to 1870 or so. I think they're H.I. accounts."

Adam scanned the shelves, and crossed to one that was packed with books of a different sort. He pried one loose, opened it. "This is a diary. 'February 2, 1867. Supper with T McConnell. A wily scoundrel, but he will take five dozen face salves. If they do well in his emporium, sales should double Mercy unwell, the vapors again. God deliver me from ailing females.'" He replaced the diary. "If they're all like that, thi guy was worse than Pepys."

"The English diarist? If that's the case, it'll take weeks to go through all this."

"Someone's saved us the trouble by burning some of them I just wonder how much has been destroyed. And why."

At this point, Pat hit the wall. All the exertions, the emotional upheavals of the past forty-eight hours became a barricade she couldn't get over, around or through.

Adam must have seen it. "That's enough. This can wait Let's get out of here."

Too tired to put up an argument, Pat started up the stairs "What time is it?"

"You don't want to know." Adam switched off the lights "You might be able to get in a couple of hours before it'll be time to get up again. Pack what you'll need for the nigh and—"

Pat stopped at the top of the stairs. "For what?"

"You're coming home with me."

"With you?" She shook her head, kept shaking it. "No Adam."

"I won't touch you, if that's what you're worried about."

She tried to quell the disappointment at his emphatic remark. "It's not that. This is a small town. You're in a position of responsibility. People look up to you."

"I don't give a—"

"You have to. Look at it this way," she persisted. "How wil you feel when Corey comes home and some big-mouthed kid tells him his father was shacked up with a lady while he wa away? No."

"Then I'm staying here," he said. "I'm not leaving you alone in this house. And you move back to Miss Hetty's tomorrow whether the roofers are finished or not."

His take-charge attitude chafed like sandpaper underwear, but Pat tried to balance it against his concern for her. "We'll see. And if you insist on staying, fine. That's the least troublesome of the two arrangements."

"I can't believe in this day and age . . ." he said grumpily.

"You're in Harland Grove. Believe it."

He scowled at her. "All right, Pat, we'll do things your way but I insist on taking the adjoining sitting room as a precautionary measure. I'd want to be close by in case . . . Get some sleep."

"Good-night, Adam. And thanks." Pat considered kissing him good-night, but rejected the idea as foolhardy. No sense in making bad matters worse. They'd had last night in the cabin—and this morning's miracles in the hammock. All things considered, she decided, she was damned lucky to have had that. Why did life have to be so complicated?

Adam, dozing not ten feet away from Pat's bedroom, heard something and was instantly awake. He didn't move, straining for the source of the sound. It came again, a soft high wail from the other side of the door. On his feet immediately, he burst into the room. Pat was sitting up in bed, gasping, one hand over her mouth. Otherwise the room was empty.

"Pat! What's wrong?"

Blinking, she looked around. Morning sunlight streamed through the open draperies, painting a bright golden streak across her pillow. "I thought . . ." She covered her face, shivering. "I thought I smelled smoke."

Adam sat down and cradled her in his arms. "You were dreaming. Everything's fine. It's only six o'clock. Why don't you go back to sleep?" He pounded her pillow, turned it over, laid her back down. It was the first time he'd seen this vulnerable side of her since that day at the hospital. Even when she'd found her way out of the hidden room, even after he saw the realization in her face that she was supposed to have died there, she'd held up well. Only now did he feel that she needed moral support.

"How . . . how'd you get in here so fast?" she asked.

"I was right in the next room, remember?"

Pat reached up, smoothed his cheek. "Poor Adam. When's the last time you slept?"

He brushed the question aside. "I'm an expert at catnaps."

"Would you like to lie down? I'll wake you at seven."

There was such innocence in her offer that he laughed. "Darling, I admit I'm beat, but there's no way I could share a bed with you and sleep."

"I meant I'd get up and let you have it to yourself."

"Pat." He knelt. "There's no way I could lie in a bed that smells of you, and sleep. That's how much I want you and probably always will."

Pat whimpered, her pupils dilating, her marvelous eyes swimming with tears. She threw back the sheet. "Get in, Adam."

He cupped her face between his hands, his thumbs wiping away the dampness. "Pat, it won't change anything."

"I know that," she said. "And I've got the rest of my life to be lonely, Adam. But it's up to you. Your choice."

Adam realized that when it came to this particular woman, there would never be a choice. Troy Lee had hit the nail on the head that morning outside the mansion. "Man, she's got you," he'd said. "You're hers." And he was.

He helped her out of her T-shirt and let his fingers wander over the contours of her body, marveling at the feel of her. She was silk, satin, suede, a beautiful, sienna brown. Slender and lithe, her breasts small, firm, perfect, fitting his hand as if it was the mold by which it had been measured.

He rushed out of his clothes and joined her between the sheets, groaning with the joy of her long legs entwined with his, her torso pressed against him. She held him, her hands traveling the length of his body, forever moving, pressing, massaging. She sought and found his lips as she pulled him onto her, parted her thighs. Testing, he found her ready, plump and honey-damp, open, waiting, seeking, her hips already surging toward him. When he entered her, she cried out, her deep voice hoarse with passion. Her arms were like straps of steel around him, clasping their bodies together.

He knew that inevitably he would somehow compare her with Ginny. He could never complain that his wife was not an active participant in the act of lovemaking. His only complaint was with the ferocity with which she went at it, as if it was something to be conquered. Pat, on the other hand, let it conquer her and in the process, surrendered all to him, a measure of trust he'd never experienced before.

Moving above her, into her, out of her, feeling the searing heat of her, the softness, firmness, the incredible grasp in which she held him inside and out, hearing her cries in his ears erased Ginny from his memory. Pat was so incredibly vocal! The sheer wonder of this woman overwhelmed him with gratitude for having met her, for having had her touch his life. She was the embodiment of the unselfish side of love, in what she had been willing to do for her great-aunt, in what she was willing to give him now.

She reached the crest before he did, and he watched her face flush, her freckles appear to darken. Then her whole visage exploded with the affirmation of the moment, his name on her lips with every movement of her hips against him, every pulsating wave of ecstasy. It launched him toward the peak and she held him tightly, still murmuring his name, urging him toward his pleasure, helping him spin it out, stretching it until it had run its course and begun to fade. Spent, he collapsed in her arms. Not for the first time he wondered how he would live without her. It would be an arid life, with no oasis, nothing to slake his thirst.

"I love you, Pat," he said softly.

"I love you, Adam," she said in return, on a whisper, a sigh. He heard the despair in her voice and was reminded that, just as he'd predicted, with passion slaked, nothing had changed. One day she would leave and he would stay and fight for the Grove. He would do it for his son. In the interim . . .

He must have slept. It seemed like moments later that he felt her fingers dance along his spine. "Adam, wake up. It's getting late, and Lorna will be here soon."

He raised his head, looked at his watch. An hour and fifteen minutes had elapsed. "Good Lord." Rolling over, he bounded out of bed, then doubled back to bend down and kiss her thoroughly, gratefully, passionately. But he could think of nothing to say that seemed appropriate, so he grabbed his clothes and went into the guest bath for a quick shower.

Ten minutes later he was dressed, and sat, waiting and watching while Pat showered and dressed in record time, with none of the agony with which Ginny had approached each morning's toilette. Pat grabbed what was convenient, shimmying into jeans and an impossibly frilly shirt. It was a ridiculous combination. On her it looked great.

She was just stepping into white thong sandals when someone pounded on the door. It was Lorna.

"Patty! Are you awake?"

Perhaps spurred by the panic in her voice, Pat hurried to open the door. "Lorna, is something wrong?"

"Mr. C.J.'s been looking for Chief Wyatt. Do you—"

Adam, who until that moment hadn't decided whether or not to show himself, went to the door immediately. "I'm here, Lorna. What's the problem?"

"Oh, thank the Lord. It's Rena. She's gone."

Stepping out into the hall, Adam placed a soothing hand on her shoulder. "What do you mean, gone?"

"Mr. C.J. said she got up during the night and went into the bathroom. She didn't come back, but he didn't make anything of that. She has insomnia and lots of time she'll just get in the Jacuzzi to relax for an hour or two, so he went back to sleep. But when he got up this morning, she wasn't there. He's called all over the place. He can't find her."

Adam's gaze locked with Pat's, but she looked back at him in confusion. Hurrying to the nearest phone, he called C.J. With no time for social niceties, Adam barked, "What time did Rena get up?"

"Two, maybe. I can't imagine where she could have gone."

"Sit tight," Adam said. "I'll call you back shortly."

"Adam . . ."

"I'm still here."

"I have a bad feeling about this."

For the second time that morning, Adam could find nothing to say. "It's early. Just hang in there." He broke the connection, went out to the cruiser and used the radio to call Bo. Bo assured him he'd seen no one on the street at all, neither pedestrian nor vehicular, and neither hood of the cars at C.J.'s residence had been warm.

"Okay, son. Call Troy Lee and Wes and have them go door to door in C.J.'s neighborhood. We're looking for Rena Harland. Tell him to keep their portable units handy."

"Ten-four, Chief."

Back in the mansion, Adam headed directly for the room under the library, Pat behind him. Halfway down the stairs he could see that it was empty. He started back up.

"Adam, wait." Pat had stopped, blocking his way. "What's that?" Squeezing past him, she ran down the steps and stopped in front of the one wall of scribbles.

He went down again, lighted one of the lamps and held it up. At first glance, the writing made no sense. On closer inspection, however, it began to take shape.

Pat grabbed another lamp and lighted it. "It's a family tree," she said, standing on tiptoe to see the names at the top. It began at the ceiling, extended from wall to wall and to the floor. "Not the Harlands, though. Can you read the names at the top?"

"Cammie. And Joshua."

Pat frowned. "That's *my* family tree! Joshua was a multiple-great-grandfather, one of the brothers who escaped to fight with the Union army. Cammie was a sister. But there are a lot more names here than are related to me." Stooping, she peered at the ones along the bottom, among them her own. "I don't understand."

"Neither do I, but look at this." One of the ledgers was wedged under the wall, and Adam pried it free. Immediately the bottom of the wall tilted up toward them. "Ah. We were right, a hidden door. This is how he got out the first time, when he cut off the power." He stepped back, lifting it to peer out into the gloom of another basement room. "Pat, do me a favor. Go out there and see if you can open it from the other side, now that we've removed the stop wedged under it."

"What if I can't? I'm not sure I could find my way to the steps to the kitchen."

"Stay where you are. I'll come get you."

"Famous last words," she said and, duck-walking, scooted under the wall.

He lowered it back into position. "Can you hear me?"

"Yes." Her voice was muffled.

"Push the bottom part of the wall inward."

Nothing happened. "No dice," Pat called.

"Okay. Be right there." He sprinted up the steps, went out through the library, foyer and kitchen. Unlocking the pantry door, he flipped the switch for the basement lights and ran down, remembering the article he'd read the night before about how to get through the maze.

He began working his way toward the room below the library. Out the door on the right, the next time, the left. Halfway there, he heard Pat scream, stopping his blood cold. He began to run.

"Pat! What's wrong?"

She didn't answer. He ran even faster, his heart pounding. From somewhere up ahead, he could hear the sounds of a scuffle, exclamations of fury, pain.

"Pat, answer me!"

He'd lost count of the rooms at six, hoping it didn't matter as long as he adhered to the pattern. Right. Left. Right. Left. The sounds were closer, then after a resounding thud, nothing. Adam darted through two more rooms and in the third almost tripped over a supine body clad in black, a black and navy ski mask covering the head. Pat, disheveled, stood over in a corner, her mouth open with astonishment.

Adam grabbed her, relieved that she was unhurt. "Honey, what happened?"

"He came out of nowhere and jumped me. I guess after last night, I'd had enough. I just hit him as hard as I could, and he went down."

"Remind me to avoid your right hook, or whatever it was." Stooping, Adam yanked the ski mask off. Blond hair swirled free and cascaded around the pale face.

"Rena!" Pat looked at Adam in confusion. "But I was sure it was a man. I tussled with her and never got any indication that it was a woman, and Rena is well-endowed." She eyed the appropriate portion of Rena's anatomy. "At least she looked like it. She's the one upstairs last night? She picked me up and carried me downstairs?"

"Rena works out with weights," Adam said. "I've seen her at the health club where I swim laps every morning."

"But why... I mean, what..."

"I can only answer part of it. Undoubtedly she has a key. She came into the house, went through the library into the room under it. I'd guess she's been burning things little by little ever since she killed Miss Harland."

"Rena killed her?"

Picking up the unconscious woman, he draped her over his shoulder. "Let's say I'm pretty sure she did. Something C.J. said after dinner kicked me in the right direction and helped me connect the dots. Come on. The pattern to follow is left, right, left, right."

"What?"

"Just stay with me, and if you see Rena waking up, deck her again."

"Gladly. What did C.J. say last night?"

"That comment about Yolande O'Connor and how the members of the gourmet club spend so much time talking about their ailments," Adam said, backtracking through the maze. "It made me wonder exactly who belonged to the club and how many might be on the pharmacy's list of people with prescriptions for barbiturates. I definitely remembered seeing Yolande's name on it. So after you left and I had time to think, I got on the phone and woke up Mariana Foy. She read me the membership roster. Three of them are on Heck's list. And Mariana confirms that they tend to discuss their physical problems and whatever medications they're taking ad nauseam. When I prodded her about Rena's complaints, she finally remembered Rena had mentioned she was taking a diuretic for hypertension. She hadn't been able to sit through a meeting without visiting the bathroom at least twice. Then I called Jim, who blew that out of the water. Rena's blood pressure is fine and Heck confirmed she has no prescriptions on file.''

''As the old song goes, I'm beginning to see the light,'' Pat said.

''Rena used her friends' bathrooms and raided their medicine cabinets. All she needed was a capsule or two from each of the three. That's why there were several different types of barbiturates in Miss Harland's system—phenobarbital, secobarbital and— Left, right?''

''Right,'' Pat said. ''I mean, correct. But why? Why would she kill Lib?''

''I don't know but I bet that family tree's at the root of it,'' Adam said. ''No pun intended.'' Exiting the maze, he carried Rena up through the pantry and out into the foyer. ''Lorna,'' he called.

She came to the railing upstairs where she'd been making up Pat's room. ''Rena!''

''She's all right, just unconscious. Call C.J., please. Tell him we've found his wife and that he might want to come over and bring a lawyer. She's under arrest—or will be shortly.''

''Oh, my Lord.'' Lorna disappeared down the hall.

Adam carried Rena into the library, lowering her none too gently into a chair. Immediately, she was up and halfway across the room before Adam caught her. He lead her back to the chair and shoved her into it. ''Stay put, Rena, or I'll sic Pat on you. She doesn't like you very much right now.''

''And I *hate* her,'' Rena spat, but she didn't move as Adam removed the cuffs from his belt and manacled her. ''She was going to ruin everything, again.''

''Me? How could I ruin anything?'' Pat demanded. ''And what do you mean, again?''

''Again,'' Adam said, ''meaning she was the instigator who got you in trouble the first time. One thing I've learned since you arrived is how much you meant to C.J. when you were here. You heard him say last night that you were the closest to a sister he ever had. Rena's a very possessive person. I'm guessing she read something else into the situation. As far as she was concerned, C.J. liked you too much. She had to get you out of the way."

"And it worked." Rena was defiant, triumphant. "I'd taken the damned ugly pendant two days before. C.J.'s mother never missed it. I had to practically lead her by the nose to the display case and mention our trip to the mansion when you came inside alone. She fell for it and the next day you were history!"

Pat looked stunned. "Rena, I liked C.J., but that's all there was to it."

"It didn't matter how you felt about him," Adam said. "What was important was how she thought he felt about you."

"Patty this, and Patty that." Rena mimicked her husband's drawl. "He was going to have to escort *her* to the prom, because she was Miss Harland High. *Her,* not me."

Pat stared at her, her face darkening. "You silly little twit. My father went to his grave knowing a Chase had been accused of theft because *you* thought C.J. had the *hots* for me? Damn you, Rena!" She hurled herself at the woman.

Adam reached her just in time and restrained her, holding her tightly. "Calm down, honey. She's not worth it. Calm down."

Dazed, Pat sank into another chair. "This is incredible. But why kill Lib, Rena, a harmless old woman?"

Rena had obviously decided she'd said enough. She clamped her mouth closed, wriggled into a more comfortable position, and refused to speak until C.J. burst into the mansion, sans attorney.

Adam had been dreading his arrival. C.J. was too good a friend for him to enjoy telling him that his wife was a murderer. C.J., however, seemed to be prepared for anything.

Rena refused to refute the facts Adam spelled out for her husband. "I admit, we haven't pinned down her motive, C.J., and I still have a couple of leads to check, but everything else adds up. You gave her an alibi for the night your aunt died, and I didn't realize until Lorna explained about her insomnia and long baths just how she'd probably pulled it off. I imagine she hoped it would appear that Miss Harland had died in her sleep. When she slipped over here to check and see if her plan had worked, she found your aunt in the bathroom, probably lying in a pool of liqueur, and decided to move her. She cleaned the john, switched rugs afterward, got rid of her fingerprints—"

"And had to vacuum the rug because she'd worn those stupid high-heeled mules," C.J. said, as if waking from a long sleep. "We have a plush rug just like Aunt Lib's, and Lorna's always fussing about the heel prints Rena leaves."

"God, you are such a ninny," Rena snarled. "I did it for you, you fool."

"For me? You killed my Aunt Lib for me?" C.J. towered over her, his face flushed with rage. Adam pulled him away. The last thing he needed was a domestic flare-up.

"I'm going to have to take her in now," he told his friend. "I just wanted you to be here when I did it."

"Take me in for what?" Rena smiled. "You can't prove a thing."

"He can prove that you attacked me," Pat said, taking C.J.'s place before Rena. "You set fire to a pile of books and you left me to suffocate or burn to death, whichever came first."

"She did what?" Astonishment and horror flared in C.J.'s face.

"She's been burning Harland family documents," Adam explained. "But she found herself trapped and couldn't leave the hidden room downstairs through—"

"What hidden room?" C.J. asked.

"I'll show you later. Her normal route was via the pivoting wall, where she'd wedged a book under it as a landmark to use from the other side to get back in. When she tried to leave last night, she found the door to the pantry locked. She had no choice but to come back through the library."

"But I was still here," Pat said, beginning to understand. "And ran into her in the dark. After I'd fallen and knocked myself out, she carried me downstairs, started the fire, and...and what, Adam?"

"She was free to leave through the library. But then I arrived. She went back to the basement by way of the pantry door, which was why we found it unlocked. She tried to get back under the pivoting wall while we were down there checking the exterior doors, but the ledger under the wall was wedged so tightly this time that she couldn't get it open. She was trapped for the night. Not that it matters, C.J., but you agree that there is just cause to arrest her?''

C.J. gazed at his wife as if he'd never seen her before. "Do it."

Adam read Rena her rights, and with her husband's help, took her off to jail. As he circled the cul-de-sac in front of the mansion, he glanced at the front door where Pat stood, a solitary figure. She didn't wave. She didn't move at all. In that instant, Adam knew that the morning they'd spent together had been her goodbye.

Epilogue

"So, honey, what do you think?" Pat asked.

Hetty stood in her living room, balancing her weight between the handles of her walker, and looked around, her eyes feasting on all the familiar things she loved. She nodded. "Good," she said. Words were still a struggle for her and her vocabulary was limited, but she could make herself understood. She had allowed Pat to take her out of the rehab center for rides, but she'd refused to come back to the Grove until she became ambulatory, or in Hetty's words, could "walk into my house under my own steam." It was her first visit home in three months.

Pat had traveled south each weekend to see her. Between visits, she'd had ramps built, both in the back and front of the house, had the interior painted, and all the kitchen appliances replaced with models that would be easier for Hetty to use. Hetty was determined to come back on her terms, which translated to mean she wanted to be able to take care of herself. At this point in her rehabilitation, her goals were the much needed impetus that saw her through her various rounds of therapy.

The local social services agency guaranteed help for Hetty several hours a day once she was home, and her neighbors promised to fill the gap. Pat, however, had decidedly mixed feelings about her being alone, and was renegotiating her contract to allow for any contingencies.

The ride home had been tiring for Hetty, but she refused to take a nap. Enthroned in one of the rockers on the back porch, with her neighbors dancing attendance, she was in heaven. Pat left her there and took a few moments to steel herself to deal with one last item of unfinished business. Hetty had almost as many items at the mansion as she had at home, among them her bible. She would not rest until she had it. Pat had delayed returning to the mansion as long as she could, even though C.J. had left the keys for her weeks before. With Hetty at home, if only for the day, Pat could put it off no longer. After making sure that someone would stay with Hetty until she got back, Pat grabbed an empty suitcase and drove to the mansion.

From the construction activity on the far side of town, she assumed Asa Tyler and his company were on their way, but she had studiously avoided any news from the Grove and had not seen Adam at all. She'd have to eventually. Rena's trial had been postponed twice so far, but that couldn't go on forever. She would be called to testify, as would Adam. She wasn't sure which would be harder, going over the events of the night Rena had tried to kill her, or seeing Adam, speaking to him, remembering, knowing the hours of bliss she'd shared with him would never happen again. She almost hoped he wouldn't come to Washington. She could not deal with him on a piecemeal basis.

There was something forlorn about the mansion. According to C.J., he checked it occasionally, but otherwise had done nothing other than maintain it. The grass was cut, the gardens and shrubbery immaculate. But Pat stood in the foyer, overcome with sadness. While it looked the same, the heart seemed to have gone out of it, as if it knew it had been abandoned. Suitcase in hand, she went to the first floor sitting room Hetty had used and began packing her belongings, a chore made simple by her great-aunt's tendency to keep her possessions in one place. She was finished in less than half an hour.

Pat parked the suitcase at the front door, then went upstairs to Lib's wing and walked through it, saying goodbye. From there she crossed to the guest wing and stood in the doorway of the room she'd used. The bed she'd shared with Adam had been stripped. There was nothing left to remind her of her last hours here with him. Perhaps it was just as well.

Downstairs again, she forced herself to go into the library. Seeing this room for the last time would close the book for her. The door Adam had shattered was whole again, the curtains replaced since the one in which Rena had tied her was now evidence to be used against her. The display case had been righted and emptied, its glass lid left unlocked. The case was no longer quite squared; her collision with it had knocked it out of plumb. Pat stared down into it. Somehow seeing it empty put an end to things as nothing else had so far.

A tiny triangle of white, easy to miss, lay in one corner, spoiling the effect. Pat lifted the lid and tried to pick it up, wanting to leave the case empty, but it was not the minute scrap of paper she thought it was. As she pulled at it, it became larger, sliding from underneath, then snagged and wouldn't come free. Whatever it was must have slipped into the breach when the case fell over. She'd have to free it from the underside.

Stooping, she peered at its base but saw nothing. "What gives?" Pat muttered, and stood up. Using her fingernails, she pried at the baize bottom. It came up easily. Pat felt her heart begin to thud erratically as she lifted it out and propped it against the legs of the display case.

The bottom was crammed with paper—old, yellowed documents in sealed plastic bags, drawings of floor plans, lists in Lib's familiar hand. Perhaps...might Lib have squirreled away the codicil with this cache? If it was here, it would be better to have a witness if she found it. Stop kidding yourself, she thought as she went to the phone on the desk, praying it was still connected. If this was the bonanza that would clear up the motive for Lib's murder, she wanted Adam with her to share the moment of discovery.

A dial tone burred in her ear. Hallelujah. She dialed the number with unsteady fingers. He answered on the first ring. "Harland Grove Police."

Pat's heart began a tap dance. "Adam, this is Pat." She heard the quick indrawn breath.

"Pat." He sang her name, a love song in one word.

Tears sprang into her eyes and she wiped them away. "I'm at the mansion, in the library. Adam, I may have found it—where Lib stashed the missing material. Can you . . . will you come?"

"Be right there." He was gone.

Relief and anticipation that she'd be seeing Adam sent Pat's pulse into the stratosphere. She dashed into the nearest bathroom and brushed her hair; she wore no makeup and now regretted it. Jeans and a sweatshirt had been the order of the day to pick up Hetty. Pat swore under her breath. Why couldn't she have opted for a skirt, anything that would do more for her than what she wore, especially since she'd dropped a few pounds. She hadn't much appetite anymore, not just for food, but for her life as she'd lived it B.A.— Before Adam. The zest was gone. She'd survived these last three months by concentrating on Hetty and her needs.

She was waiting outside the door when Adam arrived. He parked the cruiser and came up the steps two at a time, stopping to stare at her, the golden brown eyes that she'd dreamed of raking her from head to foot.

"You've lost weight," he said in greeting, and took her hand.

"Yes." She laced her fingers between his, tongue-tied, unable to think of a thing to say.

"I've missed you."

"I've missed you, too." She had no idea how much until now. Pat felt as if she was lighter than air, her feet barely touching the ground.

Evidently Adam had run out of words, as well. They stood looking at one another, unable to get their fill.

Finally he tucked her hand under his arm. "Why don't we go see what you've found?"

She nodded, and went with him inside. He closed the door, pulled her close and kissed her, the pressure of his mouth so light, the greeting of his tongue so gentle that it brought Pat dangerously close to tears again. There was love, sadness, welcome, resignation in the caress. It said that nothing and everything had changed for them both.

He pulled away. "I think we'd better stop and get down to business, don't you?"

"Yes." Longing to return to his embrace, she made do with slipping an arm through his and walking with him into the library.

He stared open-mouthed at the display case. "I'll be damned. Right under our noses all the time. We should take an inventory of this."

Pat retrieved a lined pad and a pencil from the desk. He took them from her and sat at the reading table. "Since you found it, I'll do the writing. This shouldn't take long. There isn't as much there as I would have expected."

"As long as there's enough. I guess we should list this first," she said, showing him the sheet that had led her to the rest.

"What is it?"

She scanned it. "A photostated copy of a letter dated February 5, 1862, from a Mary Hester Weems requesting two jars of Cammio face cream." It was a poor copy, probably because of the condition of the original, the ink faded, the writing the delicate, spidery cursive style of the day.

He jotted it down, then frowned. "Eighteen sixty-two? That pre-dates Harland Industries by four years. I guess this shows the demand for it before the business actually started. Next?"

Pat put it to one side, and went on to the next item, trying to concentrate on what she was supposed to be doing and not Adam's broad back and the way his hair grew in a curly V at the nape of his neck. Finally, she got a chair and positioned it so he wasn't directly in her line of vision.

Lib had stashed away a curious assortment of documents, only a few of which were related to the mansion. The plans were there, and assorted receipts for the materials with which the house had been constructed. Pat saw little reason to get excited until she'd reached the bottom layer of the pile. There she saw two battered, shredding leather-bound diaries similar to those they found downstairs.

"I'll list them," Adam said, "but that's just the beginning. We'll have to read them cover to cover. The fact that Miss Harland hid them means they're important. Let's finish the inventory first."

"Right." Pat, who'd been separating the documents into piles, placed the diaries on her left beside the copy of the first letter she'd found. Oddly enough, the next item was the original of the letter, the paper yellowed, its edges disintegrating. Handling it gingerly, she laid it atop its copy, then frowned and picked it up again. The original was appreciably more legible, the ink darker, and she saw something she hadn't noticed before. Her skin began to prickle.

"Adam, look at this."

She went to stand beside him, flattening the letter carefully. "This doesn't say what I thought it did. It's not Cammio face cream she was asking for, it's *Cammie's* face cream."

"Cammie's?" Adam stared at the writing, scrutinized it closely. "You're right." He looked straight ahead, unseeing, thoughtful. "So *that's* it," he said softly.

"What's it?"

His face suffused with animation, his eyes shining, he got up and came back to the display case. "What else is in here?"

"Not much. Another plastic bag." She opened it carefully and removed a doubled-over sheet, the paper of poor quality, coming apart at the folds. The writing was childish, labored, the hand clearly unused to pen and ink. It appeared to be a list. "'Witch hazel,'" Pat read aloud. "'Rose water, oats, egg.' Sounds ghastly." She skipped the remainder of the list, jumping to the writing at the bottom. "'Mix reel good. Let it sit in cool water. Youse nex day after you wash your face. Spred reel thin.' The spelling is atrocious. Whoever—" Pat dropped it as if the sheet had gotten hot, her eyes stretched wide. "Adam! Could this be...?"

He picked it up, nodding. "The formula for Cammio, concocted by your multiple-great-aunt Cammie, written by her or another slave. A good many more of them knew how to read and write than they let on. What's that?''

An envelope, facedown, protruded from beneath several loose ledger pages. Adam slid it free and flipped it over with the pencil but didn't pick it up. It was addressed in Lib's handwriting to Leland Stokes, the Harland family's lawyer.

Adam beamed at her, gave her a quick hug. ''Congratulations. You did find it. That has to be the codicil.'' He opened it, nodded, read it, then passed it to Pat, his eyes watching her intently. ''You'd better read it, too.''

Pat needed no prodding, scanning it quickly. Flabbergasted, she read it again. ''She can't— I mean, couldn't do this. Why would she leave her H.I. shares to me?''

''While she was rooting around looking for old documents, Miss Harland must have discovered that the original formula was Cammie's. The Harlands have lived rather well all these years off the proceeds from that face cream.''

''She said something to Lorna about restoring family honor,'' Pat said, her thoughts revving. ''That I'd be proud of her. But—''

''Pat.'' Adam placed his hands on her shoulders. ''H.I. shares have to remain in the family of the owners. Whether Cammie could be considered an owner in the legal sense, I don't know, since she herself was owned by the Harlands. It's a fine distinction, fine enough to get Miss Harland killed. In her mind, she was righting a wrong—it's a cinch Cammie never saw a cent of the money Ephraim made selling her face cream. Your name's at the bottom of that wall downstairs as the last of Cammie's issue. Rena must have found out what Miss Harland intended to do and killed her.''

''Wouldn't it have made more sense to come after me to begin with?'' Pat couldn't quite believe what she was asking.

''You weren't around. It was simpler to get rid of C.J.'s aunt and burn the codicil—only she couldn't find it.''

''Oh, my God.'' Pat's head was spinning.

''We'd better get this to Mr. Stokes, so he can figure out whether it'll stand. If it does, Pat, the chance you've probably been waiting for all these years just dropped in your lap.''

"What do you mean?"

"If this is legal, and you own those shares now, you can stop the sale to Asa Tyler. If you want to, Pat, you can bring Har- and Grove to its knees."

Pat stood in the kitchen, loading the dishwasher. It was her first time back in the Grove since her discovery three weeks before. Had it not been for Hetty's burning desire to come home for the weekend, she wouldn't be there now. She was still too mixed up, about the codicil, Adam, everything. But she'd had to come. Hetty was doing too well, and Pat didn't want to set her back.

The doorbell rang, another new addition to Hetty's house. Drying her hands, Pat went to answer it, puzzled because she didn't see anyone in front of the door. She opened the screen, and a hand gripped her wrist. Adam swept her off her feet into his arms and, carrying her, started down the steps.

"Adam, put me down," she protested. "What are you doing?"

"You're going with me," he said firmly, rounding the cruiser to sit her in the passenger seat. "Don't worry about Miss Hetty, Mrs. Ransom will stay with her until we get back."

"Adam—"

"Pat, you're going. Don't fight it, okay?"

Pat gave in, too happy to see him to resist. The scent of his cologne, the memory of his arms around her as he'd carried her, the strength and feel of him made her head swim.

He refused to say a word until they reached their destination, the bluff opposite the mansion. After removing a blanket from the rear of the car, he took her hand and led her through the brush to the willow tree. He spread the blanket for her, then helped her down.

"I want to know what you're going to do," he said, and lowered himself beside her.

"About what, Adam?"

"Don't be coy. C.J.'s talked to your lawyer. Everyone knows now that Ephraim originally set up the business promising

Cammie twenty-five percent of the profits if she'd reveal th
formula, and conveniently forgot his promise once she died.'

"It started out as Cammie's Cold Cream," Pat said wit
bitterness. "He changes one letter—the 'e' at the end of he
name to an 'o'—and in effect, wipes out all traces of her con
tribution."

"That's history, Pat. Let's deal with the present. C.J. an
Asa Tyler want to know your intent. Tyler's still interested i
buying H.I., though God knows how long it'll be before all th
legal mess has been untangled. He's entitled to a response from
you, and Miss Harland obviously trusted you to do the righ
thing. So what are you going to do?"

"Poor Lib," Pat said, staring across at the mansion. "
feel...I don't know...that if she hadn't left those shares to me
she'd still be alive."

"It's not your fault," Adam said. "It's Rena's. She went to
a great deal of trouble to kill that poor old lady. At first sh
tried to make it look as if Miss Harland was unfit to manage he
affairs by telling lies about how forgetful she was becoming
And we're pretty sure she's the one who shoved Miss Harlan
off the teetotaler's wagon, all part of setting up her faked sui
cide. That's beside the point. What are you going to do?"

"Adam, stop pushing me." It had been weighing on he
every waking moment.

"No. Jobs are on the line. And for your information, it won
be the first time everyone's livelihood was threatened."

"What does that mean?"

"How do you think Margaret Harland kept this town in lin
after what she did to you? She immediately passed the wor
that if anyone even talked about it, they'd be fired. What woul
you have done under the same circumstances?"

Pat stood up and wandered to the edge of the bank, needin
to move, needing to digest all this. Adam was right about he
For the first few years after she left the Grove, she'd dreame
of getting even. But it had always been an amorphous plan
nothing real, a childish desire to strike back. Now that she ha
the means, she no longer wished for revenge.

"Well?" Adam asked, from the blanket.

Pat didn't look back at him. "How can you ask? I'll do whatever's best for the town."

Adam's voice became husky. "I was counting on that. I'll tell C.J. Now, what about us?"

"Us?" Pat became very still, unprepared for this.

She heard his footsteps, felt his arms enfold her from behind. He pulled her back to the blanket, and laying her down, stretched out beside her. "There's something I'd like you to think about. Your work's important to you, but does it matter where you do it?"

Uncertain where he was going with this, Pat hedged. "I'm not sure. Why?"

"I've been meddling. There are several local public television stations that would turn handstands to have you on their staffs. You could even continue 'Honor Bound' from one of them down here. There's no reason you have to shoot your spots from D.C., is there?"

She hadn't really thought of it from that point of view. "I don't know."

"I do. There isn't. And you wouldn't necessarily have to live here in town, although it would simplify matters. I can't leave the Grove, Pat, and don't really want to. So it comes down to this—am I worth it? Are *we* worth it?"

Pat realized that there was little to think about. Her grudge against Harland Grove was unjustified; it was time to let bygones be bygones, forgive and forget. Instantly a weight was lifted from her shoulders, a decade and a half of toxic waste flushed from her psyche. She was free, cured, clean.

As for the rest, she'd been so close to the problem, she'd been looking at it cross-eyed. She'd wanted to be closer to Hetty, yet also wanted to continue the kind of assignments that had come to mean so much to her. Most of all, she wanted to be with this man, share his days, his nights. His children—Corey and their own. Her life would be so empty without that.

"It might work," she said, almost afraid to believe it.

"I know it will." And with that, Adam kissed her, his lips expressing emotions that went beyond words, his arms around her, cradling her, rocking her. Pat's heart lurched with joy and she moved closer, needing the feel of him again, his strength, his goodness, his optimism. This was where she belonged, here in Harland Grove, in Adam's arms. After fifteen and a half years, she'd finally come home.

* * * * *

COMING NEXT MONTH

#445 MACKENZIE'S MISSION—Linda Howard

Test pilot Joe "Breed" MacKenzie was on a dangerous mission, and he wasn't about to let sexy civilian Caroline Evans—a woman who looked too good and knew too much—get in his way.

#446 QUEEN OF HEARTS—Barbara Faith

Rebecca Bliss was used to giving orders and living dangerously—that is, until she met staid history professor Tom Thornton. Suddenly staying at home seemed the most exciting thing in the world.

#447 13 ROYAL STREET—Peggy Webb

When unscrupulous kidnappers threatened her baby nephew, Lily Cooper turned to undercover agent Zach Taylor. But the *real* trouble began the moment she discovered a burning need for Zach's passion, not his protection....

#448 THE LOVE OF DUGAN MAGEE—Linda Turner

Macho detective Dugan Magee wanted nothing to do with Sarah Jane Haywood. She was too gentle, too pretty, to fit into his world. But he needed her help to capture a rapist....

#449 EXILE'S END—Rachel Lee

From the moment burned-out, betrayed government agent Ransom Laird and lonely author Amanda Grant met, it seemed inevitable that they would fall in love—if a vengeful killer didn't get them first!

#450 MISTRESS OF MAGIC—
Heather Graham Pozzessere

Flirting with a gorgeous man while wearing a dinosaur costume wasn't Reggie Delaney's style. And the fact that the man happened to be Wes Blake, financial backer of Dierdre's Dinoland, made matters even worse....

ᵂINTIMATE MOMENTS®
™ _Silhouette_

Dear Linda Howard,
Won't you please write the story
of Joe "Breed" Mackenzie?

Ever since the appearance of Linda Howard's
incredibly popular MACKENZIE'S MOUNTAIN in 1989,
we've received literally hundreds of letters, all asking
that same question. At last the book we've all been
waiting for is here.

In September, look for MACKENZIE'S MISSION (Intimate
Moments #445), Joe's story as only Linda Howard
could tell it.

And Joe is only the first of an exciting breed here at
Silhouette Intimate Moments. Starting in September,
we'll be bringing you one title every month in our new
American Heroes program. In addition to Linda
Howard, the American Heroes lineup will be written
by such stars as Kathleen Eagle, Kathleen Korbel,
Patricia Gardner Evans, Marilyn Pappano, Heather
Graham Pozzessere and more. Don't miss a
single one!

CONARD COUNTY

Welcome to Conard County, Wyoming, where the sky spreads bold and blue above men and women who draw their strength from the wild western land and from the bonds of the love they share.

Join author Rachel Lee for a trip to the American West as we all want it to be. In Conard County, Wyoming, she's created a special place where men are men and women are more than a match for them.

In the first book of the miniseries, EXILE'S END (Intimate Moments #449), you'll meet Amanda Grant, whose imagination takes her to worlds of wizards and warlocks in the books she writes, but whose everyday life is gray and forlorn—until Ransom Laird walks onto her land with trouble in his wake and a promise in his heart. Once you meet them, you won't want to stop reading. And once you've finished the book, you'll be looking forward to all the others in the miniseries, starting with CHEROKEE THUNDER, available in December.

EXILE'S END is available this September, only from Silhouette Intimate Moments.

THE DONOVAN LEGACY
from Nora Roberts

Meet the Donovans—Morgana, Sebastian and Anastasia.
They're an unusual threesome. Triple your fun with double
cousins, the only children of triplet sisters and triplet brothers.
Each one is unique. Each one is...special.

In September you will be *Captivated* by Morgana Donovan. In
Special Edition #768, horror-film writer Nash Kirkland doesn't
know what to do when he meets an actual witch!

Be *Entranced* in October by Sebastian Donovan in Special
Edition #774. Private investigator Mary Ellen Sutherland
doesn't believe in psychic phenomena. But she discovers
Sebastian has strange powers...over her.

In November's Special Edition #780, you'll be *Charmed* by
Anastasia Donovan, along with Boone Sawyer and his little
girl. Anastasia was a healer, but for her it was Boone's touch
that cast a spell.

Enjoy the magic of Nora Roberts. Don't miss *Captivated*,
Entranced or *Charmed*. Only from
Silhouette Special Edition....

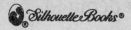 Silhouette Books ®

Don't miss this
exclusive two-in-one
collection. Silhouette
brings back two early
love stories by one of its
bestselling authors.

DIANA PALMER

COLLECTION

RAWHIDE & LACE

UNLIKELY LOVER

Look for the
DIANA PALMER
COLLECTION in August,
wherever Silhouette
books are sold.

SDP92

Back by popular demand...

TELL ME NO LIES

In a world full of deceit and manipulation, truth is a double-edged sword.

Lindsay Danner is the only one who can lead the search for the invaluable Chinese bronzes. Jacob Catlin is the only one who can protect her. They hadn't planned on falling in love....

Available in August at your favorite retail outlet.

ELIZABETH LOWELL

Silhouette Books®

SEL92